Brushes

An Erotic Romance Novel of Artistic Propositions

Un roman d'amour érotique de propositions artistiques

M. CHRISTIAN

Brushes:
An Erotic Romance Novel of Artistic Propositions
Un roman d'amour érotique de propositions artistiques

ISBN 978-1-957863-38-2

Parisian Phoenix Publishing, Easton, Pennsylvania
Originally Published by Phaze Books, 2008

Cover Image: Joan Zachary

C O N N E C T with the publisher:
 ParisianPhoenix
 ParisBirdBooks
 parisianphoenix

"Pour tous les amoureux..."
(for all you lovers)

CHAPTER ONE

Constance

I

Finger slipped carefully into the handle, heat passing through the delicate ceramic from the recently boiled drink, losing degrees of temperature to become comforting warmth, she brought the cup up gently, carefully. One inch. Another. Another. The ritual of a sip, the elegance of patience: finger in handle, cup up to mouth, a pause of fragrance, then lips touched gently to rim. Taste. Savor. Taste again to compare.

The British used it as the cornerstone of a lion-emblazoned empire. The Japanese had made it a religion. Sitting in the lounge of the Hôtel Pont Royal — immaculate linen tablecloth, Lenox kettle and cup, silver service, velvet drapes parting the view of the Saint Germain district of Paris, a waiter at the door prepared to do whatever was needed to ensure the pleasure of her stay — Constance could believe that tea was, indeed, something to fight wars over, to pray to.

Steady and refined, careful and graceful, charming and poised, it was ballet with a cup and saucer, opera with a kettle, chamber music with sugar and cream. Tea, especially tea in the lounge of the Hôtel Pont Royal, was perfect, or as near to it as anyone could come.

Then the waiter wasn't waiting by the door. Passing between her table and the window with its rich maroon drapes, he gestured to a corner table. Behind him, moving slower through the linen islands — having less of his skill in navigating the room — came the man, followed by the woman.

He was young, his body lithe and fluid, yet with the hesitation and stumbling that comes from some uncertainty in life. His hair was brown, but not common. His was a mixture of many shades, making it changeable with every turn of his head, every shift of his muscled body. His face was expressive but not comedic, handsome without being cut from cold marble. Like his shifting hair, his eyes also became many kinds of brown as he looked around the room.

She was young, her figure tight, supple, and limber, but with the hesitancy and awkwardness that came with trying to understand her own body. Her hair was blond, but not from a bottle. Hers was true shine that glowed with every movement of her lissome form. Her face was animated but not loud, pretty without being from a mold. Like her bright hair, her eyes glimmered and shone as she surveyed her surroundings.

Watching them come in and sit down, Constance swallowed hot tea — through a cold and tense frown.

* * * *

Finger slipped carefully into warm, golden metal on a hot summer day. That sensation had lingered more than many other details. More than the perfume of roses. More than what her friends — or his, for that matter — had said to her before or after the priest heard the vows. More than the butterflies that had fluttered in her stomach. More than the champagne in a flute, with its jeweled bubbles streaming up from the bottom.

Other things were long forgotten, but the ring sliding onto her finger had remained — a faithful memory of her wedding day.

Hot tea to her lips again, she scowled at the tan liquid in her cup. The beverage was excellent — as only something served in the lounge of the Hôtel Pont Royal could be — but the remembrance wasn't. Faithful, yes, because it remained close at hand, even when not wanted, but its flavor was bitter.

On her left hand, on that meaningful finger, she still had her ring. On days like today, she wanted to pull it off, leave it behind as a generous tip for superb service, but she never did. Turn it, yes, around and around, but that was all. Tarnished and cold, it still meant something. Even if it was a tarnished and cold meaning.

It was different for her husband. Clearly, for Escobar, his matching gold meant nothing.

II

"I want to capture you."

Those hadn't been the first words he'd spoken to her, but they were the ones she remembered vividly. She and Escobar had been hiking up a deceptively steep hill, the angle making her perspire. She hadn't liked that, the betrayal of her body, its descent into common sweat, but the frown she'd worn had slipped away when he, having ascended faster, had reached down to help her up the last few feet.

At the top, she still glowing from the unwanted exertion, their hands had remained together longer than was necessary for the chivalrous gesture: his skin rough, his muscles strong, his hair dark and wild, his eyes hard and penetrating. Standing on grass, hot sun above, the climb wasn't the only cause for her perspiration.

"What do you mean?" she'd asked, carefully, covertly sliding her palms along her summer-skirted thighs to dry them.

In answer, he'd dropped to the ground, uncaring of stains, uncaring of angrily buzzing crickets, uncaring of anything except for the tablet of paper he'd brought with him, tucked under one arm.

"Capture you. With this," he'd said, flipping back the cover.

From a pocket of his simple cotton shirt, he brought out a pencil. Not one an artist would use, but a common yellow thing from school. Point down to the paper, but not touching, he waved it in a meaningless round of swirls to translate his meaning.

"Sketch you, I mean. I don't like that word. I like 'capture' better. Do a drawing right and you can hold it down on the paper. Do it wrong and it doesn't stick. You know?"

She didn't, but afraid that it was just an artist's way of saying things, and not wanting to embarrass herself with ignorance, she'd said, "Well, naturally. Of course."

"Wonderful! That's just wonderful!" he'd said, tone and shimmering eyes of an even younger boy, not one just a single year behind her.

"How do you want me?" Then, realizing how what she'd said could be misinterpreted, she added quickly, "Posing, I mean. Do you want me to sit? Or maybe stand? How about this?" His gaze warmed her more than the walk had.

Too straight, too stiff, putting herself into the classical pose, posture, and position cobbled together from too many statues she'd seen in too many art books, it felt wrong. Too bony for Venus, too chubby for armless victory, on the hillside she immediately felt like what she was: a young girl who didn't know what to do.

She may not have known, but the young man with the paper and the pencil did. Grinning widely, smile too large for his roughly formed face, he coughed out a chuckle.

"Oh, I like it. A lot, really. Honestly. It's quite ... lovely. But why don't you relax? I don't want you to be uncomfortable while I do this."

"Okay. That's a good idea."

But thinking about relaxing only made her feel stiffer, her stance even more forced. Which foot should she lean on? What about her arms, her hands, her fingers — what to do with them? In exasperation, she brought up one arm, one hand, and one set of fingers, and ran them through her hair, feeling the tugs and pops of tangles.

"Perfect," he'd said. "That's just right."

His one arm began to sweep and slide behind the tablet, one hand turning and flowing across the paper, one set of fingers twirling and looping the pencil.

On that hillside, on that warm summer day, while the pretty daughter of a well-respected doctor posed, and the young man with charcoal stains drew, she'd had a tug, a flutter, a beat.

But even more when he'd turned the tablet around, showing her what he'd done: lines and curves, shading and forms, contrast and contour. Trapped, frozen, captured on the sheet was herself. Held, perfectly, by Escobar.

Sitting in the lounge of the Hôtel Pont Royal, cooling tea in her cup, young couple bubbling with joy and life so nearby, she wished she could have seen it all so much clearer: not through a haze of sweet adulation, artistic flattery, or boyish chivalry.

It was all there, but she'd been too blinded by his talent to see it.

"It's good," he'd said, eyes still bright but with a new tension in his jaw. "But it could be better. Yeah ... lots better."

He'd turned away from her, then — lost to miniscule increments, careful adjustments, redrawing entire sections, until she'd left her pose, walked the short distance between them, and put her hand on his shoulder.

III

There'd been good times. No, that was what she used to think — a habit she hadn't yet completely broken. She thought they'd had good times. Since then, her vision had improved, and now she could look back with much greater clarity.

Even though her father would have reached out his latex-gloved influence and gotten them a nice place, he, out of pride, and she … Well, it could have been spite, to be the pretty daughter of the rich, refined doctor living in a tiny, dirty apartment, but she told herself it was more to show that she could make it on her own in the real world. It was noisy, near the highway where the trucks drove — day and night — to Barcelona. It was dirty, no matter how many bottles, sponges, brooms, and mops she used. It was hot, even when the sky was overcast and rain streaked the darkly clouded windows.

As she'd done before they met, before they'd married, she worked in her father's practice during the day, leading stooped and wrinkled citizens with chubby bellies — and fat wallets — from waiting to examination. All as before, except now her father seemed older, slower, his eyes heavier with age, or maybe just the weighty disappointment that his jewel had married a poor painter rather than a man with a more pride-worthy occupation.

As he'd done before they met, Escobar worked — or said he did. Some days she'd come home to canvases stacked against the walls, each one adding wet paint — unwanted color — to the forever grimy plaster, her husband stripped to the chest, gleaming with sweat, heaving with exhaustion as he attacked his work with brush or charcoal. Other times, though, he'd be sitting in front of the cheap little TV, remote in one hand, beer in the other.

Then there were the nights. Virginity having lost its value long before her adolescence in the seventies, she'd not come to their bed inexperienced. Igualada may not have been a big city, but the world still came to it through slick magazines, American movies, and television shows out of Madrid. Boys had always been available to practice with.

It was … no, she thought, believed, lied to herself, that it'd been good. But sitting in the lounge of the Pont Royal, she had a much better view of it all. His hands had been strong, yes, but also coarse. His body had been tight with muscle, yes, but also rough. His eyes had been hungry for her, yes, but no matter what she did, it was never enough.

A memory of a morning: sleeping in while the bells rang the rest of the city to church, another thing she'd discarded with her virginity. The night before, she'd been cooking, a skill she never believed she'd ever really perfect, when he'd come up, wrapped his arms around her, pulling her away from the rushing water, the rising mountain of foam in the sink. He'd worked that day, canvases drying on his easel, on the sofa, leaning on dining room chairs. When he worked, he had a broad grin on his face. When he smiled, his hands always came to her.

Cupping her breasts, fingers knowing intuitively where her nipples were hidden, he pulled her back still more, the insistence of his erection clear to her through his pants, the fabric of her skirt.

"No," was all she'd said, shaking her head.

Women, her mother had said, should never argue.

"Dishes can wait — everything in the whole wide world can wait. I have something to show you. Come on."

A tug on her arm pulled her away from cleaning up. Drying her hands on her skirt, she allowed herself to be led from one room to another. The bedroom, she immediately noticed, was a mess: clothes on the floor, blanket wadded up, pillows slipping out of their covers. But he didn't see any of it. Pulling her through the sleep-shuffled chaos, he put her in front of her mirror.

"Here," he'd said, posing her like one of the little wooden models he studied. "Yeah, like that. Hand right here. Perfect. Okay? Now just relax."

Shoes, first — slipping one off then the other. Then her stockings, his hands reaching up under her skirt, deftly sliding fingers between elastic and her waist, before steadily, teasingly *down*.

Buttons followed, only a few on the dress she'd worn that day. A few until they were all undone and he was slipping her shoulders free, dropping the weight of the dress to the floor in a hush of falling fabric. Reaching behind her back, he found the hooks to her bra, pulled the straps and the silken cups away with steady patience. Last were her panties, also removed with almost glacial drama, the spell only broken when she had to lift one foot to allow him to take them away.

Behind her, she felt his erection even though he was fully dressed and she wasn't at all. He moved her again until she was perfectly in front of the mirror.

"I want to show you something really beautiful," he said.

Pretty. She'd been called that my her mother, her father, some aunts, some uncles. Attractive. She'd been called that by other girls, usually grudgingly. Good-looking. She'd been called that by a few boys, usually not wanting to flatter her out of reach.

Beautiful. Of course she'd been called that, probably by more than a few relatives, maybe a girlfriend or two, or even by a few boys. But after that day, whenever she heard the word, she would think about standing naked in front of a mirror. At first with a hidden, secret joy, but later — when she had been pulled out of the shade of her ignorance — with bitter tension.

But this was before, back in the days where she didn't know anything except that she was standing naked in front of a mirror. Back when she and he were a poor, happy, couple in a dirty, cold, and noisy apartment.

Back when he'd stood behind her and said one word: "Look."

And she had. What she saw had made her face sag into a weighty frown: a young woman dropping towards mid-twenties, early thirties, once high and firm breasts — petite but always well shaped — now starting to suffer under gravity, tight belly now beginning to balloon outwards, and elegantly tapered legs approaching chubbiness. A woman once perhaps worth looking at, maybe even following, possibly even the recipient of a high then low whistle, but now ... now in the past tense, all of that tightness, that buoyancy, that life behind, not in front of her.

The dropping of her face must have been clear to her husband, as his own sagged as well.

"Not what I mean," he'd said, kissing her shoulder. "Not what I meant at all."

She tried to pull away from the contact of his lips, but his hand had become firm, keeping her facing the cold, hard, silver of the mirror.

"Try to see the way I do, look at my eyes."

And she had. What she did, at first, kept her face leaden with disappointment and her cheeks burning with hate. Why would he force her to face the harshness of her own image? But then she'd looked up and away from her reflection to see him peering over her shoulder. Peering over her shoulder with bright, heated eyes. Bright, heated eyes that bounced back into the mirror, echoing a reflection of herself in his vision. Imagination wasn't a quality she'd ever really tried to develop in herself — the world being previously all she'd ever wanted, never hungering for anything that wasn't in front of her eyes. But that afternoon she really did try to imagine herself as the woman her husband touched whenever he could, kissed so often, watched getting dressed or undressed, and pressed a determined erection against while they slept in their too-small bed.

Beautiful. Yes, she was. Spry and lean, body straight and tall, deep red nipples at the tips of gently rising breasts, shoulders shapely, skin with the glow of energy and passion, belly plush and warm, legs long and tight with girlish spring, thighs robust but not too muscular — and at the base of her tummy, between those vigorous thighs and legs, a thin feather of hair that led into her now moistening depths.

"You are too beautiful for words," Escobar had said to her, his voice a bit of basso music in her ears. "Too beautiful..."

That last bit falling away, she was unsure if he'd added anything to the two words.

The burgundy tips at the ends of her breasts had wrinkled into firmness as she'd looked at herself, seeing herself the way he saw her. Her skin had begun to shine, the air in their bedroom starting to ring of salt from her sweat, and in the depths of her, where there had just been moisture between her thighs, below her belly, there was now an urgent pulse and definite, positive wetness. Listening to him, trying to pick out the exact words of his low tones, wasn't important. Having him inside her was.

Turning, she'd embraced her husband, arms snaking around his waist, pulling him tight. Clothes. They were in the way, they had to come off. Buttons first, fingers popping them away one by one, doing to him with much more urgency and the ritual that he'd done to her.

Off, his shirt. Off, his undershirt. Hands on his belt, but then his words cut through her urgency.

"I want to paint you, Constance. I want to really paint you. To get it right."

It was not a new request — after all, a flavor of it had been one of the first things he'd said to her — but it wasn't a common one. Instead, it was one that he asked only at certain moments. Like her birthday, claiming that no gift he could give her would measure up to finally being able to create a perfect portrait of her. Same for Christmas, with the same explanation. It would be a complete execution, not just a simple sketch. Color and not just pencil lines on paper.

Birthday, Christmas, she'd always shaken her head, another simple word — because even about this, women did not argue — and then a refusal to discuss it further. She told herself that it was good to keep him waiting for some things, a sizzling spice to keep him interested —

especially after that first initial taste of capturing her on that green grass hill all those years ago — but there was also pleasure in denying him.

Too hot, she almost agreed to his request, but then came to enough of her senses to shake her head.

"Maybe," came out as a throaty whisper.

It had been enough for him, and he'd dropped the rest of his clothes in a frantic clumsy strip. To the bed, messy or not... She threw herself back, wantonly spread wide, brazenly exposed.

Again, restrained and patient despite his clearly determined erection, he carefully approached her, taking two minutes when she wanted two seconds, kneeling on the ruffled covers to peer, intently and attentively, between her legs. For a man with hands that normally appeared rough and tough, he moved with a painter's precision and admiration for detail.

Labia parted, he ran a slow, steady finger from opening to the tight bead of her clit, the direct contact at the end making her legs and thighs tighten and air draw into her lungs with a long, low whistle.

A kiss then, to her other lips, and to the hot button at their top. A kiss that turned into a lick, a butterfly flutter that made her whistle into a moan, approaching with each flick of his tongue, a rippling scream.

Then she wasn't approaching. She'd come, arrived at her destination with a primal sound and involuntary trapping of his head between her thighs. The world went away, lost to a blushing flush and a body surge of pleasure.

And he was inside her, sliding himself deep into her with no resistance, either from her mind or her body. It was good. Lord, it was good. Filling her, he drove himself rhythmically and powerfully, making her breasts bounce and shake with each push, each thrust.

How long? Unsure.

Time left her, retreating against the waves and surges and ripples and bursts that came with him inside her. Without her will, her arms again were snakes coiling around his back, and her legs lifted, giving him better entry and more traction from the soles of her feet leveraged against the sliding sheets.

Then it was his turn, and with his orgasm, a new form of it for herself.

Again, a reflection: the pleasure he took in her returned to her as an unexpected and blaze of delight.

They'd slept afterwards. He in her, she wrapped around him. Two people become one, joined by sweat and semen and slippery fluids.

Good times, yes, but only because she hadn't opened her eyes. She had slept through all of those years. Not that there hadn't been signs, clues to what had been going on.

Like the next day, a Saturday, when he'd been out — dragging his canvases and sketches around town again, begging for patronage, trying to sell his work to galleries, setting up stands and easels to tempt the few off-season tourists who'd come to town — and she'd been cleaning. A smile on her face, yes, she remembered that: grinning like a young fool as she'd snapped sheets, bundled clothes into hampers, making their home a place worthy of living in.

Leaning against a wall in their tiny living room was a tilted stack of fresh paintings, just like many she'd seen and moved in the time they'd lived there. Didn't know why, but this time she'd actually looked at them, flipping one after another, seeing images of the city, their neighborhood, bits of faces, pieces of their life, and then ... and then ... and then ... a new one, a fresh one, a work just created.

On the bed, she lay, sublime and lovely, relaxed and illuminated from within. Around her, covers twisted and bunched. It was obvious, unquestionably evident, that this young woman had just experienced a powerful bodily joy.

Obvious, too, unquestionably evident, as well, that this was herself: naked and spent. Here was a portrait taken — not given. She'd never given him the permission he sought. She vaguely recalled whispering "maybe," not "yes."

By painting her regardless, he'd shown how little her wishes mattered. She trembled, feeling violated and wronged. She'd pushed his insistence out of her mind, trying to focus instead on his passion, his possible talent, his kindness — and, of course, the way he saw her, the way he'd allowed her to see herself through his eyes.

Now, though, what it was: a betrayal of trust. Just one of many.

Another sip in the lounge of the Hôtel Pont Royal, but this time her tea wasn't hot, wasn't warm, wasn't even tepid.

It was cold.

"Mademoiselle?" Not a brittle voice, that one, like her china cup, but rather rich and earthy, from honest loam and sincere soil.

At first, Constance didn't know what he was asking, so deep in her past had she drifted. Pulling herself up from the turpentine reek of pigments and the permanent dust and mold of a cheap apartment, she blinked then blinked again until she saw the then and the now: tea in a cup, pure white, linen tablecloth, warm afternoon in the lounge of the Hôtel Pont Royal, Paris, France, lots of money in her account, her face and name in a few papers, though not as many as her husband.

The here, the now, and a handsome waiter was picking up her cup, exchanging the coldness of the old with the freshness of the new. Past taken away, present laid out with elegance and grace.

In nodding to him in thanks, she appraised the waiter, really see the face and some of the body that belonged to his frank tenor, his candid accent.

Oh, my was what she thought. Then again — *oh, my* — but not a loud thought, a yelling mental voice. Instead, it was soft, a serpentine kind of attention, one that had her slowly stirring, moving her head, her hands, her arms in a steady, sensual way.

"Merci, monsieur," she said, more ashamed of her Spanish accent than usual.

To that he nodded, his darkly handsome face lighting up with a fast grin that accompanied the gesture. Turning to return to his post by the door, Constance caught a hesitation in his smooth movements, a quick casting of a glance back towards her.

Suddenly blushing, she returned to her table and the service before the obvious became embarrassingly so. The perfect summers of a young woman might be chronologically gone, her age beginning with the numeral '4' after all, but she still felt them fluttering in her belly, and thumping firmly in her chest.

With the redness in her cheeks came a chastisement of herself: proper, elegant, refined, tea in the lounge of the lovely Pont Royal. Not a place, not a time, not a ladylike thing to do. After all, she wasn't coarse, rude, improper like her husband.

Not soon after that reflective afternoon in front of that mirror, things had changed. One event led to another, slow at first and then with a dizzying momentum: the purchase of one of his paintings, and then another, then another, then another. Then a gallery showing, then another, then another, then a mention in a magazine, then another, then the cover of a magazine, and another.

Swinging herself in her chair, she glanced over at the waiter, thinking she might have to signal but instead seeing that he was still looking in her direction. A smile, warm as drinkable tea, going to her and, she felt, going back to him from her own cheeks and lips and mouth.

Success, money, and fame had rushed at them. By the second painting, she'd realized she didn't need to work in her father's practice. By the third painting, they'd realized their dirty, loud, cold, hot, mold-and-mildew apartment was *needlessly* dirty, loud, cold, hot, moldy, and mildewy. Their next place, a two-bedroom — one room as Escobar's studio — wasn't any of that. Bathroom all polished metal and fine marble, floors all glowing hardwood, a view of more than the next apartment block out the window; it was a move from shame to pride. People came to the new address. Men and women sat in the living room, talking about color and shape and texture, who dropped certain names and places, who seemed to have strolled from glamour magazines and into their home.

"Mademoiselle?" the waiter asked. "Is there something I can do for you?"

"Oui," she said, then said nothing, leaving the word hanging out there. Dark eyes, very dark eyes. Hair, too, jet black, not like fireplace soot. It was like he'd brought a moment of a hot night with him, mysterious but still comforting. Looking at him, she imagined a fireplace, fine champagne, a fur rug. Fantasy borrowed from a magazine. She chastised herself for her lack of imagination, but she couldn't think of anything more perfect, more apt for him.

It'd been what she'd always wanted. Those beautiful, important people would come into their home, take them to parties, write about them in the newspaper, tell her husband that he was a genius, and say that clearly she must be his inspiration.

Her husband, though, while he'd enjoyed seeing his paintings hanging where he'd always dreamed of them being shown, had taken even more pleasure in fading into his studio, emerging for the soirees, the photographers, the reporters, and the journalists with paint under his nails and an untamed beard with crumbs of a rushed lunch caught in it.

Pearls around her neck, a fine silken gown draped around her, gold and diamonds on one finger, platinum and ruby on another, she'd entertained them— laughing, charming, elegant, refined, and as perfect as she could be, telling them things like "Artists, you know how they get lost in their work," and "Poor fellow, nothing's as important as his painting, except maybe me."

"Mademoiselle?" the waiter asked, kindness sing-songing his accent. "Can I get you something? A menu, perhaps, or something else?"

"Something else, I think," Constance said.

The crudeness of her next thought was too brazen, too quick for even another blush, or for her to hide behind the white linen tablecloth, the Pont Royal's refinement, or even the façade of her carefully prepared elegance. She wanted this man. Wanted to kiss him, to stroke his chest, to put her arms around him, pull him close, feel his erection straining for attention.

What would it take? Very little she knew, she could tell that about the atmosphere, about him. The right few words, a few hours for him to leave work, her to go to her room. No fireplace, no furred rug, but champagne and hot kisses.

Champagne and hot kisses and then fewer and fewer clothes, his and hers dropping away until they were nothing but twists and tangles of cloth and elastic. Tea-colored, that's what his skin would be like, tea with very little milk. A nighttime experience, he a nighttime man.

On her knees in front of this stranger, his cock in her mouth. Still crude and vivid: taking him down her throat, the plumpness of his circumcised head sliding in and out of her. Still no blush, no shame in the desire. Yes, she could invite this man back to her room, she would drink with him, she would suck his cock, she would lift her dress and bend over the bed, she would let the waiter fuck her.

Fuck him, yes. Strong words, dirty words, soiling words: let a stranger, a tea-colored waiter fuck her.

As she'd spoken to the waiter, as she'd thought about what she could do with him, she'd slipped a finger back into the fragile china handle of her cup. No memory of it, no conscious will to do it, but she suddenly became aware that she was holding it. Looking down, she saw the dark liquid ringing back and forth, the tremor of her hand broadcast to the liquid.

Fuck him, yes, she thought, taking a breath to steady her hand, her mind. Not the waiter, no. Not the tea-colored man standing by her side. That was why she'd hadn't blushed again, why she'd rushed into the coarse fantasy, why her heart was pounding and her hand was shaking.

"Please tell me the time," she asked the waiter. "That's all."

"Of course, mademoiselle," he said, glancing quickly at a gold watch on one dark wrist.

He said the hour and minutes before nodding politely and fading back towards the door. She blinked quickly. Lost in her mind, it seemed to be much later.

What she'd fantasized hadn't been about desire. Originally yes, a flush and a flash of arousal, but not anymore. It had become different, changed, twisted — turning as cold as her tea had been. A fuck not to the waiter, but rather a 'fuck you' to her husband.

Staring down into her cup, she watched the rings of tremor steady and fade away. The Pont Royal lounge, excellent tea, fine silver, clean linen — a mantra of calm and refinement. Her own life might be have been soiled, broken, and sour, but for now, she was seated in elegance, wrapped in refinement.

Then the couple by the window began to laugh, hushed giggles punctuated by musical chimes of delight. Her hand on his one moment, his hand on hers the next. Eyes bright, shimmering with play, with happiness, they were in their own two-person world, a globe that extended to the limits of the tablecloth and no further.

* * * *

Wasn't it what they'd wanted? Paintings hanging on famous walls, being written about in famous journals, appearing on famous shows, money in their account, driving an expensive car?

After their two-bedroom apartment, they'd bought a house, a stone landmark near Lourdes, and with it, a new way to spend their money: new plumbing, new wiring, new appliances, antiques, and art. Their days were spent apart, she touring nearby towns and villages for just the right thing for just the right spot in their new home, at night entertaining men and women with perfect teeth and flashbulb-dazed eyes.

Escobar painted.

A few times a month they'd get into the upholstered sophistication of their car and drive to Paris, he to meet with Marcel, his dealer, and she to shop. It was on one trip, after Escobar had spent most of the morning in Marcel's gallery discussing commissions, installations,

14

publicity, and all the other things he always hated about art, that she'd discovered the lounge of the Pont Royal. A new treasure she'd wanted to share with him.

They'd been sitting where the young couple were sitting. Constance on the right, Escobar on the left. Tea had been brought, in china, just like the one still in her hand. Looking across at him, she'd wanted him to feel what she felt about it: the delicate chiming of spoon against teacup, the perfume from the kettle, the perfect plain of the linen — a visit to a time, a world, of grace.

At the time, she'd smiled and enjoyed what seemed to be his enjoyment, too, at having tea. At the time she'd dismissed the faint feelings that they hadn't been sitting together, that there was a gap between them. Now, though, looking across the room and back five years, she could see that'd been right, that they'd traveled far apart on a tortuous road from an obsession with a sketch, to a stolen moment of her life in paint, to looking at him across the tablecloth and seeing his nails still filthy with paint.

In the here and now, the couple were still laughing. What could they find so funny for so long? What could be so delightful in the world, or just the lounge of the Pont Royal, to generate such peals?

Again, she examined them, trying to see a chink in their youth, their glowing skin, their bright eyes, the endless possibilities in front of them. Not finding anything immediately, she distracted herself from them by pouring herself more tea.

The first clear crack had been the new series. Not a fool, she knew many artists had done the same, but when the models arrived, stepping into his studio after polite kisses on her cheek, praise for their home, admiration for her privileged place in the genius painter's life, she found herself tightly clenched with less-than-sophisticated feelings.

Champagne, caviar, the high intensity stares of television cameras, pretty people on cell phones, journalists with pocket recorders, the exhibition was an in-the-tanned flesh fantasy from glossy magazines. On his arm she arrived, stepping out of a limousine to applause and bright glare. Marcel's *L'Art* was a small venue, so the guests had been picked with surgical precision. The movie star, the politician, the director, other well-known artists, the models — they'd grinned and bubbled, kissed and flattered them both. He for his genius, she for providing inspiration.

During an eye, a momentary quiet, she'd stepped towards the refreshments, leaving Escobar to animatedly discuss philosophy or technique with another painter. Looking at the table, she remembered trying to decide if she was really hungry or just wanting to eat to ground herself in a mundane, everyday thing, return to earth from the land of fame and fortune by biting into a cracker and some cheese.

No, she'd finally decided. Living in the clouds with angels cut from the covers of *Vogue* and *Le Monde* was too much to give up with a single crumbling bite. The world, she'd thought, was good, brilliant, attractive, and rich.

Then, with a look at the walls, it changed: cracking, cooling, and soiling.

The couple stopped laughing. *Thank you*, Constance thought, certain that if they'd continued, she would have begun to cry.

It wasn't that the pictures had been nudes. It wasn't that they'd been of women with bodies tight and smooth with youth, or with bigger breasts, finely tapered legs, sculpted thighs, or prettier faces. None of that. It was much worse.

They were reflections. Stolen from her or not, the painting he'd done of her had been revealing, personal, intimate. It had captured too much of her, exposed more than just her body. What hung on the walls felt the same. Not just nudes, but portraits — too-intimate portraits.

Pictures only a lover could paint.

V

The woman ordered. What she ordered, Constance couldn't hear. All that came across the lounge were the musical notes of her voice, but not the words. The waiter, standing next to her, nodded and turned to the man, who also ordered, also not loud enough for Constance to hear details.

The waiter left, carrying their order to the kitchen. When he passed, Constance felt herself shrink a bit in shame, neck pulling down, chin dipping.

It was a posture she'd developed over the last few years, one she was getting used to performing. Beginning with that night at the gallery, she'd started to work on the little details of it. What had happened, and what continued to happen, cracked it all, broke her love for Escobar, their success, and their lives into jagged pieces. The more she looked at their days together, the more she saw evidence of his betrayals.

The woman carefully slid her hand across the table. In unspoken response, he put out his own, gently cupping her fingers. It was an automatic gesture for both of them, a habit of trust and affection.

Constance frowned. It wouldn't take much. Not much at all. Just looking at him, she could tell he was weak, easily bent towards any obvious opportunities. Get him alone somewhere — say an elevator, say a hotel hallway — with no immediate obligations, and he could fall right in. All it would take would be a touch of his arm, a few buttons undone, a sensual voice, the warmth of a body standing too close.

Then there were the rumors. Furtive, at first, but then with more daring, circulating from foul web sites to between the lines of better print publications. Young artists taken advantage of. Blatant seductions.

Then there were the models. Touching him at exhibitions; batting big, inviting eyes; using push-up bras to try winning appearances on museum walls. Their names were a roster of unearthly beauty: Miranda, Evey, and, of course, Jacqueline. She'd be a fool to think that they were only naked for his brush, only passionate for his talent.

The man began to stroke the back of the woman's hand, fingers flowing neatly between hers. Constance felt a shiver as she watched them — a jolt of familiarity. The same table, another time. A husband she thought had loved her.

Looking away from their hands so gently touching, she found herself looking intently at the man's face. The glow was there, the same he'd walked in wearing: excitement, kindness, vulnerability, but also a force there as well. A will that would come out when they were alone: an erection at the sight of her bare skin, at a kiss of her lips, even the sound of her voice if she said certain things.

Constance wanted him, too. She wanted him hotter, harder, more intensely than any fantasy involving a member of the wait staff. The fantasy was quick and remarkably detailed, culled from the darker parts of her imagination: he gets up to use the bathroom, she waits the briefest of moments and then follows. With only movies and television to guide her, she quickly projected toilets, mirrors, urinals, tile, metal stalls, and a trash can.

Washing his hands. Yes, that's what he's doing when she arrives. Washing his hands in the sink, sleeves of his shirt pushed up, glancing at her. Odd expression on his face, oil and vinegar mix of shock and puzzlement at seeing a woman like herself walking into a men's room.

Standing in the doorway, she unbuttons her blouse, sensually but quickly, undoing with one hand, stroking the curve of her breast with the other, conjuring a nipple to appear through the satin.

Off goes the blouse, onto the counter. Off comes the bra, to join it. Breasts bared, she walks towards him. Her breasts, she knows, are still good, lovely in form and texture. Firm enough, soft enough, nipples hard enough, despite the *four* in front of her age.

He watches her approach, eyes darting around for witnesses but also drawn back and down to the beauty of her breasts. Up to him then, she reaches down and takes one of his hands in hers, lifts it up, and places it on one breast. With his fingers she massages the tender, soft skin, making the nipple stand out even more aggressively.

But she has two hands. With the other, she then reaches down to take hold of the long, hard muscle of his cock, well-defined and firm even through the thick fabric of his pants.

Turning, breaking his grip on her breast, breaking her grip on his cock, she faces the way out, offering her ass to him. To make herself clear, to rip away any hesitation on his part, she hitches up her skirt, exposing her panties.

He tugs them down, dropping them to her knees.

Next? Of course, what it's all about. In he goes, sliding straight into her hot wetness. It would be a fuck from the best pornography, full of sounds and movements and grunts and groans, her breasts swinging free with each powerful thrust.

Hot and quick and hard, ending with a jet into her depths.

It's not over yet. Oh, no. There's the best for last. Clothes on, she leaves him spent and exhausted on the floor of the restroom, pants around his ankles, dignity ripped and shredded, remorse twisting his face into a crying baby's.

Out then, back to her table, to look across the lounge of the Pont Royal lounge at the woman and meet her gaze, Constance licks her lips, showing how much she's savored the destruction of their happiness.

* * * *

"Excuse me," the man said to the woman, rising from the table. "Be right back."

To this the woman just smiled, sweet and bright and innocent and alive.

18

No, Constance thought, shrinking even deeper than she had when the waiter had passed. *No*, again, and again still, a ringing refusal so loud it had to come out somehow, if just as a firm shaking of her head.

Picking up her purse from where she'd gently lowered it, she dug out her billfold, removed a clutch of money that could have been too much or not enough, and stood.

"Mademoiselle?" the waiter said as she moved towards and then past him, her only response an even more vigorous shaking of her head.

Outside, traffic rushed by, candy-enameled and chrome-highlighted, too-coarse engines sounding furious. Her gasps brought exhaust, smoke, and dust into her lungs, then out in a hard cough.

Steadily, her hands stopped shaking, her breaths came in slower and deeper draws. Intently not looking to the right as she began to walk, she avoided seeing the lounge of the Pont Royal and its comfort, refinement, elegance, and calmness. The way she was feeling — the way she'd been thinking — she wasn't worthy to sit in there and drink tea from fine china on a white linen tablecloth.

A few dozen meters away she realized that she'd had the car parked for her, that she'd have to return to the hotel to claim it. Not yet, though.

Eventually she had to stop walking, her feet in her new Italian shoes hurting too much to continue. Choosing a café at random, she walked in and sat. It could have been one of a hundred small bistros in Paris, but it could only have been in Paris— cigarettes burning in ashtrays, brass fixtures, and frosted glass windows.

She ordered a sherry. It came quickly.

"Merci," Constance said, nodding to the young waitress.

Fallen, that's what she'd done, through the fine tile floors of the purity of the Hôtel Pont Royal and down into a clamorous, smoky, crude café.

Looking into the rosy liquor, she felt like crying. It was one thing to want to hurt her husband, to try and make Escobar feel like she felt. But it was another to want to do it to a pair of strangers, to ruin their love as well.

Slowly, though, as she sipped her way through one sherry and then into another, her mind began to clear — or at least become reflective, lit by a good, inward glow from the liquor.

This was not where she wanted to be.

She wasn't happy. But she wasn't happy anywhere — not at home, not at a flash and dazzle party, not even in the lounge of the Pont Royal.

Happy? When was the last time she'd been happy?

Happy was laughter, happy was warmth, happy were hands on her body. The Hôtel Pont Royal was good, even special, but not because it made her happy. It'd been good, special, because it'd been a good place to hide — a cold china, frozen linen, icily elegant retreat.

Happiness meant not caring if the world was dirty, cold, or noisy. Happiness meant not caring if you were rich or poor. Happiness meant not caring — good or bad — about being recognized in the street.

The phone came out of her purse, still a strange silver plastic object to her. A memory slipped into her mind: he so patiently explaining its functions to her, how she could call his studio, call her mother, call her father, call anyone at any time. Constance hadn't liked that, because to her, calling out just meant that someone might call in, and she hated to be interrupted, but the shine of his eyes, the quickness of his grin, the beautiful tones of his voice had entranced her into sitting through his instructions long after she comprehended any of it.

Flipping the phone open, she nervously scrolled through the numbers. Telling herself she only wanted to hear his voice again, she heard the hollowness of her own thoughts, recognized what was deeper, below her surface: a need to laugh, to be warm, to have his hands on her body.

About to push a button, about to connect — no, reconnect — with her husband, the tiny machine buzzed, an irritated insect, and rang, a flat mechanical bell. The number displayed wasn't familiar, but she answered it anyway.

Clumsy, lacking richness or subtlety, the woman's voice spoke a version of French learned in a classroom. She introduced herself as Sheri, English obviously her first language, and her uniquely flat tones labeled her as American.

"Would you mind if I asked you a few questions?" the woman asked.

Usually self-conscious of her own accent, Constance found that the reporter's awkwardness made her less so.

"Now is not a good time," she replied.

"This won't take more than a minute."

"Very well," she found herself saying even as her thumb remained over the phone's red button. "But I can't speak for very long."

"I understand. I'll keep this short."

The reporter explained that she was scheduled to interview Escobar, but wanted to talk with Constance first.

"Since you know him better than anyone."

"Yes, I imagine that I would," she replied, unsure.

"What was he like before he was ... well, 'discovered' is the word everyone uses."

"My husband has always been a painter. His recent success only gives him a wider canvas." *Yes*, she thought, *that was good, a well-spoken lie.*

"Well, I ... I mean, I've heard that he's very focused, but he also has a very real sensuality about him. Aren't you worried about him being tempted?"

"No," Constance said, noticing that she was rhythmically flexing the fingers of her right hand. Consciously, she held her fingers flat on the marble table. "Because whatever happens to either of us, we will always be together. I love my husband and he loves me."

"That's nice, especially considering how many other couples seem to fall apart when one or both of them becomes famous."

"I wouldn't know about that."

"That's remarkable," the reporter said, her sly tone beginning to seriously annoy Constance. "I'd even say it was very, very rare."

"I love my husband and he loves me," she replied, then realizing she'd repeated herself, quickly added,"Yes, he is very sensitive, as all artists are, but he is also a kind and honest man."

"Oh? But even the best men can fall when presented with opportunity. Not that I'm saying that your husband has, but I do know it has happened to many men like him. It's not that unusual."

"Escobar never would," she said, knowing she was acting, on stage for the journalist as well as herself. "I do not appreciate what you are insinuating."

"No, no," the American said hastily. "I'm only saying that I've heard ... I mean it has happened to other people. That's all."

"I must be going," she said, thumb down hard on the button, the call silenced, the reporter gone.

In a nameless café, a place of full of hustle, bustle, clanging dishes, harsh voices, a gargling espresso machine, she sat, a chipped glass in front of her that used to contain cheap sherry.

Phone in her hand, ready to call.

But she didn't.

CHAPTER TWO

Jacqueline

I

Café latté before her, steam rising into a cool morning. Her phone rang with the first few bars of a top ten hit that had slid from number two to number eight just that morning. She took it out of her purse, silver and slim, and put it up to her ear.

"Oui?"

The voice on the other end was tight, professional, asking if she was Jacqueline — to which she replied with another "oui" — then identifying itself as a secretary working with a writer at *LeMonde*, and would she, Jacqueline, be available for an interview scheduled for later the next day, in the evening?

Wrapped in the latest fashion, trying to make themselves look less giggly and clumsy, two young girls four tables over chittered and chattered behind their menus, with careful, wide-eyed glances towards her.

"Oui," Jacqueline said to the young man on the phone. Details were exchanged: a date and a time.

"This number okay?"

"Oui," Jacqueline said.

They chatted for a bit, professional pleasantries, cooling latté on the table, then it was over. The phone went back into her bag.

The girls were still there, baby fat faces hunched down, voices soft yet sharply excited, looking at each other when not watching her.

Leaving her now cold, untouched coffee, Jacqueline paid and left before they could work up their courage to talk to her.

The day was hers, but there were always calls that could be made. From the bistro, she headed towards the Boulevard des Italiens. As she walked, she talked to Henri to see if her schedule had changed.

"Glad you called," her manager said, the clicking fingers on a computer keyboard in the background. Brusque and quick, he told her of a new appointment for a week later, some up-and-coming photographer wanting her for an outdoor shoot.

Henri wasn't one to chat so the conversation was short, but before he rang off, he said, "Keep up the good work."

Jacqueline grinned.

Next call was to Bois, to check on the dress she'd ordered. Putting a creased frown on her face, she got his creature, a lithe child who managed to sneer with each word she spoke.

"I'll-tell-him-you-called."

If he wasn't the best, Jacqueline never would have put up with that kind of treatment, but he was, so she did.

At a corner, the engines of traffic making progress difficult but not impossible, she checked her messages, the voice sounding far away even though the phone was pressed tightly against her ear. Henri, asking her to call, sounding even more professional, even more wound up, and, if possible, even tighter. Delete. A rambling voice, nasal accent making it difficult to understand came on next. It finally dawned on her that it was that British designer — Joan-Hart, was that it? — reminding Jacqueline they'd met at Lauren DeBarge's party, and on and on and on and on and on and "it would be so lovely" if Jacqueline had the name and number of some woman who'd been at the opening. Delete.

Next, a sharp-toothed voice, leaving a simple message: "Call when you can." Delete, then another punch of the tiny button to make sure.

That was all. But before she called her sister back, there were a few other calls to make. Across the street, traffic quieter now that it had stopped for the light, she dialed her friend Simone. It was only after her musical voice sang to leave a message that Jacqueline remembered Simone was probably still out on her shoot, modeling for Camille — *the* Camille — and she hung up without saying anything.

Pausing to look at a purse in a window, moving on when she decided it was just a bit too gaudy for this season, which was heavy on smooth Italian designs and simple hues, she next dialed Colette. The up-and-comer who'd asked for help in learning the business had seemed pleasant enough, and a chat with someone with wide, adoring eyes was just what Jacqueline needed, but there, too, she was greeted by a sing-song voice asking her to leave a message. Again, she did not.

About to dial again she was interrupted by a ring, the not-the-top-of-the-charts tune making her sigh. *Might as well*, she thought, answering it.

"Allo?" she said, knowing full well who it was.

"Bonjour, Jacqueline," said her sister, words cut and precise. "I hope I haven't caught you at a bad time."

"No, no," she said, transferring the phone from one hand to the other. "Just on the way to another posing, Audrey. Sorry I haven't called you back."

"I know you're so busy, Jacqueline, but since Maman was asking about you, I thought I'd give you a ring."

Knowing what the answer would be, she asked anyway, giving her sister that much, "How's she doing?"

"She's old, Jacqueline. She doesn't have a lot of time, but you know that."

Merde. "I know that, Audrey. I do. It's just that things have been so busy, what with the sittings and shoots and all. In fact, just the other day, Camile … Maybe you've heard of her? She was just saying–"

"We're proud of you, Jacqueline. Maman reads the papers and the magazines, or I read them to her if she's too tired. She was very excited by that painting of you, the one they say is good enough to hang in the Louvre."

"Oh, *that*! Escobar is such a sweetheart, a perfect gentleman. I'm so happy for him, of course. Have you seen the painting? Last I heard it's still on display in that gallery, the one near the Rue Christine. It's really nice, but then he has been described as a genius."

"No, I haven't seen it. I have to stay here with Maman. I hope I can see it sometime, though. I'm sure it's quite beautiful. Maman and I were just saying how you are too–"

Walking down the street, talking on her phone, Jacqueline danced around a rasta-curled boy also walking down the street, also talking on his phone. Walking, talking, dancing, she missed the last part of what her sister had said, replying as if she hadn't.

"I know I have to see her, Audrey, and I will. How about next week? Is that good for you?"

After a long moment, her sister said, "Anytime is okay. Come when you can. It would mean a lot to us."

"I promise, Audrey. I'll be there before you know it. I have another call coming in, darling," Jacqueline said quickly, even though she didn't, slipping her finger across the button to disconnect the call.

* * * *

A few lights, a few streets from the Boulevard, she stopped again, pulling out her phone and flicking through the address book for people to call. Names and numbers scrolled by on the tiny screen: this model, that friend, this photographer, that painter. She almost dialed, but then her fingers didn't complete the action that would ring *the* painter, and she went back to names and numbers flashing by.

Later, maybe later.

A newsstand on the corner displayed a copy of *ArtNews*. An old copy, last month's copy. *The* copy.

Just like every other time she really couldn't recognize herself in it, at least not the Jacqueline she saw in a mirror. Reds and blues, mostly. Strong strokes. Bright colors. Eyes, a nose, lips, ears, hair. A background that looked like fire. It didn't look like something that might hang in the Louvre, but that's where some people were saying it belonged.

Not that she'd argue with them. Never.

"How much for the copy of *ArtNews*, Monsieur?"

Lifting his grey-flecked beard from where it was folded up against a sadly faded sweater, the owner looked up at her from the racing form he was reading, eyes bloodshot.

"Eh? What did you say?"

"*ArtNews*," she repeated, reaching down and sideways to the rack, pulling the copy free. When it came, it took a copy of *Marie Claire* with it, causing *Claire* to tumble to the ground and into a small pool of water.

"You have to buy that," the owner grumbled, red-streaked eyes narrowing at her, daring her to argue with his pronouncement concerning his tiny kingdom.

"Of course," she said, holding the *ArtNews* so it faced him, her hands not obscuring the painting on the cover.

Not recognizing her, or pretending not to, he made her change, and went back to his form. Before she turned to go, she glanced down at the other magazine, the one swelling up, pages wrinkling as it soaked up old rain. Its cover, brand new, this month's, was a photograph, not a painting. A photo of Simone.

Holding her *ArtNews* close to her chest, Jacqueline left the newsstand and began to make her way slowly down the street.

* * * *

Home. She really didn't want to go home. Not yet. The sun was still in the sky, though lowering towards the rooftops; calls could be made, though none of the faintly glowing numbers or the people attached to them appealed to her. There were shops to browse, though none of the silks and satins, beads and belts, appealed to her.

So, sun lowering, phone stuck in her purse, the shops of the Boulevard des Italiens exhausted of potential new outfits, she resigned herself that home was where she should be heading.

But she still didn't want to go there. On a corner, watching glass glide by, the lights of the city reflecting in their windows, she caught a new kind of illumination. A coffee, she decided, seeing the windows of the cafe, would be nice.

"Bonjour, Madame," said the hostess as Jacqueline entered. Against the growing dust, the inside was too almost dazzling: polished brass, pale marble, frosted glass, the too-bright smile on the young woman waving her towards a table.

"Café latté, si vous plait," Jacqueline said, making herself comfortable. She pulled her chair closer to the polished table top and set her purse on top of the table, *ArtNews* lay next to the purse, her face as seen by Escobar, peering up at her.

How long did she look at it? Long enough to make a coffee, obviously, as a cup and saucer suddenly clicked and clacked down onto the marble. "Oh, that's beautiful," said the hostess.

"Pardon?" Jacqueline said, looking up from the swirling dark liquid, its steam adding to the sauna spilling from the nearby bubbling brass espresso machine.

"That. Your magazine. It's a beautiful picture."

"Thank you."

That was it. That was all. The hostess, as sparkling and bright as the café where she worked, moved away to chat with other customers.

Feeling warm and glowing, from the compliment as well as the coffee, Jacqueline stayed until she finished her cup. Then, purse over her arm, magazine in her hand, she left some coins and stepped towards the door.

Hand on the handle to push it open, she realized something, a shiver like the night outside. Madame. The hostess had called her Madame.

Then her phone sang that less-than-popular tune again. Pulling it quickly out of her purse, she glanced down at the screen, the text message there from Annette, another model, another sort-of friend. PARTY? it said.

II

So, home it was.

From the cab, returning the driver's grin and handing him a generous tip, she went to the foyer door. Bernardo, the doorman, as always showing his old man teeth as she shuffled to the door, turned the gleaming steel handle to let her in.

"Bonjour," he said, dipping his head as she swept past him and toward the lift.

Then up to the clean lines of the hall, the clean lines of her door, the clean lines of her apartment, the door shutting behind her with a soft hush of expensive precision.

It was a beautiful place: a glowing wooden slab of a coffee table, polished swirls and perfect knots; floor-to-ceiling prism windows, the clear blue of thick protection, the view beyond a faery kingdom of late twilight Paris. Terzani lamps hovered high above, glimmering crystal throwing brilliant perfection all around. Against one wall sat a Campaniello sofa, creamy leather as soft as a blown kiss; on the other, a Matteucci-designed sideboard, tranquility in luxurious teak.

It was a place to show, to stroll through in silk. The few pictures that hung were of her. Subtle, only the most transparent of ghostly arrogance in black and white photographs.

Heels clicking on the Italian flagstones that led from the entry to the bedroom, she carefully laid her purse on the bedside table, cautious that it would not fall back against the stiff cream diamond shade of the Estiluz lamp, turning its perfect placement into clumsy misalignment.

Wood and steel, crystal and stone, bright and flawless. It was a beautiful flat and she was proud of it. With a few practiced pushes of buttons on the lacquer-black stereo system, a mix of the most popular songs of the week surged from hidden speakers, bass and treble putting dance into her movements as she slipped off her dress, a satin descent adding a drum fan to the thundering music.

Then there was the shower. She was proud of the apartment, the way it had all come together from her suggestions and an expert decorator's skill, but she loved the bathroom. Bra and panties neatly lowered into the hamper, she stepped into the elegant, obsidian-tiled stall and, with a few turns of a well-tooled Rohl faucet, the water roared down onto her, drowning out the teeth-on-edge chilling lines and eternal coldness of the apartment with warm splashing.

On *her* body. Out there, it was theirs; in here, it was hers.

Water jetted a steaming massage on her face, down her neck, between her breasts, onto her belly, on one thigh then the other as she shifted and moved. The building had an old outside, but the plumbing was brand new. She had plenty of hot water.

Hand roaming, she brought a mild soap to her face — something benign that wouldn't argue with her usual, more serious regimen. It came off when she put her face under the spray, lather rolling down her belly and then spiraling down the drain. From the same tiny shelf came another bottle, a dollop that cost as much as a good dinner out. It was health in a pearlescent plastic bottle, a specially formulated glow of sensuality. All so she'd look like a goddess for the cameras or the brush of a master painter.

It also felt damned good. The wraps and plucks and peels and astringents and masks and cucumbers and the rest were okay sometimes, painful others, but that little bit of slipping and sliding felt wonderful.

Fingers spread, she applied it everywhere: her belly and around and around the perfect dimple of her navel, the gentle rises of her ribs to her thighs, along the tight muscles of her slim neck, the bumps of her spine to the sculpted rises of each rear cheek, shoulder to shoulder then down to the upsweep of her breasts.

Clean lines carefully maintained and perfected, everything in its place: an ideal form. The apartment as well as herself.

But in the shower, they were just breasts that felt good to touch, an ass that was thrilling to caress, and between her thighs … That was the best place of all to touch or caress.

In the shower, she could. Once, after the apartment had been finished, she'd tried, sprawling out on the vast black, silk-sheeted bed, but she couldn't. It was only in frustration when she'd taken a shower to relax that she realized, away from the cold lines and precise corners, for the first time, she was actually comfortable.

Hot water. Lather, rinse, repeat. Under the pounding spray, Jacqueline put everything aside, except her hands and her body.

Cupped, then squeezed, then kneaded, then thumb and forefinger to nipple, then pull, then pinch, then squeezed hard, the right then the left then together, putting her face into the stream of water, opening her mouth to let the jet pound her tongue — her breasts.

Caressed, then slapped, then spanked, then gripped hard, then walked apart, then hand down between the right and the left, touching the back of her lips and running a finger from where they were swelling up fat and plump past the wrinkle of her anus and then up to where they blended into her back — the cheeks of her ass.

Slicked, then relished, then stroked, then spread wide, then a finger seeking the tiny hard point among slippery hot folds, a dance, a tinkle, a stroke, a rub, a circling, then to make it last longer, away from it to explore the much hotter, much wetter depths of herself.

From one to another then back again, one hand on a breast, another between her legs, to one hand on a breast and another fondling herself from behind, to both hands on her breasts pulling and rubbing her nipples, to both hands exploring the molten heat and throbbing clit of her quim, to both hands rubbing and squeezing the muscles of her ass.

Which fantasy? They bubbled and roared in her head. Bent over the railing of a yacht bobbing on a too-blue Aegean Sea? On a beach in San Tropez at midnight, priceless skirt hitched up around her hips, alone except for the rock star kneeling between her legs? Masturbating in the changing room of a boutique while a famous photographer snapped shot after shot of her performance? Naked, maybe, on the runaway, the applause of the crowd like a million hands on her tight and fine body?

Knees buckling, breath wheezing, eyes closing, hands out to catch an-almost-collapsing fall, she moaned in thundering release, an orgasm that brought stars to her eyes and quivers and quakes to her legs.

Sitting in the bottom of the black well of the shower, she panted for a few minutes, letting the body rush fade to a general bliss. Then, strength returning to her legs, she got up, soaped and lathered again, and stepped out of the shower. Taking dozens of controlling, calming breaths, she looked in the mirror, frowning at her wet disarray.

Hair, facial, makeup — so much to do if she was going to be presentable for the party.

Without a smile on her face, she set to work.

* * * *

The cab driver knew the way, so the trip was quick and efficient; merging elegantly with the city traffic, gliding up to and then away from lights, never getting too close or too far from the cars in front of them, and not a single tap of the horn.

Getting out of the taxi as carefully as he'd driven, Jacqueline stepped gracefully out and away, stylishly turned back, and carefully opened her little purse. She passed him a neat fold of bills: the fare and a handsome tip for his eyes surreptitiously watching her in the rearview mirror and for never once calling her Madame.

Annette lived away from things, on a barely lit street in a nearly forgotten corner of the city that, only a few years ago, would have been dead to everything but the rumbling and quaking of late-night trucks hauling this or that. The avenue was still mostly dark, but possessed a mischievous hope of life. Music faintly played and scurried, bouncing between the heavily shuttered warehouses, as stretched shadows danced on their plastered walls.

Closer to the party, the tune got louder, identifiable as a techno beat, and the shadows shrank to a handful of men and women who'd spilled out of Annette's brightly lit doorway, smoking and chatting and drinking and laughing.

"Darling!" came Daniel's chiming laugh as Jacqueline walked up.

The royalty's here, Jacqueline thought as arms wrapped around her and a pair of lips landed in a flighty kiss on her cheek. Kings as well as queens.

"Now all the pretty people are here!"

Letting Daniel lead her inside, she laughed and smiled and kissed and hugged her way through the pressing crowd that was either leaving early or arriving fashionably late.

"So glad you made it." Annette was elegant and simple, a nymph wrapped in Audrey Hepburn purple, with a blast of Monroe lipstick. "It wouldn't have been a good party without you."

"I was just telling her the very same thing," the dresser said, uncoiling himself from around her arm. "Now you two chat or

31

something fashionable while I go mingle and get me some of those wonderful canapés before some fat cow eats them all."

Air kisses and he was gone, sliding between a photographer and a junior set designer from the opera.

"So how have you been, Jackie? Bet things have been crazy since that posing."

"Oh, you know how it is," Jacqueline said, who hated to be called anything but her full name. Annette, she knew, didn't know *how it was* as she was new to the profession. "Phone ringing all the time, one job after another."

"I can imagine," the other woman said, waving past Jacqueline's shoulder at someone moving through the crowd. "But being busy has got to be better than not having anything going on, right? Wanted rather than not and all that."

"I guess. But to be honest, things have been so crazy lately, not having something would be a nice little vacation."

"Well, I hope you get a break. Don't want you to be working too hard."

"In fact, just today I got a call from Henri for a new assignment. He always seems to be calling me for one thing or another. A new photographer. Jorge, I think his name was."

"Oh, I know Jorge! Such a sweet man, and very talented. I saw him ... two weeks ago, I think? Did a lovely set with him. In fact, he said he wanted me to come back and see him, and maybe not just to pose again, if you know what I mean."

Jacqueline did, but didn't say. "That's very nice, Annie," she did say, knowing the other woman also didn't like to have her name trimmed down. "I'm so glad for you. I hope Jorge and I will have just as nice a time when I see him."

"Oh, I'm sure you will, Jackie. I'm sure you will. He even told me he was looking to work with someone ... more unique."

Face flush, face hot. Jacqueline knew what Annette meant, but still didn't say. "Well, they say being unique is far better than being common, Annie."

Then, before the other woman could say something, Jacqueline pretended to see someone behind her. "Oh, look," she forcefully gushed and chirped. "Isn't that Depaulo? I must say hello to him. See you later, Annie."

Stepping around her and away into the crowd, she turned to look behind her, catching Annette's eye and, with a royal wave of her hand, Jacqueline said, "Thank you for inviting me, by the way. It looks to be quite a lovely party," before a curtain of men with drinks and women laughing like musical instruments came between them.

* * * *

Toasted fresh shrimp set in a bed of tapenade, on a tiny wedge of dark rye; some kind of rich pate on a light cracker; carefully manicured cones of fragrant cheese; summer pears dusted with cinnamon and sugar.

She'd drifted somehow, or was moved by the unconscious Brownian motion of the party, from the front room to the hall and eventually back to the kitchen. Kisses and hugs had preceded her retreat — or exile, but she didn't think about that — through the low-ceilinged space. Compliments were fluttered and gossip was acidly whispered to her as she shuffled from one area of the apartment to the other, bubbles of amusement between the two. Escobar's name came up often, as did the possibility of his portrait of her hanging in the Louvre, but all the flattery couldn't melt the frozen smile on her face.

Inexplicably tired, she rocked back and forth in her heels, stretching one foot and then the other, trying not to let the spikes of either catch in the tiles that floored Annette's kitchen. Unlike Jacqueline's clean and cold lines, the other woman's apartment was tight and cluttered. Wrought iron shelves up against thick plaster walls, curls and coils of sometimes fake brass and veined blue glass, and sometimes real vines; plates painted with scenes of pastoral simplicity. It looked more like the rooms of a dowager artist than a runway walker.

The food looked tempting, but even though she ached to do something, anything, other than just stand there, she resisted. It was one thing to be someone who'd drifted from the living room to the kitchen, an added shame to be the one there stuffing her face.

"Pardon! God, I'm sorry. I didn't mean to stare."

Not having noticed him come in, she started, catching her heel-teetering before it turned into an embarrassing stumble.

"N-no, it's alright," she said, shooting her smile towards what she thought was a warmer and more sincere one.

"Nothing looking appetizing?" he replied, stepping all the way into the tight kitchen.

"Oh, no. It all looks fantastic. I'm just not all that hungry."

"At least let me get you a glass of wine."

33

Did she really want some? Older than she was by what looked to be five maybe even seven years, he moved well, like he knew at all times were his elbows and knees were. Salt and pepper beard, salt and pepper hair, but with a face that said the spices were premature. A ready and bright smile, blue eyes that flashed with light humor. He was dressed down, in just a pair of jeans and a similarly blue denim shirt, which could have meant a lot of things, but what she took to suggest the kind of comfortable that came with success.

"That'd be nice."

"An impertinent little vintage," he said, choosing an unopened bottle from the white linen catering table and filling two glasses. "Cheers!"

The chime of their toast rang loud in the tiny kitchen.

"Merci," she said, trying to figure out exactly where he fit in, casting him in quickly flickering roles of agent, director, photographer, journalist, painter, designer, hairdresser. She rejected her casting as he was too nice, too polite, too sloppy, not sloppy enough, too smart, too charming.

"Very nice," she said, after having a sip.

"You know, I actually had to fight to urge to say 'not as nice as you.' Beauty," he sighed, "always makes me a fool."

Laughing, she swirled the contents of her glass. "But you did say it."

"Merde. So I did. A fool. A complete and total one at that. See what I mean?"

"I've met worse."

"I could say 'I bet,' but that would imply that you're surrounded by legions of fools. But what I would have meant, if I had said that, is that you're so handsome that you must reduce other men to being that way. Fools, I mean."

Banter, not nerves. Had it been the latter, she probably would have put the cold smile back on, maybe even pretended that she had to be somewhere else. But it wasn't — at least not completely — so she didn't.

Instead, she said, "We're all allowed to be fools sometimes. Even the best of us."

"That I find very hard to believe," he said with staged solemnity. "I'm afraid you've reduced to me other clichés. I know I've seen you somewhere. You have to be part of the business."

"Very possibly," she said. "I am."

"I knew it! But you are far too beautiful for that, unless you're legendary and I am simply too much of a fool to be aware of it. A fact we have already established."

Banter, not smarm. Had it been the latter she absolutely would have put the frozen grin back on, definitely pretended she had to be somewhere else, fast. But it wasn't — it didn't feel that way at all — so, again, she didn't.

"I'd hardly call you a fool."

"Normally I wouldn't either. But tonight, mademoiselle, I am a complete and utter one."

Sipping his own glass, he seemed to take a deep breath at the same time.

"Believe it or not, this isn't easy."

Raising a perfectly executed eyebrow — one that Rodriquez had called, pausing in the middle of a barrage of machine-gun rapid strobe shooting, 'the best in the business' — she said, "And why is that?"

Slowly, almost solemnly, he answered, "You're unearthly. Almost too beautiful. The first time I saw you, I really didn't know what to think. If I were a painter, I know I wouldn't be good enough to paint you. Same if I were a photographer. I'd never be able to do you justice."

The banter had been fun, a little circling game. This was ... different, but she still didn't feel the need to retreat. If not painter or photographer, then maybe an agent, director, journalist, designer, hairdresser?

"You are too kind. I'm really just a woman."

"I would never call you 'just' anything. But then, by now, you must be getting tired of these asinine compliments."

Flushed, she laughed to cover it and swallowed a bit more wine to cover it even more.

"I wouldn't call them that. You're very sweet."

Salt and pepper rose at the corners, his grin wide and animated.

"It's my pleasure."

Breaking off from looking into her eyes, he glanced to the left, out of the room.

"Things seem to be dying down a bit. All and all, I think it was a success, but you usually can't know about such things until the morning after."

"Well, I had a good time. If that helps."

"It's the only thing that matters," he said, taking a bow. "I should go make a quick check, I guess. Shake some hands. Kiss some cheeks. It's been a true pleasure. Honestly."

Extending his hand, she saw elegant fingers, clean nails. No rings.

"Luc," he said. "Luc Bressan."

His grip was light but present. Lips to the back of her hand, dry, firm, and elegantly and respectfully quick.

"It's been a pleasure," she echoed, meaning it. Feeling the need to say something else, she added, "Jacqueline Montelle," even though she suspected he already knew it.

Hands parting, he looked up at her, catching, but this time holding, her gaze.

"Jacqueline Montelle," he said, saying her name with careful weight. "I will hate myself more for not asking this than for saying so, but would you like to have a drink with me?"

Choices visualized and dismissed again and again with cinematic speed: home, staying at the party, dinner alone. Puzzled, then: what was he if not painter or photographer or agent, director, journalist, designer, or hairdresser?

Whichever, he glowed and smiled being around her, which did the same to her.

"Oui," she said, putting out her arm so that he could lead her out.

III

The wine bar at the end of the still-dark street was swollen with similar refugees from Annette's party. To get in and get glasses would have meant sliding shoulders across shoulders and mumbling too many "pardons," so by unspoken mutual consent, they moved towards the distant traffic flashes of a major Parisian artery.

As they walked, he occasionally made a quick witty remark about the party, to which she responded with a short pulse of laughter. His arm, still around hers, was warm and strong.

Even though they hadn't had that drink, and she'd only had two small glasses at Annette's, Jacqueline floated, drifted, bobbed along at his side. Had it been that long since she'd been wobbly on the arm of a man?

It hadn't. Not really. Nameless gropes and sometimes more at other thundering and pulsing parties, hands on her body, between her legs, cupping her breasts as techno vibrated her bones. A long afternoon only a month or so ago, sliding between the sheets at a moderate Roman hotel with Bertoli, a smooth-chested and muscled pretty boy. But that had been nothing but a sticky and slick release, the stress of them both parading for the editors of a new Italian fashion magazine, let go in cocktails in the bar then growling and scratching in his room.

Afterward, they had returned to the gliding steps and haughty demeanor of their professions, weighing the value of each other's company on what could be gained, or harmed, by their association. Bertoli hadn't called afterward, but she hadn't called him either.

Traffic, the roar of cheap cars and the purr of expensive ones, and she looked up from where she'd been looking into herself to see they were at the Avenue. A few meters towards the rushing traffic was another café, this one with only a few couples bent over tables. More than enough room for one more evening pairing.

"How about here?" Luc asked, with a nod towards the door.

"It looks nice. Let's," she said, with a smile towards him.

At a table, a bottle and two glasses soon brought, they chatted with short, grinning bursts about nothing — or nothing she remembered. Looking at him, at his honest black and white hair and beard, at his sincere laughter, she tried to place him yet again, to figure out what he was.

But despite her confusion about his role, she still didn't ask.

"This is quite amazing," he said, eyes twinkling at her over the rim of his glass.

"Actually, I think it's more than a bit average," she said, thinking he meant the vintage.

Shock and disappointment were there on his face, a lowering of peppered eyebrows, a turning down of the corners of his mouth.

Before he could say anything, a laugh came up and out of her with loud sincerity that made the few other late-night sippers and chatters turn towards them.

"The wine, I mean. Not you."

"Merci," he said, relief evident on his face. "Had me worried there for a second."

It continued from there: chatter, chuckles, smiles, then a surreptitious touching of his hand on hers, hers not moving away; she pouring for him, he pouring for her.

If not painter or photographer or an agent, director, journalist, designer, hairdresser, then what? It was important to her, but that

night, his opinion of her as the most beautiful woman in the world
was all that mattered.

* * * *

He lived nearby, or at least within a reasonable walk. When they
left the little café, she thought about Danielle. A vertical line of a girl,
streamlined and frightfully purposeful, she'd told Danielle one day as
they sat in the bar during a hiatus in a long Danish swimsuit shoot
that it was all a game: the industry, her appearance, people, the world,
everything. It was a something you either lost or won. Her way of
winning one battle was to make a man beg for her, to put herself on
top of every facet — from flirt to kiss to strip to fuck. To make him
wait and wait and wait until he'd practically explode, then after he'd
had a taste, make him do it all over again.

Luc's arm was around her waist, a nervous daring that made her
want to laugh loudly again. Playfully, she took his hand away, waving
a warning finger at his panicked face.

"Not too forward," she stage-whispered.

It *was* a game. Gone from it after she lost by marrying some
third-rate director of commercials, Danielle was right, even if she was
a poor player. Maybe not a painter or a photographer, but perhaps an
agent, director, journalist, designer, or hairdresser, Luc was dangling
at the end of her hook; and although she wasn't going to make him
beg, she was enjoying her own version of Danielle's competition.

But by the time their walk ended at a heavy oak door in another
dark and half-forgotten curl of a Paris street, she had to admit to
herself that he was scoring considerably as well. Eyes shimmering
with both desire and awe, his touches were equally warm, then heated.

At the door, they kissed for the first time. Not planned, not
strategized, no rook to king, no grand slam, just an occurrence: his
key in his lock, a turn to look at her, she moving in, he moving in,
then lips to lips.

Danielle would have been disappointed. Jacqueline wasn't.

The game was completely abandoned beyond the very modern
and very heavy metal door: a narrow flight of stairs climbing steeply
upward, diamond-plate steps, and a brass railing completing the
industrial ascent.

On the first few steps, they moved in unison but apart. As the stairs
narrowed, it pushed them together — an architectural matchmaker.

Whose hands first? Hard to say. Maybe at the same time, but definitely different places: her fingers sliding between the buttons of his shirt, tips touching the curls and swirls of his coarse chest hair; his dropping down to the flat of her back and then the rise of her ass. In response to her, he grinned and leaned forward for another kiss. In response to him, she pulled herself closer for another kiss.

It was hot, it was wet, it was strong, and it traveled from her lips and tongue down her body, ringing her already aching nipples and down between her legs where it released a weight and warmth of readiness.

As the kiss continued — hotter, wetter, stronger — she felt Luc's own response against her, persistent, long, and very hard.

Before she was even aware, she'd slipped her hand from between those buttons and had dropped it down to, instead, a zipper. A grip told her that her initial reaction hadn't been exaggerated: indeed very long and very, very hard.

He moaned into her mouth, breaking the seal between them to give a quick series of pants. His hands went from caresses to fervent squeezing of her ass, which made her even more daring in her fondling of him.

Somehow during all this, the door to the street had been closed, which she realized was good because she was burning far too much to have cared if they had an audience or not.

For some reason, what was happening struck her as funny, and she went from hissing between her teeth in her own melody of excitement to giggling into his shoulder.

"Shouldn't ... we get upstairs?" she whispered into blue denim.

"Oui, oui," he said, his own stammer deep and rough.

Turning away was very difficult. Their hands had become powerful magnets, not wanting to break from their touchings, holding, strokings, and kneadings.

Leading the way, she took the steps slowly in her dizziness. Holding the railing tightly — instantly wishing it was his own muscular pole she was gripping — the attraction between them grew too strong again, especially for him, as she almost immediately felt his hands cup and then grip her ass. Stopping, each foot on a different step, she hissed and pushed into him.

Fine silk sliding. She felt like she was going to pass out. Thankfully, she did not.

Knowing what he would be seeing as he slid her dress up made her even hotter, even wetter. She hadn't selected the lacy thong with the intention of it being seen, had made no plans to show it to anyone, which made it all the more exciting. The thrill of their mutual surprise; she for being revealed, he for seeing.

A kiss, one on each cheek. A ritual. Holding back for two simple gestures of affection. Then his hands, one on each cheek, and a gentle parting — and as he did, she felt herself further, and almost completely, liquefy. She might have been showing him the silken thread of her panties, but she also knew she was also showing her very plump, very wet lips.

Knew, as well, because he touched them. Again, slowly, cautiously, almost respectfully: one single finger beginning at the top then down and going down, then in the barest amount.   The contact, that barest touch, was a bolt of lightning. It made her gasp, hiss, and moan from there, her clit, to *there*, her lips.

Spreading her legs, giving him permission, demanding his attention, she pushed toward him.

At first, she thought he was going to drive her completely insane. He rubbed her swollen lips, played with the muscular ring that introduced her vagina, tickled where quim became anus, and then circled but not quite touched that pulsing button.

Just when she was about to scream in frustration, to stop her heavy panting to yell at the top of her lungs, he stopped his teasing. Tap, tap, tap, rub, rub, rub, he went, playing her, and in playing her, drawing out steady deep-body moans instead of any kind of demand.

It came — her coming — unexpectedly. Normally, even with the most sophisticated of partners, she had to descend into a fantasy, picture instead of boyish models, anonymous fucks on pulsing dance floors, or sweaty managers in dressing rooms, someone else and somewhere else. Places of refinement and sophistication, fine silks on her back, jewels around her neck, and men rippling with muscles or immaculate hair. This time, however, in a stairway off a cheap street in a cheap part of the city, she screamed louder than she ever had before.

Knees failing, she collapsed onto the stairs, at least partially. She would have collapsed all the way onto the steel steps, but Luc put his hands under her, supporting her until she could see, breathe, and carefully pull herself up onto her feet.

Then, he took her hand and led her to the top.

Not really looking, not really seeing, she didn't perceive the apartment as anything but quick images, tiny details that slipped past her glistening perspiration, fluttering heart, weak legs, panting breaths. Huge, very modern kitchen — all polished brass and chrome, streaked marble, and blue tinted glass — full of well-used pots and pans, and plastic bins full of greens and even some browns; huge dining table roughly hewn out of what looked like one huge slab of mahogany, surrounded by mismatched chairs. Low bookcases containing a jumbled chaos of bright covers, then the bed, a great pad of an unmade futon.

Then, the bed. On it in a tumble of hands and lips and clothes. She licked his fingers, tasting herself. She nibbled his lips, tasting herself there as well, though not as strong.

He sprawled, shirt unbuttoned, head between his own huge pillows. Eyes glittering in the low light, looking entranced, hypnotized.

Hypnotized, by her. She knew that, understood that. It was more exciting to her than any cold tryst with plucked and waxed models, any ham-handed gropes or bathroom blowjobs in clubs, any career moves on her knees in dressing rooms — far better than any gleaming fantasy of yachts and gold and jewels and applause.

Jacqueline was the woman he'd heard about, read about, seen in magazines, walking the runway on television, and hanging on gallery walls as immortalized by a true and spectacular genius. She was the woman in the portrait by Escobar.

Here and now, just for him, she was the legendary Jacqueline.

While sitting on rumpled sheets, she strolled into his most intimate of dreams, of fantasies, by reaching down and taking hold of the hem of her fine dress and carefully, almost cruelly, pulling it steadily up and up and up and then off, to fall loosely to the floor.

No bra. Hard nipples. Shimmering sweat between them. His expression said it all: awe, delight, amazement, and most of all, total and complete desire.

Rising slowly up from where he'd been sprawled, he gazed at her with every climbing inch, clearly drinking in her renowned beauty, absorbing every detail of her body, ending up nose to nose, looking deeply into her eyes.

Locked together, she saw herself reflected in his gaze: saw herself the way he saw her.

Perfect.

Flawless.

Ideal.

Beauty.

Then his clothes were gone and he joined her in nothing but skin and sweat. From a corner table, a quick moment of reality, a tiny plastic wrapper tossed to the floor, a condom rolled down the length of his cock.

While he lay on his back, bobbing with desire, she climbed on top of him, positioning herself carefully so that he was just *there*, at her entrance.

Down. In. Together. His dream, his fantasy, made real.

And hers — in being his — as well.

IV

During the night, two more times. Twilight hands, twilight bodies, not enough illumination from the street outside to see much beyond the smooth rise of a hip, the halo of uncombed hair, a hand outlined against the soft gloom, the gleam and glimmer of eyes in delight, or teeth in passionate smiles.

Then sleep, heavy and deep. Warm, wrapped right in thick blankets and satin sheets, it was dreamless and still. No tossing. No turning.

Sunlight woke her, intense brightness coming through those same windows, a hard day heading straight into her rapidly blinking eyes. Rubbing them, she sat up, a sudden sharp concern with it that she was alone in the bed.

Eyes clearing finally, she saw him at the far end of the room. Naked, on the phone, he paced back and forth in and out of the kitchen.

Watching him, she grinned, trying to decide how to draw him back to bed. She never felt more beautiful. More perfect. Agent, director, journalist, designer, hairdresser — whatever he was, she liked being his ideal, his dream come true.

"I'm happy you liked them. I did think they came out especially well," he was saying into his tiny silver phone. Seeing her see him, he grinned back and blew her a kiss, his eyes as wide as his broad gesture.

"Sorry I didn't hang around to check in with the cleanup," he continued, stopping to listen to a response. "Excellent. I knew Marie would take care of it. She's wonderful."

More that only he could hear, then, "Jacqueline? Why, yes, we had a wonderful time. Thanks for asking."

Still more, still only what he could hear. Finally, "Well, I'm very pleased that you're pleased. If you're having another event, please keep Pomme in mind for all your catering needs."

"Good morning, beautiful," he said, stretching as he walked back towards the bed. Closing the phone, he set it neatly on the dining room table as he passed. "That was nice. Annette said the party went wonderfully. I'm glad because normally I hang around to make sure, but Marie is very capable and ... well, with you on my arm, I really couldn't think about anything else."

At the edge of the bed, he sat, arm reaching out to stroke one of her bare legs. "She asked about you, by the way. Hope you don't mind if I said we had a nice night. No details, mind you — I do try to be a gentleman in such matters. No gossip! You know, if you ever want to quit waitressing, I would be more than willing to take you on, as it were. I always need servers, and, well, my food would taste like the ambrosia of the gods by just being near such a beautiful and amazing woman ... I'm sorry, did I say something wrong?"

* * * *

Her feet hurt, but she kept walking. She didn't know where was going until she turned one corner and recognized the neighborhood.

The day was busy, lots of people about: doing this, doing that, on the way from some things, going to other things. Jacqueline knew she must not have looked her best, with the same dress she'd worn the night before, scuffed heels, smeared make-up, hair frayed and wild, but even though she still cared, she was too lost, too alone amid all the bustle and rush to do anything about it.

A caterer.

A police car rushed by, its wailing cutting through any the other sound that day. It made her stop on the corner, and with the stop came a few other sensations with the ache in her ears from the gendarme's siren. Her eyes burned and smarted, swimming in close-to-crying tears; her feet hurt, a pulsing throb from her toes to her ankles and then up her legs; her chest ached, muscles fisting in her rib cage.

She'd gone home with the caterer.

Breathing in, breathing out, biting her lip, she fought the battle of her tears. One battle won, her nose pulled a surprise, end-run strategy

43

and began to run freely. Tissue, she needed a tissue. Her purse, there was probably one in there. Swinging it around, she popped the clasp and began to dig.

She'd fucked the caterer.

Cell phone, sunglasses case, makeup, wallet, keys, miscellaneous slips of paper, tissue, wadded, wrinkled, torn but well enough. Stepping away from the edge of the curb, back close to but not touching the wall of a dry cleaning establishment, she dabbed, then gingerly blew in what she hoped, prayed, was a dignified, ladylike manner.

Annette knew.

The damp tissue went into a nearby trash bin. Taking a deep breath she tried to release some of the tension, to shake it away, to push it out. Fingers through her hair, she tried to tame it, snapping knots carelessly, not caring in her rush for tsk-tsks from hairdressers in the future.

The neighborhood was familiar. She was real close. Why not? She might as well stop by. Yes, that was a good idea.

Across the street, down the avenue. In the near distance, just a few hundred meters or so, the pure white of the façade. Was she presentable? Suspecting she wasn't, she decided to go ahead anyway.

A waitress.

L'Art, that was the name of it — the name of the gallery — the memory bubbling as she walked up to the door. A small place, known for the pomposity of its name and one recent discovery. Four months. Was that how long it had been since she'd been there last?

Flashing cameras, lenses turned towards her; tart champagne in fine crystal; black beads of fine caviar on fine porcelain; journalists asking questions; beautiful women. Faces dark with jealousy: Escobar looking uncomfortable — his wife looking even more uncomfortable.

Four months? It felt like only a few days. Jacqueline wished it really had been four days since the party, the unveiling of that new work, a month later the cover *ArtNews* with the same beautiful work gracing its cover.

The painting. Her portrait by Escobar.

Seeing it again would be good. No, it would be wonderful. It would make her feel better. Not like a woman who'd fuck a caterer. Who people thought was a waitress. It would make her feel beautiful; make her special.

Adjusting her dress, trying to sweep off a few of the more noticeable wrinkles, she held off opening the door and going in — like a present where the anticipation was almost as precious as the contents.

But then she stopped smoothing her silk. *L'Art* was small, just one large, pale-walled space. To one side was a desk, a slab of heavy blue glass. On the other, a narrow ascent of stairs to probably an office.

It was still early, the gallery clearly just having opened. It was empty aside from the owner, a man whose name she couldn't remember. Large and slow, yet dressed in a finely tailored suit, he busied himself with papers and documents, wide back to her and the front window.

One wall was that glass; the other two were for art. On one of them — she looked once, then again and again — were the explosive colors, brilliant sweeps, refined compositions of Escobar.

But none of them were her. None of them were the painting he'd done of her. It was gone.

A waitress. He thought he'd spent the night making love to a waitress — a plain, ordinary, waitress.

Not Jacqueline.

V

During her second shower that evening, the phone rang. An expired, tired, past-its-prime tune. Even though it came as hot water was smashing down on her, steam clouding the room, she still quickly twisted off the flow and jumped out of the bathroom to grab it.

"Allo?" she said after flipping it open, droplets from her wet hair tapping onto the tops of her bare feet.

"Jacqueline?" came the voice on the other side, flat with an American accent. "It's Sheri of *LeMonde*. My editor said you were available for an interview...?"

"Oui, oui!" she gushed, automatically wishing she were dressed in something fine as opposed to her damp skin. Crooking the phone between ear and shoulder, she rushed back into the still-steaming bathroom, quickly pulled her towel from the bar, and began to wrap it around herself.

"Of course, I remember. How are you?" she said, a spontaneous stall as she pulled and tugged the towel into place.

"Um ... I'm fine. Is this a good time? This won't take very long. We're planning on featuring Escobar in an upcoming issue and it would be great if we could get some comments from you as one of his models."

Sitting on the edge of her bed, not caring for the moment that she was getting the Miazaki spread wet, she answered, "I'm so flattered! Thank you for thinking of me."

"Well, I'm trying to give the piece some depth. I just got finished talking with his wife, Constance."

"A wonderful woman. Of course, I've only met her once or twice. But she's always struck me as being very ... dignified, I guess you could say. I always got the impression she hasn't been very comfortable with her husband's — well, his life as it's become. Maybe even a bit jealous of him and me. I was just saying to Simone — you know Simone, right? I was just saying how this life, the life of art and artists, I mean, can be wonderful, but how it can also sometimes bring out the absolute worst in people."

"The worst? Yes, I could easily see that. I guess I should ask what Escobar was like to work with?"

"Escobar? Oh, he was wonderful, darling. Absolutely fantastic. A genius, of course, and like all those kinds of people, completely focused on his work. Not that he was rude or anything. Not at all. Treated me like a princess — if not better, if you know what you mean. Always made sure I was comfortable, brought me drinks, rubbed my neck when it got sore. Posing takes some time, you know — that kind of thing."

"Um, yes. So you'd say he appeared to be conscientious?"

"Oh, more than that. Much more than that. But then artists, especially great artists, are like that. Very sensual people. Guess it must have something to do with the way they look at the world, eh? Always trying to make love to everything with their art..."

"So you and he were actually ... intimate? Can I ask that?"

"Well, you can ask it, certainly! But a lady would never tell, and I may be a lot of things, but I always try to be discreet."

"Oh, I think I understand."

Not great, just good, but Jacqueline could still hear through her French that the woman did understand what was being implied.

"It also sort of agrees with what I've heard."

"Now, now," she tsked into the phone. "Mustn't gossip."

The journalist's laugh was rough and loud. Very American.

"So, Jacqueline, what was it like to have the privilege of being immortalized by a master?"

"It ... it was good, but while I know the painting's been considered a masterpiece and all that — I've even heard talk of hanging it in the Louvre, if I remember correctly — it's just something to hang on a wall. Being with Escobar, a man like that ... to have that kind of experience ... well, it can change a waitress, say, into a princess."

"But what was it for you?"

"It was magnificent. Truly magnificent."

CHAPTER THREE

I

No one else was there, no one he could ask, so he couldn't say. It didn't have the passion of Picasso, the spectrum of Monet, the delicacy of Manet, the composition of Mondrian, the whimsy of Kandinsky, the elegance of Sargent, the tranquility of Hopper, the precision of da Vinci, the strength of Michelangelo, the madness of Van Gogh, or the music of Cezanne.

It was ineffective, clumsy, inelegant — or maybe just ugly.

Through a window, at the end of the pure white box of the gallery, was a single work. Small, only maybe a meter square, it had color, form, balance, structure, but it wasn't genius, though that's what everyone had been saying about Escobar. Reflected back was Philip's own face, a semi-translucent mirror superimposing his narrow nose, high cheekbones, close-cropped black hair, over the artist's distant work.

A wry smile on his ghostly self-portrait. *Better art by accident*, he thought at his reflection.

The gallery was closed for the evening, small incidental lights dully lighting the rest of the works hanging on its walls. Only one high-intensity beam shone, singling out the bright colors and mad streaks of that one painting. From the side, from a niche filled with a glass-topped desk, a man walked out. Dim in the closed gallery lighting, details were lost, but Philip could see he was big, not exactly heavy. Thinning gray hair. The posture, the age, of an owner — not an employee. A small clipboard in one hand, short fingers curling around the edge. Philip couldn't see where the man was looking, but his shoulders and posture broadcast dismissal as he turned and walked out of Philip's sight.

Sucking his teeth in disgust, Philip went back to the Escobar. The gallery was a little out of his way, a stroll from the off-site Sorbonne classroom — where he'd been substituting for a vacationing professor — down the Rue Christine, and eventually to his little plaster box apartment in Montparnasse. Normally he wouldn't have turned that one corner, walked down that one avenue, to take himself past the pure white geometry of the gallery — called, in supreme arrogance, *L'Art* — to look in the window.

The name had been rare a year or so ago, and then only uttered among long-haired students trying to impress each other with the more outré or less-known painters, sketch artists, and sculptors. Then the name had worked its way to the end of a long list of new talents muttered by aficionados and those who thought, worked hard to be in the know. A few months later it had been whispered in the halls, professors saying it with excitement.

Finally, the name had appeared on a few respected web sites, then in a magazine, a small print caption under a small picture in a distant, high-numbered page corner. More time and *Escobar* had been on the cover of the magazine and other respected publications. Now he was spoken of casually, by people without pigment under their nails. People with television cameras in their faces, with sincere yet plastic smiles. Jeweled people who held champagne flutes filled with rare vintages during receptions dazzling with paparazzi strobe lights. People with checkbooks and tax attorneys.

People who decided what would hang on the modern art walls, within the pipe and conduit-covered Pompidou Center.

In the back of the gallery, at the end of a pure white tunnel, a single light shone on one painting. Confused, muddled, sloppy, disproportionate. Not Picasso, not Manet, not Monet, not Mondrian, not Kandinsky, not Sargent, not Hopper, not da Vinci, not Michelangelo, not Van Gogh, not Cezanne. But, according to those students, the professors, the editors, the critics, the gallery owners, the patrons, and the press, this artist was just as good if not better.

Philip turned away from the glass, his image revolving with him. It had rained that afternoon, the cobblestone streets of Paris still littered with muddied reflections, putting the darkened sky above, below him, at his feet. Looking down, he saw his as a Picasso profile, the glowing plastic Cinzano sign outside a little bistro as one of Monet's water lilies, a stream trickling along the gutter of the Seine by Manet, the shadows on the cream-colored doorway the precise lines of Mondrian, in the streaks of taillights the delightful creatures of Kandinsky, a movie poster under a streetlight a portrait by Sargent, the night and the street done by Hopper, his hands — when he looked down at them — painted by da Vinci, or cut in stone by Michelangelo, stellar streetlights by Van Gogh, the perspective of a rue ordinaire by the knife of Cezanne.

But not Escobar. He was nowhere to be found. Philip was alone on the street.

II

Not wanting to go home just yet, he let his feet lead him from one illuminated pool to another, Saint Germaine (the Seine and Notre Dame in front, to the left) to Saint Michel (Eiffel behind and also to his left). He had some vague grumblings in his stomach but didn't want to eat just yet. Seeing Escobar hanging on that supremely white wall stirred up another hunger, one that would only be satisfied by a destination at the end of a familiar walk closer to the river.

Soon the dark water and the tall spires of the cathedral were still to his left but much closer, as he strolled along the slick pavement of the quai. The bookstalls were shut, their shutters padlocked, proprietors in nearby bars and bistros clicking down their centimes. Where he was headed would still be open, its hours much later, the bookstore staff spending their paychecks at hipper hangouts and eateries.

If it had a name, it'd been forgotten by everyone except for the staff who drank their wine or ate their meals with the old men who ran the stalls. To the rest, it was just Biblio. From the outside it was a glowing rectangle of a doorway on a dark featureless street that curled up and away from the heavy, slow waters of the river. Tourists missed it, even people who'd lived in the city all of their lives missed it — unless they read more than they ate, turned pages more religiously than they said their prayers, felt paper more often than the skin of another person, or knew more about titles and authors than what was good on any menu.

Stepping through the darkness, trying not to trip on any loose stones, cracks in the street, or uprooted pavement, he moved towards the light, the glowing rectangle hovering in pitch black. All around it was nothing, but in the brilliance was the end of a wooden bookcase, and in front of that, a precarious pile of leather-bound albums. The rest was hidden.

50

Then he was inside — cool night behind, dust and bindings surrounding. Hesitantly buzzing fluorescents in yellowed plastic covers with the bodies of moths seduced to a powdery death high above. In a niche to the right, behind an ancient desk, was one of the staff, a thin rake of a student with a crest of greasy black hair, leaning forward on bony elbows, skeletal fingers gripping a lurid-covered paperback with white-knuckled concentration.

Everywhere else was books. More rough-hewn bookcases lined the cracked or stained walls, crowding the aisles and forcing patrons into a sideways scuttle, every shelf packed tight. But there was more, piled on groaning tables, stacked like attempts to honor the trees dead to make them: volumes, editions, folios, paper- and hard-bound, loose and tightly stitched, old and new, precious and impenetrable, or — like the page noisily turned by the rooster-topped boy behind the counter — cheap and easy.

Walking down the tight avenue inexplicably between ceramics and popular biographies, Philip streaked a hand across spines — some gold leaf, others cheaper typography on torn paper covers — as library grime darkened the swirls and vortexes of his fingerprints. For the allergic or the illiterate, it was a nightmare, puzzling symbols on rotting paper, cryptic knowledge mixed with mold and mildew.

Slapping his hand on his pants, little clouds of knowledgeable dust falling behind him as he walked, he turned at Cooking (a well-worn and possibly tastily stained edition of *Larousse Gastronomique* catching his eye) and climbed a steep pair of steps, carpeted in what once could have been rusty gold but was now threadbare, before heading down the deep canyon of paperback mysteries, almost toppling a tower of Simenon mysteries.

Another step, this one protected by haphazardly nailed tin, into a new section, and he let dirty fingers fall on one book. Not looking at the title, he balanced it in one hand, letting the book's covers fall apart where they would.

Glossy paper, gleaming even in hideous lighting. Soft colors carefully applied, clear lines marking reality. Straw hats, deep blue figures. Dancers in the middle ground, seated men and women in the foreground. Faces delicate and perfect. You knew these people, or at least would like to. A good time with friends, laughter, and champagne during a *Ball at the Moulin de la Galette*. Renoir, student of Delacroix for color, Monet for light. The book didn't — couldn't —

reproduce the reality. For that, he'd have to cross the river and pay to see the original in the Louvre. It was good enough, though, to spark his memory when last he'd seen it hanging. He recalled a gaggle of third-year students, poker faces on while they walked hallway after hallway of brilliance. With the professor off that day, it had been up to Philip the Assistant to play shepherd.

Recollection of a hot day, the bliss of air conditioning, sunlight geometry on the museum floor, and there it was: those happy people captured by brush and sight and mind. Happy forever, smiling for Renoir. He didn't remember much else from that day, even the name of the girl he'd been hoping to lure away from the group, offer coffee or supper to after the field trip was over, the museum closed.

Same book, different page, identical methodology: balanced in one hand, he let it fall open at random. Ballerinas and a smile — dancers precious and young, girls more than women. One of them so like Dorothea. Cascade of red hair tumbling over bare shoulders, a triangle of freckles that he liked to connect — dot after dot — with a slow finger as she lay sleeping afterward. Plump breasts with huge dark nipples, areolas like teacup saucers the color of coffee with too much cream. A swell of belly above the thin streak of hair below.

It'd been at the end of the relationship: hours of chatter deteriorating to leaden silences, held hands becoming arms folded, long kisses becoming chaste pecks on the cheek, nights and afternoons of fingernails on his back becoming days then weeks then a month of excuses and feigned exhaustion. The night before, they'd tried, one last time. She, on her stomach. He tried to connect them one more time, but her hand reached around, slapping him away from her freckles.

They'd been traveling, a little vacation to try and return the spark. They'd found a small town for lunch. In it, not really a museum, more like a shrine to local artists and maybe a few from some masters, paintings not good enough to hang on a city's much more discerning and demanding walls. A brick and thatched building beside a green-coated canal. Right inside the door was a ballerina in bronze, hands behind her back. Adolescent and lithe, ready to step from her marble pedestal and pirouette for her mother's applause.

As they'd walked in he'd said, "The ubiquitous Degas ballerina. Must hand them out to any place with pictures and four walls."

She'd snorted with laughter, making him grin for the first time in that long, slow final month of them being together. The next day, over mussels and wine that'd tasted of ashes and iodine, she'd cut the last cord.

Degas was brilliant, even if he'd given every gallery and museum in the world one of his dancers. That wasn't why Philip closed the book and took a carefully drawn breath. It couldn't have worked. That small bronze statue had just been color, form, texture.

"Pretty" was what she'd said, after she'd stopped laughing and actually looked at the sculpture. That's all any of it was to her, coffee house girl with the funny-shaped nipples. It was all just pretty and nothing else — no depth, no analysis, no perception, no intellect. She was just pretty and nothing else. It never could have worked, but that didn't dull the ache.

"Pardon."

He looked up from dancers sliding slippered feet across polished wood and bows preciously tied in auburn hair to meet violet eyes in a pixie's face: pointed nose and thin lips, high cheekbones peering out from under tumbles of black, twisting hair.

"I'm sorry," he said, befuddled.

Hands weak, *Les Artistes Francais* tumbling, pages flapping like bird wings too bound up to fly, slick pages landing hard on the dirty floor.

Kneeling down, trying to save the book, her hands across the cover, long thin fingers with glittering purple polish alongside his.

"No, I am. I made you drop your book."

"Not mine yet. Don't think I'm going to buy it."

He didn't know why he said that, the confusion knitting his brows before he could stop it. It always bothered him that he had an animated face, one that could never hide anything from anyone. The world could read his mind.

"Why not?" In their fumbling, the book had ended up in her possession. It was odd to see the plates in someone else's hands, Degas upside down, ballerinas balancing expertly on their heads. "Seems like a good one to me. Maybe a bit mundane."

She was tall, a few centimeters shorter than he was but not much more than that. Lithe, long. Most of her was behind the curtain of a simple black dress that ended just above her thighs. Below the hem, coal tights and a pair of brass buckled shoes. The toes, he noticed, were scuffed: the leather abraded, common brown beneath. Over the hem, far above the hem, a simple gold chain around an elegant neck.

"Some would call it *classical*," he said in theatrical bravado, but not a good performance — nerves making him too hurried, a squeak punctuating the last word.

She smiled, cheeks springing up, her eyes shining. He broke down their color: a bit of emerald, a hint of amber, a measure of azure.

"Not the painters, the book," she said. Her emeralds, ambers, azures dropped down. The smile curled, playfully, and she turned the book around to show him. "What an eye."

The colors of life, astute composition: blue sky, flowers blurred with the intensity of their spectrum, a girl with a parasol. He might be able to understand the eyes of the young woman in front of him if he could study them long enough — the thought of that pleasurable to him right then — but he could never, ever copy, analyze, properly understand the colors in the painting she was holding up to him.

"Very good," he said, his face showing his embarrassment at becoming a graduate student again, a boy playing professor. "I mean the quote. I mean ... Cezanne about Monet. 'He's nothing but an eye — but what an eye.'"

"Merci," she said, her complexion rose-ing. "I try to be clever. Don't always succeed, I'm afraid."

"I'm sorry," he said to the pause that had grown too long between them. "You wanted to get by." He moved, backing up against Architecture, Frank Geary digging into his spine.

"That's all right. I'm not too sure what I'm looking for anyway," she said, book still in her hands. She turned a page. "Besides, I'd better get going. Have to get to work."

"Oh, okay. Have a good night then," he said, waiting, but she didn't ask, so he couldn't say. His face had probably already betrayed his hope and desperation.

"Small city, small world. Who can say? Here's your book."

Purple nails on the cover, her fingers obscuring the title. He'd just seen it, but already he couldn't remember it. Taking it, he tried to think of something else to say, but by the time he'd opened his mouth, she was walking away.

After a stretched moment, he was back to being alone in the aisle. He looked at the book. It was nice, but he wouldn't — couldn't — buy it. Looking at Renoir, Gauguin, Pisarro, Seurat, at least in those pages, would make him remember her, his clumsy tongue, the missed opportunity.

So, back on the shelf it went. Now his hands were empty, his mind wrapped in thick heavy blankets. He needed a distraction. Putting out a hand, he picked up the first book he touched. He opened it and tried to put his mind aside, lose himself in hues, tints, contrast, composition. Something perfect and balanced, something he could hold onto — even if it was just on a printed page.

Chaos of pigments, watercolor wars, acrylic nightmares, jarring forms, clumsy assembly. Amateurish, boorish, infantile, pompous. Mad vomits, like embarrassing stains after a voracious dinner. Pollock had more restraint. De Kooning had more skill, Rothko more elegance. Page after page, again and again trying to see what those students, professors, critics, buyers saw. He failed. Hesitating, he stopped at one: a square of blue, a face in red — blood on a frozen sea. Heavy jaw, leaden lips, invisible eyes. It looked like an American footballer, a Neanderthal's face broken down until it was nothing but shadows and light, a graphic representation. The brushwork was rushed and clumsy, mixing a riot of techniques, none of them working together. A painter deserving ignominy — and nothing else.

Even though no one was there, he still mumbled out loud as he closed the book and shoved it back into the stacks: "Merde."

"Pardon."

He started, turned. There: much better choice of colors, an elegant dance of hue and tint, shade and texture. Such lovely eyes, such a lovely, lovely face. "Oh, hello," he said, and again was sure his face was as clumsy and obvious as Escobar's paintings in the book he'd just held.

"Can I see that book again?" the girl asked, holding out a thin hand.

"Oh, sure." He turned, hunted for a second, mumbling, "Just had it here," and there it was. Pulling it out, he presented it to her, wishing as he did that it was a flower, a special trinket, anything but a cheap art book with a slightly torn cover.

"Thanks," she said, whimsy making her smile even broader, her cheeks and color more festive, adding more emerald, amber, and azure to her eyes. There was a pen in her hand, a cheap ballpoint. A few strokes on a page and she passed it back. "Just me trying to be clever again. Let me know if it works?" The last spoken soft, low.

He didn't say anything — just watching her walk away from him, disappear with a turn behind the stacks — not because he didn't know what to say, but because he knew it would be better not to. It was that kind of moment: a girl with a parasol, ballerinas stretching before a recital, friends dancing with friends. A classic moment.

When his heart slowed, he opened the book, riffling through the pages until he saw it, quickly written in the white border surrounding one of the plates. Smoke haired beauties sitting on the grass, skins dark and sensual. Eyes innocent yet seductive. A tropical paradise of passion fruits and languid days spent in pleasure. Gauguin — one of his tropical, Tahitian series.

The painting was beautiful. The painting was wonderful. But he didn't have eyes for it as much as what was written above: a phone number and a single name. Madeline.

III

Three days. That seemed about right, the formula for when to call. He knew he was obsessing about it, but he still didn't confide in anyone. Not his students, his professors, or even the few of either that he may, maybe, *sort of* considered friends. It was a quiet fret, a silent mental loop. It wasn't that he couldn't tell them — they'd certainly bent his ear over their own problems — but, like the silence when she'd handed back the book, it was too important. Trying to tell them, having to explain it, would have taken off some of the gloss, the shiny illusion. Made it common: just a name, just a phone number, just a girl, just a date.

His voice caught when he called. A hitch when he left a message on her voicemail. He'd rehearsed it all that afternoon, just in case. A cell phone soliloquy. Hopefully witty, flirty, charming. He hoped, but worried and worried and worried some more that his voice had scratched, coughed too much. Desperate. Pathetic.

Then she called back. Washing dishes in his sink, his phone sang from the next room and he'd rushed in, fumbling with the silver plastic, his hands slick with more than soap and water. "Hello?"

"Hi, there. Enjoying the book?"

Her voice was light and singing, an intake of breath away from laughter.

"Very much. Thanks for suggesting I get it."

"All I did was put my name in it."

He didn't know where it came from, but there it was: "That was the best thing in it."

Her voice grew low and soft, almost hard to hear.

"That's too sweet."

"I mean it. I'm glad you did," he said, and this time his voice didn't halt or stumble.

"I hope you don't think — I mean, I don't do that a lot. Give guys my phone number and all. It just seemed like the right thing to do at the time."

"Well, it's never happened to me before."

Stupid. You'll sound like a loser.

"We're a pair then. I mean ... we have that in common."

"Guess we do. Probably a lot more. Maybe a lot more, I should say. I mean ... I don't want to presume...?"

His mouth was running too fast, his mind blazing white.

"It's okay," she said, the laughter coming at last. "I'm sure we do. The trick is just to figure out what. Hey, you hungry?"

The remains of a cheese omelet was what he'd been cleaning up. "Definitely. I'm open to anything. You name it."

God, what am I saying?

"Great." Her voice bouncing and playful. "I know a nice little place. Good but not too pricey, near Hôtel De Ville. Seven good for you?"

She had to have known he was barely hanging on, a breath away from being a jabbering wreck, and either thought it was cute — which made him instantly miserable — or didn't care — which made him frown — or thought that there was something in him worth looking at.

With that last in mind, he said, "Seven it is."

"Looking forward to it," she said, then rattled off a quick series of directions that he tried to memorize. "See you there."

A cool dial tone purr in his ear, the girl gone. He closed the phone. Deep breath in, deep breath out. Doubts aside, nerves momentarily forgotten. All those thoughts, the static in his head, the shivering in his hands and body gone for a while because she'd asked, he'd answered. A bite to eat, at seven o'clock.

* * * *

Hours later and a fee paid to the Metro to get him close enough. Hours, when really only one would have been enough. He jogged up the marble steps, into cool night from the station, more out of breath from nerves than from the exercise. A taxi pulled up on his right, interior light showing a stocky man with a bald, brightly polished head. The passenger got out, paying the driver with bills pulled from a fine leather billfold. Philip had stepped up from affordability and had emerged into posh and polish.

He hoped her scraped and well-used shoes meant that she knew the value of a euro, and that the place wouldn't take the twelve he had left in his faded and inexpensive wallet. Even a quick side trip to a teller machine was out, as it would just tell him what he already knew. He had nothing left.

With more than a few minutes to kill, he found a darkened shop window. Surrounded by clocks silently marking time and hovering over Louis XIV painted porcelain, he patted down his close-cropped hair, made sure there weren't any shadows of missed shaving. He tried a smile, but then frowned when his reflection turned into a cartoonish grin.

Calm, he thought, cool and collected — wanting, just once, not to wear an idiotic puppy dog expression for all, especially her, to see.

The place looked nice, even from where he stood across the Rue de Rivoli. Cut glass windows, trimmed in filigreed gold leaf. Flowers like tiny fireworks on virginally pure tablecloths. It was trapped in amber, a relic from the 50s. Traffic was harsh, cars passing by like meteors. Finally, a gap and he was across. As he got to the restaurant, his wallet already seemed empty. He felt a tiny, guilty stab of anger at that, her lack of consideration. He would have picked somewhere cheaper.

It wasn't busy, only a few diners in the place. As he closed the door behind him, a waiter broke away from serving an elderly pair, two gray heads down and studying menus, to say, "I'll be with you in a moment, monsieur."

"That's okay. I'm with her."

He smiled at her from across the room. Euros didn't matter. Fine gold lines on clear glass didn't matter. Flowers on spotless linen didn't matter.

"Bonjour!" she said, waving, her voice sharp and loud.

The old couple looked up from their decisions, the man scowling at the interruption, the women smiling in sympathy.

Pulling back a chair, he sat. There was a tiny brown mole next to her nose, like a single point of punctuation: a stop between eyes and mouth. Her lips were unpainted, naturally rose. They weren't full, but not thin either. Blue, her eyes were blue. A deep cerulean, laugh lines streaming from the corners. He never could judge someone's age — it was a trick he'd never learned — but he thought she was in her late twenties, a few years younger than he. Either she was wearing the same dress or one too close in color and shape for him to tell it from the old one.

"The place is a bit pricey," she said, leaning forward in a conspiratorial whisper, explaining what a girl like her, or at least what she appeared to be, was doing in a place like this, "but the croque madame is incredible and very affordable."

The waiter was at his elbow, face tense, disapproving.

"I'll have the croque madame," Philip said, "and cafe au lait."

"If I have a coffee, I'll never get to sleep," she said when they were alone again. "But I can't start the morning without it."

Her hair was pulled back, but it wasn't about to be so easily tamed. Wild strands framed her face like a halo. He didn't say anything for a moment. She was beautiful.

"I-I'm lucky, I guess. It doesn't affect me very much."

"You don't remember me, do you?"

Her voice serious but not leaden.

Rummaging quickly through his mind, he flicked through his past for her. Only thirty years old, but too many places, names, jobs, schools to go through. Middle school? The halls of Saint Germain Academy in Montelione, freezing on winter nights, sweltering in the summer, and always smelling of bleach? Early years at the Sorbonne? Learning where everything was and who was who. Dropping books, saying the wrong things. Working for Professor Largrasse, for whom he could do nothing right? Had she been a student in one of his classes? Seen him roared at for being too slow passing out exam papers? Working for Professor Arrounaf, who'd really opened his eyes about what art was and what it could be. Had she been in the library when he was wheeling away cart after cart of heavy books? She was beautiful, but he didn't remember her.

"That's okay," she said, laughter playing with her voice. "It was just one class. Intro to art a year or so ago. Real basic stuff. I was hanging out with a first year friend so I tagged along. Afterward I told you I really liked it."

He'd taught lots of classes. Way too many. One face in an auditorium full of faces.

"I'm sorry."

"Don't worry."

Her hand was on his arm.

"I didn't think you'd remember. But I did like it, especially when you said that Van Gogh was either mad because he was an artist or an artist because he was mad."

"I'm sure I stole it from someone."

He liked her hand on his arm. Without thinking, he returned the gesture. Her skin was hot like freshly baked bread.

"I'm good, but not that good."

"It scored points with me. But then I'm a sucker for anything having to do with artists. Hits close to home."

Rolls arrived, slid onto the table by a dusky busboy, the intrusion breaking them apart. Putting his napkin in his lap, Philip covered a strange moment of embarrassment, like they'd been discovered doing something more intimate than just touching each other.

"Do you get your hands dirty?" he asked, lips quickly tight. The reference was too snobby, a professor's way of separating researchers from practitioners.

Fanning out her fingers on one hand, she playfully rubbed her nails with the other, pretending to clean off the remains of favorite mediums.

"Charcoal, acrylics, watercolor, even tried airbrushing once or twice. Too scientific — and I kept putting the thing in my mouth when I was thinking."

He really laughed.

"I could see that. I wish I could do it — paint, I mean. I like what I do, but I think if I picked up a brush, I'd be stuck. Too many other artists leaning over my shoulder."

Surprise at that: it really was what he thought. He'd never told anyone before.

"It's not easy. It really isn't. But I don't try to be what they are — were. I just try to have fun. Not exactly a great philosophy, but it works... most of the time."

Her brush was a fork. She sketched the air with the tines.

"You like what you do?"

"Well enough. There's a lot to know. I spend way too much time in research. It's nice that I get paid to teach, though. I like telling people about art."

And he did. He might not create any of it, but there was something special about opening students' eyes, revealing wonder and beauty where they didn't know there was. Next best thing. He didn't know, but guessed.

"I can see that. I'm the same way, I guess. When I do something, it's like I'm telling them about something — something that only I can see. I like seeing their faces when they get it. If they get it, that is." She sipped her water, eyes turned down for a moment.

"That's what I adore about it. It's like they aren't just showing a sunset or a river or a flower or whatever it is that's *there*. It's more than that. We're looking through their eyes, seeing the world the way they see it. Crazy colors of Van Gogh, like you said. They are putting all of themselves down on the canvas. It sounds like that's the same for you," he added, sensing himself slipping into the too-comfortable insulation of teacher, professor.

He didn't want to do that with her. He liked being Philip with her. She nodded.

"That's me. Maybe I'm crazy, or maybe I'm an artist so I'm crazy, right? But I see the world like I have to paint it. Do it all the time. Like you. What do I need to do to get your lips right. That little curl at the ends. What shade do I use for your eyes. Your short, stubby hair, like your head is fuzzy, out of focus. The way you hold your hands."

She ran a finger around her half-empty water glass, losing herself in the slow orbits. Then she looked back up.

"From the first moment I saw you," she said finally, "I wanted to draw you."

IV

Paris is a city. A very big city, and like other mazes of stone and iron inhabited by many, many people, parts of it were simply falling apart. Stone cracked and crumbled, iron rusted away, and people sunk to their lowest possible level. Madeline lived near the Arab quarter, not the bottom but uncomfortably close to it.

She seemed to be comfortable with the area, which was good because Philip wasn't. Once he realized the direction they were headed, his hackles rose and he began to eye each pedestrian through a filter of potential problems — and bad American action films. After another street, though, he found himself relaxing, following

Madeline's buoyant stride, and remembering who she was, which was lovely, and what they were going to do, which he didn't know but had his hopes about.

He had his suspicions that although she was used to the neighborhood, she was nervous about what was coming because as she led the way, she'd occasionally turn back to him with a smile and "not long now," "just around the corner," "almost there."

Then, they were. On a darkened street, both of them alone except for a black cat all sinew and matted fur slinking by, head down, tail up.

"Home sweet home," Madeline said with irony.

As he climbed with her up the stairs, he tried to interpret her body through her simple black dress. She talked in fits and starts, with loops and trailing edges, but she moved carefully, precisely. Taut, firm, he decided. Thin but without sharp edges and protruding bone. Breasts? He'd been trying since he first saw her, but they were as much a mystery as the rest of her.

He was excited beyond the thought of where they might be heading. When he thought about it, he hoped he wasn't naive. Dorothea, Anna, Francesca, Willa that summer in Berlin, Lizabeth in early college (and still a lot of pain to go with the name and that time in his life), Jeanette in middle school (a developing breast under one of his hands, a precious memory), and he guessed he should count the few times with the women walking the avenues near the Moulin Rouge.

But with Dorothea, Anna, Francesca, Willa, Lizabeth, Jeanette — even the affordable release of streetwalkers — he'd approached them all, walked up his or their stairs, with a determined erection. With them, he was excited but didn't feel that physical demand. He was nervous now, not because he wouldn't be able to perform, but because he was hoping this would be something better than, more than Dorothea, Anna, Francesca, Willa, Lizabeth, Jeanette, and everyone else had ever been. He didn't know this girl, but she had something over all his other lovers, and it had nothing to do with his flickering fantasies of her body.

She was fun and funny, smart and quick, creative but not shallow. He liked talking to her, he liked hearing what she had to say, and she apparently liked what he said. She'd also asked. No one had ever asked him before. Even if drawing him was all she wanted to do, she was the only one who'd ever asked. The other girls, the women, hadn't asked. They'd assumed and treated him accordingly.

He liked her. He really liked her.

Her hallway was dark, the carpeting threadbare and dirty. Her apartment door was dull green. Her key was in the lock and then she was opening her door. "Home affordable home," Madeline said.

Heart beating faster than it had ever beaten before. He followed her in.

* * * *

"Just like that. That's great. That's perfect."

His foot was falling asleep. His back was starting to hurt, low down, where his ass hit futon. But he didn't move.

His face itched for a grin, but he kept the muscles there locked down tight. It really was what she wanted, for him to sit still for her darting pencils, the strokes of her charcoal. At the door, a few formalities — "Please excuse the mess. Believe it or not it's usually a lot worse." "Coffee, some tea? I have some Orangina, too" — she nervous, he nervous. A tight little dance in her cluttered little bedsit. Philip thought about putting his hand on her, a touch to show that he was interested. Something to push them over the edge of her sagging futon covered with clothes and coats, but his hands stayed by his sides.

Shyness was part of it. He'd always had a hard time taking that first step. Yet here he was enjoying himself. If it happened, it happened. Not that he wouldn't mind if it happened. Not at all. But if it didn't, it wouldn't be the end of the world. There'd be other times. Maybe. But what if she wanted him to make the first move? Then he should fight his hesitation, turn her towards him, move for a kiss. She'd like that. He'd like that. Not that he wouldn't mind if it didn't happen. But maybe she wanted him to do that. His hands — still — stayed by his sides.

Pad out, her pencils hissed across the paper. Madeline didn't need to tell him to smile. Despite the thoughts racing through his mind, chasing their mental tails, he smiled naturally, if a bit stiffly.

Frozen, he had nothing to do but pose, think, and look at her. Her nose, he noticed, had a little bump halfway down its length. The tiny mole danced when she laughed. Her eyebrows were bushy, but narrow enough that he supposed every once in a while, she plucked them. Madeline wasn't much of a reader, but she liked art books. Stacked in the corner were a few of his favorites.

She wasn't much of a housekeeper, but then neither was he. Dishes were piled in the sink, a few bottles of cheap red stood by the door. No ashtrays, so she didn't smoke, which was okay with him since he didn't either. He suspected she wasn't self-conscious, but a pair of her panties — silk, not cotton, he couldn't help but notice as he tried his best not to stare — draped over a chair by the single small table confirmed it. A bra was on top of a pile of what he hoped was washed laundry in a far corner, but he couldn't see what size it was.

"This is wonderful. Thank you so much."

Her blue eyes peered over the top of her pad.

"Anytime. Do you want me to change position?" he asked, letting his face unlock into a grin.

"Um, sure. I don't know if you want to, but I'd, um, if you could pose a bit more naturally that'd be great."

Her voice was sweet and light but with a huskiness on the vowels.

It took him a second to realize what she was asking.

She'd asked, so he said, "Whatever you want."

Shoes, socks, shirt, pants — even though the little apartment in the bad part of Paris was warm, his hands were shaking. Underwear. Naked, he still wasn't hard, though he could feel the muscles in his lower belly, his groin tensed in preparation. He still didn't know the rules; if she just wanted to sketch him or if this was a game she was playing. It was confusing. What surprised him the most was that he didn't care. He was having fun.

"Just like that, push your back out a little. Perfect," she said, looking back down to her pad again. Folded neatly, she sat on the floor, long legs curled under her. "Beautiful."

Hands flying, sweeping gestures, moments of vigorous shading, she worked. There was something about Madeline's concentration, the way she peered around the sheets to take him in, that struck him as intimate, passionate, and powerful. It was like she had a minute, just a minute, to capture him. Her self, what she was and what she saw and experienced, was focused onto one tiny square of paper.

Then, before he was even aware of it, he was hard. He didn't look down, but he knew he was. He could feel it: the swelling, then the familiar stiffness, the deep muscular ache. He was embarrassed, but also relieved. It had happened, and it was either going to be over or it wasn't.

"Oh, my," she said, peering above the pad. "That's not just pretty — that's gorgeous."

He smiled, pushing against his suddenly tight face. Thumping in his chest, beating all the way down to his groin, his pulse was quick and forceful. He should get up, he should say something, he should touch himself, he should…

The paper came down. Sparkling blue, and very wide, eyes.

"Stay there."

From sitting to hands and knees, a smile inching towards him. Her hand came forward, and neatly wrapped around him. For a long, long moment she felt him — sliding her hand slowly, carefully up and down his shaft. He almost came, then and there, not because what she was doing was so perfectly done — in fact, she was a bit rough, her ups and downs too fast, her grip a bit too tight — but because he was watching her face.

His cock was a brush in her hands, a new artistic tool for her to play with. Madeline was fascinated, enraptured. The way she was looking at him, the way she touched him, he could see that. Orgasm was looming, a pressure in his body, his balls. He didn't want to, so he closed his eyes and stepped back, away from what was happening, to save himself.

Then her lips were on him — and everything changed. The action was a shock, a bolt of warm, soft, wet bliss that pushed him to the brink. A kiss at first, just a slow wet introduction. Pulling back, she rolled a thumb across the head, easy oscillations — getting to know the territory, he thought.

"Pretty," she said, lips returning for another slow kiss.

Then, he was inside.

She moaned, a deep primal sound working its way out her throat and around his cock. The vibration made him moan as well, which surprised him into opening his eyes even wider. Then, she couldn't make any noise at all as she eased him all the way down. It wasn't a long trip, a few slow, tight, warm, wet strokes before he slid easily out of her hand and then out of her mouth.

"Whoa," she coughed into her one hand, the other never leaving its firm grip around his base. "I love that. Can't do it long, though."

"It was wonderful," he said in almost a whisper.

"It's going to get better. I can tell."

Knees this way and that, she climbed unsteadily up. Hands

behind her, pulling a zipper down, then they went to either side, on the hem of her dress. Up it went as she wiggled her hips back and forth to free the clinging fabric. Off. Lean, lithe. A naiad stepping out of a forest glade. A Greek figure freed from marble, blessed with translucent skin. Teacher and student even then, he tried to put her into a painting, recognize her from some classic work.

Then he couldn't. She was too pretty. She was lush and glowed with a gentle tan, a uniform light caramel that made him think of summers on the beach, relishing warm sunlight on every inch. Blocky shoes still on her feet, she kicked them off — each landing with a heavy thud. Black tights, from her toes to her hips, a darker elastic waistband pinching the gentle swell of her belly. Beneath it a pair of bunched panties, precious blue flowers on yellow cotton fabric.

Her bra was black, without lace, just black and simple — something an art student would wear. It made him smile. She reached around again, working some clasp magic, making an art student's bra fall away.

Lovely — that was the word. *Lovely.* Firm and impudent, petite and upswept, firm, with only a whisper of shadow underneath. Perfect handfuls, with nipples like little brown nuts that would peek out mischievously between fingers, playfully begging for kisses.

Thumbs then, down into the tops of her tights and a funny little dance getting them off. Several times, the length of her threatened to topple, but she always righted herself and always with a spatter of infectious giggles. Maybe not a lot of women in Philip's life, but enough — or so he hoped — and while some of them had smiled, a few had laughed, none of them had actually giggled, and none of them had ever made him want to giggle as well.

She was naked. The panties had come off, down and gone with the smoky tights. A long body, tight and defined. This, he realized, was what she really was: the clothes were on top of the real her, obscuring her natural self. The lithe nymph in front of him, the sun-worshipping artist as naked as her model, here was the real Madeline.

If he could have, he would have simply stared at her all that night. It wasn't just the beauty of her body, but rather how Madeline shone through her skin. He had liked her before, but seeing her in her real element, the real girl, he knew what he was feeling was more than that.

Looking down at his bobbing erection with a hungry, almost feral desire, she flopped down on the lumpy futon in a playful tangle of arms and legs.

"You're so pretty, Philip," she said, putting her hand around him again, stroking him once then twice.

"You are," he said, his voice tight and squeaking. He coughed into his hand to cover it.

"Stay there."

Rolling over, she began to dig feverishly through a pile of clothes and books and bags, eventually coming up with a wicker ball. No, a little round basket. Flipping it over, she shook a bright spray of foil packets onto the floor.

"Got you."

Green, like the body of an Egyptian beetle. Tearing one open, she popped a condom out, swung around and — tongue sticking ever so slightly out — rolled it along his length.

"Sorry," she said. "Maybe after I get to know you better."

"It's okay. I understand."

It was important to her and so it was important to him.

On hands and knees she crawled up to him. Up close, her face was even more elegant, even more elfin. Her eyes, half obscured by passion-heavy lids, still gleamed and glimmered. Leaning forward, lifting his head from the futon, he kissed her. Her lips were so plush, so soft they felt like a hint — just a suggestion. Touching, they opened their mouths together, began a hot dance of tongues.

It felt like eternity — long, stretched time of rapid heartbeats and rapid breathing. She broke the kiss first. "Mon Dieu," she growled, reaching back between her legs, then wrapping a hand slick with her own wetness around him.

A little dance with her legs and hips, positioning herself just right. Then she was on him and he was in her. Even through the safe insulation of the latex, it was wonderful. In the back of his mind, all through the night, he'd been seeing the colors, the shapes, the textures of what was happening. Seeing it all through an artistic filter. Flicking through mental catalogs, picking masterpieces to compare to the glow of her skin, the flickers of her eyes, the sheen on her cheeks, the dark chaos of her hair. Exact titles or artists weren't there, but the landscape of his art appreciation was: a rolling comparison of color, form, technique, style, composition, tint, shade, line, stroke, until that moment when she went onto him, and he went into her. Then, there, he was gone.

It *was* eternity. She took the lead, lifting and settling her hips, relishing in their contact. Dimly, he was aware of the sounds they were making as their bodies slicked and slid together. Abstractly, he felt her small, firm breasts and her tight nipples gliding across his chest. What he was aware of was her face. He watched her as they moved, as they moaned, as they enjoyed each other.

She was the most beautiful thing he'd ever seen.

Then it happened, beyond his ability to control it. A deep body rush, a shudder, then a bolt that arced up and through his body and mind. Echoing him, playing the same sound, she collapsed down on top of him, their ragged breathing coming together, mixing into dual pants of release.

V

"Rembrandt?"

He kissed the top of her head. She was absently twirling the sparse tangles of his chest hair.

"Dark but real. You want to touch the plumes on their hats, polish the brass of their buttons. I've always wondered how he could paint them, by just sun and candlelight," she said. "Mondrian?"

"A master of form, the supreme elements of composition executed without human reference yet imparting emotion. His direct impact is negligible, but he showed how far abstract could travel and still remain fine art."

Her hair smelled of sweet soap and salty sweat. His hand was almost to the small of her back; the bones of her spine lay under his palm like a row of marbles.

"What about Bosch?"

She seemed to be fascinated by the corded muscles of his thigh. It took her a stretched minute to respond.

"Twisted. Like a traffic accident you have to slow down to watch. What's worse is that he does it so well. Like a meticulous execution painted with a single hair brush." She shuddered gently. "Botticelli?"

"For my Venus?" he said, putting another touch of lips on the top of her head. Cooing in response, she hugged him tight, mixing their heartbeats before he continued. "The definition of Renaissance without the hammer of the church. The slightest touch of the artist yet conveying the purest and most puissant of statements. Its power has not diminished for the centuries. Chirico?"

Bells and flutes, her laugh into his chest.

"Either you're in a dark mood or you're testing me," she said. "The poor little girl. I know the monster's out there, but I keep hoping that she'll just roll her little hoop right by him. I like happier pictures. Like... oh, I don't know, Lautrec?"

"The first true marriages of commercialism and expressionism, the birth of the graphic arts. Life and desire distilled to bold forms and outlines: a pair of crimson lips, a pair of stockinged legs, a dancer's billowing skirt. Statements of eros, but distant and unattainable. Understandable considering the situation of the artist."

She was studying his face. Bending gently forward, he touched his lips to hers. Warm. Soft. Silken. Touch going further, a meeting of tongues. He felt himself stir.

"But he's wonderful. Really," he said when they came apart.

"Mmmm..." she cooed. "I like Klimt." She stretched, a young cat stirring before a nap. "Like a jewel. All those golds and sparkles. I've always wanted a dress of him, something to wrap around myself and be the prettiest girl in all the world. Dazzling."

"You are prettier than any picture." He coughed suddenly. "I like Manet. By altering the course of art and painting forever with his *Olympia*, he will always represent the daring and passion of the artist. He did what he did not because of what anyone might say, but because he needed to give us all his unique and wonderful vision of the world. I wish I could have been there when it was first displayed, to feel everything change in that one instant."

"I like him, too. He paints people, real people. Freckles and all. But he makes them pretty because of that. Bet he could do wonders for me," she said, grinning up at him.

"He would never need to. You are beautiful," he said, looking down into her eyes. His chest felt tight again, like something was trapped inside him. "How about Lichtenstein?"

"Oh, now you're being silly."

"Not at all." Mock serious, pomposity on pomposity, he said, "I'd love to hear your thoughts on the pop art master."

Snort. "Awful. Wish I could paint up a bunch of cartoons and hang them in a museum. Should put the real artist up there — he deserves it."

His laugh was loud and fast, startling them both.

"You're wonderful," he said when he'd caught his breath. "Okay, what about Rothko?"

"Oh, please! Throw a bucket of paint on a wall and get a billion

Euros. I've seen better stuff at the bottom of a pan after I've been cooking, and you have no idea how bad a cook I am."

Madeline dropped her head down into his chest, quiet and still.

Philip thought for a moment she'd dropped off, drifted off inexplicably. Then her voice, almost a whisper, drifted up to him.

"What about Escobar? What do you think of him?"

She asked, he answered.

"Horrible garbage," he said, rolling fingers over those marbles of her spine. "I hate his work and everything it and he stand for. Clumsy, poor composition, no sense of craft or control, no elegance or beauty. Just color and form with no balance or meaning. Drips and drops, streaks and smears. When I think of other artists, what they've created and accomplished compared to him and his cult of pomposity and arrogance without a sign of true brilliance or talent... He and his work are deplorable. I'd be happy if he and his hideous works were never seen again and he'd go back to waiting tables or polishing shoes — positions he'd be much more qualified to do. I don't say this much, but for him, I'd yell it from the highest rooftop: he is an appalling artist, with nothing to contribute to the world of art."

Madeline was looking up at him, her face frozen, as if trapped in cold stone. Then the ice softened, the stone cracked, and her eyes filled softly with tears.

"Let..." she began, then stopped to breathe slowly. She tried again. "Let me tell you about Escobar."

VI

"I like you. I like you a lot. You're really damned smart, you're funny — or at least I think so — you seem a very nice guy, and you're lots of fun to... fuck," this last a giggle, eyes turned down. "But you don't do it. Get your hands dirty, I mean." Fingers spread, turned towards him. "You can break it all apart, but you can't put it together."

His proximity to her passion was heat on his face, like a candle too close to his lips, or a too bright summer sun in his eyes. This was important to her — very important. So important his heart raced alongside hers, making the room small and tight and confined. Hand resting — just resting, not stroking or fondling — on her tightly muscled thigh, he clenched her gently, a kiss of fingers. A reminder that he was there, with her, as she spoke.

"When you do it, when you pick up a brush and start to work, it's like... it's like... I don't believe in God. I hope that doesn't upset you. I don't feel him. I close my eyes and it's just me, in the dark. But when I pick up a brush, I feel I'm doing something that's beyond me, something really amazing. When it's good, I mean."

Cold water shock then, realizing she was leading towards something deeper, even more special. He didn't know if he was ready for that. Mouth open, he was prepared to say something, anything. His voice was just about to begin — anything, anything at all. Quotes, maybe, or stories of other artists he'd read about, other legends of paint and canvas who'd written about their inner life and turmoil. Rembrandt, Mondrian, Bosch, Botticelli, Lautrec, Klimt, Manet, and others. He'd tell her what he'd read, studied about the trials of the great ones, the diaries of the almost forgotten ones. He was about to, but didn't.

"When it's good, you're painting with God — or something like that. But when it goes bad, it's you that's bad. So you tear up a piece of paper or whitewash a canvas. You can do it again. Try to be better. But it's worse when you think you've done it, that you maybe created something really good — not great, not wonderful, just nice — and then you show it to someone... and they don't like it. It's not a sketch they're frowning at; it's you, all of you. They don't like you."

Her eyes were wet, he saw. Reflections in gleaming cerulean blue. Like Kandinsky, fresh on the canvas. Like the reflective skin of El Greco. Like the ground gems in a Titian. Maybe he should say that, speak of him working mortar and pestle, crushing mere jewels to create something of greater value? He was about to, but didn't.

"I had a show. Nothing big or fancy — a few things in a little place near the Pompidou. Must have been about a year ago, I think. I'm not very good with dates. Anyway, I told my friends, some of my family — that kind of thing. A few emails, a couple of postcards. I knew it was early for me, but I really liked some of the pieces. My best work, I thought. I even got some cheese and some cheap wine, 'cause you don't want anyone hungry."

Maybe a laugh there, a different kind of story? Tell her funny tales of creators and their creations — abstracts hung upside down, absent splashes becoming masterpieces, the wit and subsequent grins of gallery dandies and studio fops. Wives and mistresses telling tales out of school, peeling back washes and patinas of pretension, revealing stiff and proper geniuses as men, just men, who liked to laugh at it all.

"People came. That was nice. Chit-chatted with some, but mainly I watched. I saw them look at my stuff. One of them, this sketch I did of the Arc de Triomphe, when I was done I just stood there on the street and I cried. It was right: I knew it. But they just looked at it. They just looked at it. They drank my wine, ate the cheese, and talked about the movies they'd seen, or what an idiot the president is. A few stayed, most were just polite. I knew they'd forgotten what I'd done the instant they walked out the door."

Her lips became tight, pink compressed to white. The pale bone of a Fabritius cloud, the deathly sheer of David's Marat in his tub, the alabaster luminosity of Michelangelo, the whispering sands of O'Keefe. A catalog flipped through mental fingers, comparing the tightness in her lips to master after master, work after work — hiding in stacks of books, in musty schoolrooms.

"I sat in the back, after everyone had gone. Just sat — and did nothing else. Nothing seemed worth doing, you see? Nothing mattered. Then... then the door opened. It had a bell. I looked up at the ring and there was this man. Middle-aged, wild head of dark curly hair, wearing blue jeans and a tweed coat. He'd stand and look at a picture for a really long time, then he'd nod or shake his head and move onto the next one. I knew he was looking at them — I mean really looking at them. No one else had done that."

Then, the pallor was absent; lips back to the deep ruby of a Caravaggio, vanishing with relaxation. The reds lifted a weight off his chest, he breathed — in and out — slow and steady, with her. A smile, he allowed himself that, and another squeeze of her thigh. The grin slipped a bit, though, when he realized where he'd gone, where he slipped away — withdrawing once again to stacks of books, retreating to musty schoolrooms, hiding among the masters and their techniques. Quotes and anecdotes lingered in the back of his mind, voices not from lessons and professions, but — heat on his cheeks now, not from her passion but rather his shameful memories of Dorothea, Anna, Francesca, Willa, Lizabeth, and Jeanette. Just about all of them, at the end, as they walked away. He never asked why, but they said it anyway: *You were never with me. You just watched. That's all you did.*

"He said that he didn't like most of them. Just like that. Other people say they like them, but that's all they say. They don't mean it. It was okay that he didn't like them because he could say that. At least he'd really been looking. The others hadn't. Then he said he liked one of them a lot.

The Triomphe. Said that it was better than anything he'd done at my age. He wanted to know if he could give me something for it. He asked for my sketchpad and I gave it to him. Then he tore out a page and drew me a sketch. It was a simple little thing, just a sketch of a doorway, some little piece of the city in pencil. It was beautiful. So beautiful."

Not wet, her eyes were. He didn't know what to think of the way her eyes looked right then. He could have compared them to works he knew. Paintings he'd seen in books. Seen hanging on walls. Names on pages, notes and breakdowns, critiques and analyses. Catalogues and studies. Papers and monographs. Data and information. Knowledge. He could have looked at her the same way he'd looked at Dorothea, Anna, Francesca, Willa, Lizabeth, and Jeanette. But when he looked at her, then, he didn't see data and history, analysis, and dissection. He was with Madeline in that tiny room. A woman he liked, loved, and wanted to honestly, completely understand.

"He kissed me — no, not like that — on the forehead. I didn't know what to do, what to say. For a moment, I thought it was a game, a way to get into my pants. Flatter the poor little student; make an offer for some modeling or a night of instruction. But that's all he did. That's all he did. He traded me my work for his sketch, I wrapped it up, he kissed me on the forehead and ... and he said, 'Thank you.' I have it, of course, the sketch. But I don't show it to anyone. It's not that you're not special or anything, it's just ... mine. When I draw and it doesn't come out right, or when a professor, or just a friend, or some idiot on the street looks at what I do, and says 'not good enough,' or 'needs refinement,' or 'amateur,' I take out that little doorway, those few simple lines, and I remember what Escobar told me after he kissed me on the cheek."

Classes and tests, insights and examinations, awards and degrees. There was a gap in his education. He didn't know how. He was ignorant. She was on one side: he was on the other.

"He said... he said something very special to me that night. I keep the sketch hidden, here in my room, but I always carry his words with me wherever I go. But you're not an artist, so I guess you wouldn't understand. Would you?"

She asked.

He answered, his voice weak and whispering, "I want to know."

* * * *

"Like this?"

"That's good, but you're holding it too tight. Relax. Let your wrist go limp, but not too limp." Bright and shiny, her laughter was bubbles trickling from the bottom of a champagne flute. "Flow, that's the word, just let it flow. Be natural."

"I don't know what I'm doing."

"Got a secret for you. No one really does. I think it's the great dark secret of the world. Everyone is just trying to do the best they can. Sometimes it works, sometimes it doesn't."

"I'm really worried about messing up. Disappointing you."

"You won't disappoint me. No one does it right the first time. I wasn't good when I started out, and sometimes I think I'm still not very good, but I know I'm better than five years ago."

"I'm not doing a very good job, I'm afraid."

"Sure you are, for a virgin. You're doing something you've never done before. Be gentle with yourself. This isn't easy."

"No, it's not. I can see how it would be hard to keep going."

"You mean not giving it all up?" A giggle like sweet wine again, jewels rising and the tickling of a nose. "But if you give up, you'll never get to the good part."

"It's hard to think of a good part right now," he said, looking at the table, the few lines he'd scratched there. This was a mistake, he thought. He knew his place and it wasn't to be on *this* side of the canvas. Rubbing the end of the charcoal, Philip smudged his thumb, darkening the swirls of his fingerprints. Instantly, he wanted it gone. To be clean again.

"But there is one. Like I said, when it's good ... no, sorry, that's probably just words to you — especially right now."

They were sitting on the futon, he at the very edge, she in the middle, he facing her, she facing him. Both of them still naked. In his lap was her tablet, her sketch of him flipped over and hidden. His own page was blank, except for a few sweeping black lines.

A mistake. He didn't need a catalogue, a professor, a study guide to tell him that. From the paper he glanced up, saw her eyes — her eyes watching him.

"But it is good," she said, shifting her body, breasts swaying, lithe legs stretching out. Between arms and hands, a flicker of pink nipple, tight and firm. "Keep trying. You'll see."

A big mistake. But she was there, face lighting the room, body warming it. A glow from a fire. Back to the tablet, charcoal returning to paper. He wanted to understand, but it didn't seem to be working. The paper was just paper, the lines were just lines. It wasn't anything close to what she was.

"I didn't tell you something. I said about when it was good, yeah, yeah, and when it was bad. But there's something else. No, don't stop — keep drawing."

Lines, a new one. Not a good one, but he forced himself to keep going. Her lips curled like that, her face was shaped like this, there was a shadow next to her nose, her brows were dark commas so he sketched them like punctuation. It wasn't good. He knew that.

"It changed me. It really did. I know what you're thinking; I'm another billowy art student with too much pigment in her veins. But it did, it really did."

It wasn't her. Brushing some charcoal aside, a wayward streak became a brutal smear. A frown at that. Anger at that. He wanted to flip the page, begin again. He wanted to put it down, give it up. This wasn't him. This wasn't something he understood. He felt naked — more than naked.

"You're not just painting a picture. You could take a photo and do that, but that's cheating — or something like that. I thought that's what I was supposed to do, at first. Probably what you're trying to do now, right?"

Warmth of skin contact, her hand on his thigh, a reach from where she sat to touch him. A smile at that. A line at that, then another, trying to pull her out of the paper, bring her to life in paper and charcoal.

"Uh huh," he mumbled, not knowing what to say.

"But that's not what it's about. You can't do it right, because there is no 'right' to any of it. I know what the books say, how some are better than others, all that stuff of masterpieces, but that's just a professor's opinion. Sorry."

"That's okay," he said, looking over the top of the tablet to see her eyes again. Blue. So blue — and all he had were black streaks and blurs to work with.

"It's like Escobar. I know you don't like his stuff, and that's okay, because it isn't about what he paints."

He looked, tried to see what she was, bring her out of the paper with what he had. In the back of his mind, a chorus of masters and teachers jeered and hissed at every stroke, every touch of tool to surface, but all he had to do was look up and see her there, on her cheap futon, in a bad part of Paris, to remind himself why he was there and what he was trying to do.

"Pictures are nice, and I love them, probably as much as you do, but what touches me ... what gets to me..." she paused, the moment followed by a firmer squeeze on his thigh, her voice speaking of looming tears "...is what they were trying to do."

Suddenly, a part of his drawing — just a part — the way her nose looked in the poor light of her little studio, wasn't that bad. Looking at it, he felt the smile, his own bubble of laughter. Who would have thought? But he realized it wasn't right. That wasn't the way her nose really looked; he hadn't captured it at all. He'd failed. He'd failed. Fingers clenching at the edges of the paper, he felt again the impulse to tear it up, wad it into something honest: garbage.

"It's not what you make. It's never about just making pretty pictures. Escobar showed me that. Funny, now here I am, trying to teach the teacher the same thing."

No, it wasn't right. It wasn't correct, that one part of the sketch. But then he knew something else, and it all fell away. It wasn't accurate, but it was true. That tiny fragment wasn't a perfect description of Madeline's face. It wouldn't incite dissection, examination, a paper, a treatise, a critique.

It was how *he* saw her, how Philip viewed Madeline.

"It's not the painting that matters. It's what you feel when you do it, and how that comes across when you've put down the last of it. That's why I do it. Because it makes me feel wonderful to show the world what I feel."

His face ... his face was hot. His breathing quick and shallow. Drops, on the page, circles of moisture wrinkling the marks he'd drawn. His hands were gently shaking.

"What did he tell you?"

"Escobar? He said that anything done with the heart, with the love of the doing, is always beautiful. Just like what you have drawn tonight."

Then she was wrapped around him and her tears joined his, the sketch he'd drawn falling to the side to make room for their touches, and then their kisses.

* * * *

The same place, a different time. Days later, looking through that thick glass window, down the white tunnel of that gallery.

After a kiss of parting, he'd left her little apartment and floated down through the rough and tumble streets of the quarter, unafraid of anything. No dates had been exchanged because he knew they didn't need to. She'd call, he'd call, and they'd be together again. He'd felt good before, he'd felt giddy and light before, but never this good, this giddy, this light. He liked it. He *loved* it. He felt free.

A lightness, a smile on his face, but deep inside him was a weight, a downward pull that kept him from floating off into the dark evening sky. That last kiss had been warm, not hot. A kiss between lovers, not just between a man and a woman who'd shared a night of orgasmic fun. Her eyes had been wet, her cheeks gleaming with tears. Matching his own. He'd couldn't remember crying with anyone, ever, before.

Street to Metro, Metro to … for some reason, he didn't want to go home, at least not yet. It was late, only a few cars sliding by, only a few other people stumbling along with him. He had things to do in the morning, classes to teach, papers to grade, meetings to attend, but he kept walking. It all seemed so unimportant.

He walked for a very long time. Chest getting tight, legs feeling packed with iron shot, he kept moving. At one dark corner, a tiny café shut up tight, a kiosk shuttered, a garage closed, he stopped to catch his breath. He didn't recognize the neighborhood. Looking down one street and up a nearby other, he felt an old familiar reflex, hunting up artistic comparisons: the night sky by Delacroix, torn posters against one wall by Duchamp, streaks of old paint on another by Ernst, a red-lit window and gently billowing shade by Grosz, again the Philip reflected back up at him from the oily street at his feet by Picasso, again the streaks of taillights the fanciful creatures of Kandinsky, the quiet night and architecture by Hopper, his hands once again by da Vinci, in marble by Michelangelo, Van Gogh's stellar streetlights, the perspective of this ordinary part of the city by Cezanne. But this time, unlike the last time he'd stood and simply looked at a dark Paris street, he wasn't alone. Thoughts of Madeline kept him company.

Walking again, turning here, there, then a few quick recognitions: a landmark in the distance, the name of an avenue, the awning of a shut-up patisserie. He knew where he was. Serendipity? Had his feet known what his mind hadn't? Did the world turn just so, to put him at that very intersection of avenues? He didn't know. But recognizing where he was turned him, pointed him towards a destination.

Then he was there, standing in front of a window, looking down white walls at the end of a gallery. It had been raining the last time he'd been here. He remembered the smell of wet concrete, the mad reflections of water, the shushing of cars driving through shallow puddles.

The painting was gone. It had been hanging in the back of the gallery. He remembered it; colors without form or complement, clashing tones, warring hues. It had been a riot, an explosion, a splatter of pigments. There'd been no control there, no skill, no refinement, no vision. It had hung on the wall, simply taking up space. It had been ugly — and that was being polite.

But that was before. Before Madeline. Before his own hand sketching on a pad. Before it had all changed.

"It's gone."

Philip wasn't alone, so late at night, in front of *L'Art*. Next to him was a short little man, stocky, with a brush of gray hair. He looked compressed, weighed down by more than just a heavy, fur-trimmed coat. His accent said far eastern Europe, Croatia or maybe even Russia, his words a simple inquiry.

"The painting that was there back there, did you see it?"

"I did. I saw it," Philip said, looking past him, through the window, at the blank wall where the Escobar had hung.

What had he seen? Paint on a canvas, but much more than that. Invisible before, visible now — not just pigment, but art created from within, reflecting what was inside. What Escobar was: a portrait revealing the entire spectrum of the artist.

"What did you think of it?" the man asked.

"It was lovely," Philip answered.

CHAPTER FOUR

Marcel

I

"You're not listening. Be quiet. I said be quiet. Didn't I just say I only want the five ... the *big* five? Didn't I? Don't you dare bring up Desparimou. I'm well aware of how much that boy paid for that ghastly Guillaume last year, but you are obviously ignorant of the fact that he hasn't paid close to that amount since. He might look like he has a checkbook, but it is Papa who handles the funds. I said I want the *big* five and that's all I want. Yes, I know how difficult it may be for you to get them together, but that's what I pay you for, isn't it? Maybe I should hire someone else to make the arrangements. Or is a commission on a new and undocumented work not interesting enough for you? Good, I thought that might restore your concentration. I think sometime next month would be good, before they scamper off to their villas and yachts on the Azure. No, I don't think that's impossible. In fact, I think for what I have here, it's more than possible. You simply do what I'm paying you for and tell them what I've told you and they'll come. Understand? No, I'm not willing to discuss it. I've told you what I want, so make some calls or whatever it is you do."

Returning the phone to its cradle with a soft, ghostly chime, Marcel took a deep breath, a slow intake with closed eyes to steady his jangling nerves. Again, it seemed, the way of the world — in sight of the heavens yet dragged back down to earthly soil by someone else's ineptitude. Still, he wasn't going to let Gerard completely overcast his mood. His secretary would do the job, for better or more than likely, as always seemed the case, for worse, but even if he got only three or four of the bidders, that should be enough to get a heady financial battle going.

As he picked up his clipboard, the neatly ordered papers slid under his fingers: invoices, shipping orders, insurance forms, schedules — sheaves of business minutiae. This artist, that work, this buyer, that invoice. Any other night he'd add it all up, make it balance. In the end, black or red ink would determine whether it would be a night of champagne (black) or cheap wine (red). But tonight he didn't need to.

The lights were out, except for a single bright halogen sun set high in the ceiling. Everything in *L'Art* was shadowed, shaded, obscured, but one square of paint and pigment was brightly revealed.

Stepping away from the glass-topped desk, he turned and glanced out front. Outside, looking in, a young man stood — maybe student, maybe green-stemmed professional, maybe even child of the very nouveau riche — eyes bright in reflection from the halogen. Marcel almost waved him away, a gesture to dismiss him back to his coffee houses, clumsy collegiate seductions, pretentious cinemas, fumbling musical performances — the frivolous life of an adolescent, arrogantly assured that they would never have thinning hair, an expanding waistline, or dentures in a glass by the bed.

The wave went unexecuted. Instead, Marcel turned to the revelation of that bright spot on the wall. Small, yet excellent: a perfect example of the wunderkind's style.

Three, four, or perhaps all five would come, but only one would walk out with this new, undiscovered work. The real winner, though, would be the owner/operator of *L'Art*. The numbers, after the five came, the five bid, and one paid, would be nothing but black for him.

Sitting at the reception desk, he'd matched the corners and edges of each invoice, shipping order, insurance form, and schedule. That done, he'd aligned the clipboard with the edge of the desk. After that, it was time for the pens: one after another until they were a row of candy-colored plastic.

Everything aligned and uniform, he'd done the last task of the night, the call to Gerard. Executed. Complete. Nothing left to do. No more stretching out his anticipation. Time to go upstairs, open a bottle of very special champagne, and celebrate.

From the desk to the young man standing outside, from the young man to the work on the wall. It was bold, overbearing, egotistical. It was bright, vibrant, and ridiculously strong. It was contemptuous of traditional techniques, cheeky with genius. It was the portrait of the artist as a success, a sensual dynamo — a name to be remembered. From the Escobar hanging there to the stairs in the back and up to his office, but before he put one step on the narrow stairway, he looked back, at the little meter square of lively reds, passionate yellows, sensual greens. Marcel, the gallery owner, frowned, deep and bitterly, at the painting.

* * * *

Home was a lovely house on Rue Condorcet he'd paid a small fortune for. It was a place to eat simple meals, watch dull television shows, listen to Brahms, sleep in a big bed, put on his suits and tie his ties. It was not a place for celebrations.

Up the narrow stairs. At the top, a tight landing twisted him into the office. It wasn't a big space, a few meters smaller than the gallery below because of a storage room at the back, but it was big enough for the black marble slab of his private desk, four file and two narrow, drawer print cabinets, and even a ridiculously plush, upholstered cloud of a sofa. On the walls were framed prints of exhibitions — two from his, three from other galleries — that every time he looked at them he thought about taking down, replacing with something new, but never did.

Looking at his own desk, he considered picking up those pens, those other papers, the leather-wrapped pencil cup, and organizing them as well, matching edges and straightening corners, but just as with the prints on the walls, he didn't turn thought into action. The prints were left because he didn't have anything better. The mess on his desk existed because he simply couldn't wait any longer.

Sitting in the chair that had looked so good in the office supply store but always made his back ache if he stayed in it longer than four hours, he opened the desk drawer, reached in, and pulled out a pair of address books. The first, in red, with furry edges from many page turns, contained the names and numbers of artists, agents, shipping companies, insurers — the people of the business that was *L'Art*. It went back into the drawer.

Many people suggested that he make the climb into the twenty-first century, abandon paper and clipboards and phone books for a machine that would do it all and more for him. They even came in designer colors, computers did, with tasteful schemes that would fit even the elegance and simplicity of his gallery. But Marcel liked paper, the weight and reality of it. Although everyone told him they were there to stay, they just felt too ... temporary and mercurial to him. So, his files, clipboards, cabinets, and phone books remained.

The other address book was smaller, less well thumbed. He didn't open it. Not yet. Impatient excitement was a stiffness in his back, beyond even the bad chair, but he only tapped the cover of the little book with one finger.

One name in that other book was Escobar, one of the first names he'd put in. Five years ago? Six? He could look it up if he wanted to, the date of that first purchase, the morning that scruffy little Spaniard came in. Was it a newspaper, some art journal, or just general chat over coffee? Marcel rubbed the bridge of his nose, trying to remember how he'd first heard of the new artist, the one with the vibrant, lively style. In the end, though, it wasn't important. What was important, the only thing that mattered, was what hung on the walls of his gallery, and what lay in a folder in one of the filing cabinets: exclusivity. Escobar was his. Escobar belonged to him.

Tap, tap, tap on the cover. The trash bin next to his desk, he noticed, was still full: the bright leaves of magazine pages, fanned and crumbled in a Swedish modern bin. Four days ago he'd taken the stack of new issues and swept them with one close-fisted, tight-muscled sweep off the desk and onto the floor. It was only after many deep, controlled breaths that he'd been able to collect himself enough to get down on the tight nap weave of the office floor and collect them all, then drop them where they belonged, in the bin.

"The artist of the new century," "a true visionary," "the best of the best," "showing us things we should all see, in ways we could never expect," "beauty in all its truest forms," "a powerful vision," "glorious visions," and simply "genius."

But that was four days ago.

Since then, things had changed. Eyes blurring, he grinned as he opened the little book and began to studiously turn pages.

II

"Didn't you hear me? I didn't say Michelle, I didn't say Zazu, and I clearly didn't say Claire. I said Josephine. That's who I said and that's who I'm making an appointment with. Yes, I heard you, but what I don't understand is why there's a problem. I thought I had an understanding with your agency that my needs would be met — and this is clearly not recognizing my needs or our relationship. I don't care that she is *not* available, because she *should* be available."

No soft ring this time when he returned the handset to its cradle. His office phone was better than the stylish, though inefficient, one downstairs. Deep breaths again, jangled nerves returned. Heaven obscured once more because someone simply didn't do their job.

No, he wasn't going to let this ruin his celebration. Josephine was who he wanted, but because of stupidity, couldn't have. The new girl, Zazu, was available, and so he simply had to deal with the disappointment as best he could and try to enjoy himself.

Standing, he smoothed his shirt, vanishing wrinkles with a few sweeps of his hand. An abrupt look around the office didn't reveal anything that needed his attention, nothing embarrassing. Home was for dull yet filling meals, watching common television shows, listening to the lovely compositions of Brahms, sleeping in his big brass and silk bed, putting on his expensive suits, and neatly tying his ties — but not for celebrations, especially celebrations for *L'Art*. For that, his office was just too appropriate.

Selling a work was more than enough cause, but because of the work hanging below, lit by that firm brilliance of a spotlight, this was more than special. After six years of hanging his work on the walls of *L'Art*, he suspected, then knew, that Escobar wasn't honoring that special term in their contract. *Exclusivity* might not mean anything to the painter, but to Marcel it was more than fifteen percent. It meant honor, it meant respect. Mind returning, back and back and back, to his suspicions that had been nightmares and anger, ulcers and many deep, slow breaths — until a man walked into *L'Art* with a meter square of canvas wrapped in dirty newspapers.

Glancing at his Rolex, Marcel stepped around his desk. The new girl would arrive soon. The smooth voice on the phone had said that she'd be leaving immediately, and although Paris was a snail-vortex of roads, it was possible for her to get from her point A to his point B fairly quickly, no matter where that starting point was.

Where was the thing? He remembered walking in just that morning. He'd put it down... there, on the print cabinet, hiding behind a blue glass lamp in the shape of a crescent moon. A celebration required many things, but special celebrations required special things. A phone call made from his book was one, an appointment made, a fine vintage was another. Brown paper rustled as he rolled it down the heavy bottle. The label was gold and elegant, the price had been impressive, but it would be worth it. Pulling a couple of glasses from the bottom drawer of a file cabinet, he put them and the bottle neatly on his desk, making sure the two small circles of the flutes and the larger of the bottle made a near, and suspenseful, triangle. Hope then, that Zazu would be as acceptable as the sparkling bubbles and cloying flavor of the champagne.

The city snail moved faster than usual, for the buzzer immediately sounded, shockingly loud, much more so than he remembered. A glance at his reflection in one of the prints — a Monet exhibition two years ago — confirmed that his thinning brown hair looked respectable enough and that his suit wasn't too horribly wrinkled. One, after all, should inspire respect — even from late night, expensive visitors.

Down the stairs, the glare from the halogen dazzled him. For a shaved moment of a second, there was nothing but brilliance and the painting on the wall. The Escobar. The power and the color and the beauty of a master at his peak, a painting that should have been brought into his gallery by the artist himself, a work of vibrancy and sensual mastery that should have been sold through proper channels, sold through *L'Art*. But it hadn't been. Instead, its bold composition and skillful use of color had been delivered to him under the arm of a little Russian man, an unknown and uncatalogued work sold by the artist to the matriarch of a White Russian family, a family now in desperate need of money.

When he managed to forget for a second the shame and anger embodied in that little bundle that had come under the arm of that Russian, he could see it for what it was and he didn't have words for it. It was a lovely work, amazing and moving. It was exquisite. But remembering its objective beauty was rare, so instead it hung on the wall, lit by an unblinking light, showing not art but revealing a portrait of the artist as ugly, deceiving, and dishonorable.

The door — yes, the door. Tonight was a celebration, the sale of a work that would bring Marcel not just a percentage but every single franc he was due — and nothing for the ugly, deceiving, and dishonorable artist. This evening would be champagne and the treat pressing the front door buzzer again.

Tonight would be a night of enjoyment, of a different kind of beauty, a different form of sensuality. A celebration for Marcel. A celebration of victory over Escobar.

Then he noticed as he approached the door, that her hair was vivid purple.

III

"Late. Sorry. Couldn't find my purse, traffic was crazy, road work everywhere, lots of folks out and about, Metro was a zoo, it's a full moon, so forth, so on — but here I am."

Hand around the chrome handle, he held the door open. Half his mind said to tell her she wasn't wanted, that he'd take up with the agency his displeasure over this replacement, as was his privilege as a favored client of many years. The remaining half told him to resign himself to the moment, put on a brave countenance, celebrate as much as he could with this — what was available and immediate — then swing the door wide, telling her to save her excuses and enter.

Neither half of his mind got a chance to do anything. Ducking under his arm with a remarkably quick and elegant dance step, palm on the glass door, pushing it wide, she was in before he could say or do anything to her or about it.

"Magnifique."

Throaty and deep, her voice sounded like she inhaled a pack of Gitanes a day, or maybe it was just the prelude to a long and throaty purr.

"What a place."

At her feet, dropped spontaneously, was a huge black leather purse like an upholstered gourd. As she'd swept in, something heavy had struck his leg. The bag was an obvious suspect.

"Très chic," she said, pirouetting in the middle of the gallery.

Purple hair like a precisely cut helmet above a body hidden by absolute black, she was tall. But beyond her height, the rest of her was effectively camouflaged by a voluminous coat of cheap leather, worn to a yellowed fringe at the hem. Elfin, firmly edged cheekbones drawn forward to a narrow nose, above a pair of thin lips the color of her hair. Her face was animated — jumping, leaping, springing from dulled world-weariness when she'd stood outside to mischievous merriment as she darted in, to struck amazement as she stood and spun in the middle of the space.

Irritating, every last bit: her appearance, her momentary brusqueness, her mercurial whimsy, her fleeting wonder — and irritation wasn't what he wanted, or, more importantly, what he was paying well-deserved francs for. It was supposed to be an evening sipping a rare vintage from a crystal flute, refined entertainment, elegant arousal — not growling vowels and cheap hair dye.

She shrugged off her coat with a few quick gestures — one shoulder, then the other, finally folding it over one arm. Under, and now exposed, was still more black, even more purple: a short dress, tight and hugging, not revealing but at least suggesting a voluptuous body, an hourglass with sand in potentially attractive places. Continuing below, a pair of lively stockings the color of her hair and lips hugging a pair of excellently turned legs, down to a pair of clogs a waitress might wear to serve her customers.

Refinement and distinction, a superior bottle of exorbitant champagne, a night in the company of a courtesan of expertise and dexterity — supposed to be, should have been, was requested, instructed, and most importantly of all, deserved.

That thought was one half, but the other half appraised her as the coat came off. It was that half, the one that saw the sand in her hourglass that spoke.

"Oui, you are late," he said, closing and locking the door with a quick twist of the bolt. "As you admitted a moment ago, I requested Josephine and, as a favored and regular customer of your agency, I expected to have my reasonable request honored. I was very disappointed to learn that your agency obviously does not respect me or my business as they have sent me someone obviously unsuitable. No, let me finish. While I am displeased by this situation, I am an understanding, and in my own way flexible, man, so I am willing to attempt to salvage this evening by retaining your services. Do you understand? Am I making myself clear?"

"Yeah, sure, whatever," Zazu said, a wide grin, rows of bright teeth, cheekbones high. "This place got an upstairs?"

IV

"Hey, that's a ... god, what's his name? *Escobar* — that's him, right?"

She suddenly asked as they walked back towards the stairs. The *that* she was looking at was pinned to the wall in the harsh light of the spotlight.

"The guy everyone's talking about."

Foot on the first step, he twisted to see where she was looking. Allowing that he was impressed, admitting it in the tone of his voice, would give her an advantage, tip the scales between them.

But as he said, "You are quite correct. I'm his exclusive world dealer. In fact, that's a very recent acquisition — only this week. A fine work, if I may say so myself. I expect it will bring in quite a large sum at auction," he knew he'd surrendered his advantage.

Yet if she was aware of the tip of the balance between them, she didn't seem to notice. Instead, she stood — just stood — and looked at it. Coat over one arm, heavy bag dangling from the other, cat eyes focused on the square of colorful canvas, it took her an elongated moment to pull away and back to him.

"If you are quite ready?" he said, gesturing up. This time he cut his vowels, leaving behind a sharp, impatient edge.

A response was expected — gutter shot, snide retort, or even a simple quick profanity — but she followed him up the stairs in silence. Rounding the top, he nodded to the sofa.

"You may put your bag there. I have to ask you not to touch anything while you're here. I'm sure you'll understand. I deal with many very important clients and artistic works of significant value."

More was queued in his mind, but he bit back the words. Why this sudden need to impress her?

"Oui, oui," she said finally, dropping all of it on the couch, the cushions springing and squeaking in complaint. "I've got it. I know the drill." Bright purple bangs swayed above bright eyes as she twisted her head and sighed as she released the burden of her heavy coat. "You know it, too, right?"

The soft pop of the cork echoed in the room, the round-edged sound bouncing back and forth off the walls like an acoustical rubber ball. The neck of the bottle was cool, not too cold. Bubbles threatened to spill, but he poured at the right moment, sparkles only into the glass.

"Yes, we have an understanding, that is correct. I'm familiar with the terms of your employment. I hope the agency has instructed you with regard to my needs as well?"

Accepting the glass with a smile, she took a quick and delicate sip. "Nice."

The planes and angles of her face wrote an emotion he couldn't quite read. Wry humor? Wicked intent? Sympathetic knowledge?

"They're good that way — never have to go in anywhere without knowing a bit about the client." Crossing her arms, glass still in one hand, she glanced around. "Not that I couldn't have guessed. I mean, merde, look at this place: can you be more obvious?" Purple lips to glass, a long drink, then away, a ghostly set of prints remaining on the edge. "You like to watch, right?"

Her bluntness staggered him. Foam came close to the top of his glass, an impending spill.

"I would not put it as *commonly* as that."

Stalling for composure, he put the champagne down too carefully, absently falling again into the ritual of aligning the bottle with the corner of the desk.

"I enjoy it, yes, but I prefer to consider my interest as a refined and aesthetic appreciation of the female form."

More words again waited, but once again stayed in his throat. Why did he need to explain himself?

"Same difference." Stretching out, she rested her flute next to the bottle, ruining the symmetry. "I think I've got the picture. So ... you ready?"

Josephine would have sat on the edge of the settee, alabaster fingers tipped by pearlescent nails around the crystal, eyelashes rising and falling in a gentle ballet of grace, discussing — perhaps — the newest twist or embarrassment in the world of fashion or the failings of the current theatrical season. Josephine's legs would be crossed, her own superb choice in dress revealing, with a whisper of silks and satins, the hint of a perfectly sculpted leg. Josephine would have laughed as she spoke, as she moved her legs to reveal and then temptingly obscure her body, like the stemmed flute she held; a sound that chimed with sophistication and, despite the anticipated progression of the evening, dignity.

Zazu grinned wide, showing teeth white as plastic yet just-so, kind-of uneven. Kicking, she sent her clogs tumbling in an end-over-end of common leather, missing — but only by the slightest margin — one of the legs of his black steel desk. Zazu kneaded her stockinged toes, working the nap and weave of the carpeting with feet shadowed by purple silk.

"So, you're going to sit there?" A nod towards the desk chair. "And you want me ... here, right? Is that the plan?"

Sighing as loud as he could without bridging the gap between communicated disappointment and theatrical embarrassment, Marcel walked around the desk.

"Yes, that is correct. I will remain behind the desk the entire time, and you shall be approximately there."

With Josephine, it had all been understood. No words needed to be exchanged. Carefully sitting — again wishing the chair's comfort was on par to its complement to the decor — he moved her glass to a point equidistant between the bottle and the edge of the desk.

"At no time do I require you to approach me."

"You're paying the bill," she said. Josephine had never mentioned money. "Guess I'll start then. That okay with you?"

Josephine had known when to begin and what to do.

Marcel looked down at his desk, not at the girl. Heaven, again, was far away. He'd been held down by the leaden idiocy and sluggish minds of others. This, what should have been a night of sparkling delight and orchestrated bliss, was only a heavyset, middle-aged man, pathetically paying for the company of a common prostitute with purple hair. He almost told her to leave, so he could try and fade the memory of this night, to move on. He told himself to open the bottle some other time and entertain himself in a more satisfactory manner.

But then he recalled the genesis of this evening, his celebration. A Russian with a painting under his arm, proof of what Marcel had suspected all along: that the man he'd sponsored, the artist he'd nurtured and brought out into the world, had betrayed him.

Thinking of Escobar made him angry, and so he looked up from the heavy slab of his modern desk and said to her in a voice unlike his normal glossy resonance: "Take off your damned clothes."

* * * *

"Like I said: you're the boss," Zazu said.

If she was insulted, she showed no sign of it. If anything, the smile that fluttered and played on her sharp features was more wry, wicked, or even sympathetic than before.

"If you want me to do something special, you just ask — otherwise I'm just going to do a little act for you, okay?"

Fanned fingers ran down her dress, smoothing the fabric, giving the suggestion of the firmness of her hidden body.

"I also like to talk a bit."

He almost told her to be quiet but didn't. The departure from composure had made his heart beat much too fast, made his face much too hot. A breath in, a breath out, and everything slowed, eased, calmed. But still he didn't speak, frightened of what he might say or how he'd say it. Instead, he merely looked at her, agreeing with a quick nod.

"Bien," she said with a hidden teeth grin. A steady spider walk, her hands then went to the hem, her thematically shaded nails bouncing up and down against the dark fabric backdrop.

"Quiet can be so oppressive, don't you think?"

Oppressive for her, perhaps, but at that moment, Marcel was praying for a bit of it — an island of stillness in his darting, clanging mind, his pulse a fluid rushing in his ears. What had happened to his orderly, precise, and wonderfully calm life?

Her hem lifted, inch-by-inch, knee revealed, thigh exposed — then the revelation that she didn't wear hose, but true stockings.

An arrangement of black finery and silken-stitched filigree that jarred against her brusque and jangling persona as well as her shockingly colored hair and lips. Beneath the fabric, her legs were firm, smooth perfection.

Up and up it rose: the hose topped by a band of finely stitched charcoal flowers, stays ascending, belt hidden by the rising dress.

"I should be humming something, shouldn't I? Like stripper music? Can't sing worth a damn, though. But I have other talents."

Who was he? What was he threatening to become? Was a boorish lout just around the corner? A coarse and primitive man? A soccer and popular music fan? Who was he? He thought he knew: a connoisseur. A gentleman of refinement and taste. A man of intelligence. The respected owner and operator of *L'Art*. The sole agent and dealer for many celebrated artistic talents. The sole agent and dealer for one special artistic talent.

"See my panties?"

More dark flowers, fine workmanship of thread and fabric. More not there than there, they hinted at a flower of fine hairs, the rise of a plush pudenda. They suggested a gentle sweep up to fine hips.

"Aren't my panties nice?"

He was four walls: a venue. He was where people went to see the artist's work, the man who took their money. Was that all? Or was he even less than that — a broker not even worth the consideration of being told of a new commission. A fluke, that was all, that Russian with an unknown Escobar under his arm and he never would have known. The deception exposed, but now his true position in life obvious: he was Marcel, he was only four walls:

just a gallery owner. Middle-aged, alone, sipping champagne with a prostitute.

Without anger, he stared down at his desk through half-shut lids, weights on his shoulders, life losing color and resolution, washing away to gray.

"I like showing you my panties," she was saying, "but I want to show you more than that."

The rustling of fabric. The sound of heavy cloth falling to tight-napped carpeting. He lifted his gaze from the marble surface of his desk and stared across the tight span of the office.

No sound, no motion. A memory: a young man standing in soft quiet and staring in rapt awe at a work of brilliance, of captured paint and pigment splendor. He'd been in his early twenties, a student with nowhere to go, taking classes to fill his life. Then, an assignment to visit the Louvre. He'd been before, of course, with his parents, other students, girls he was seeing, but that time it was different. The way the light behaved that day, a certain combination of place and time, perhaps he himself in a new stage of being. Why that time and not the others, he didn't know.

She was beautiful. No other word. No other way to say it. Before it had just been a word, easily tossed around without anything to anchor it, to give it firm meaning. But then, as he stood and gazed, the word was there: beautiful. She was beautiful.

The picture was gone when he went back, returned to whomever had loaned it to the museum. But it stayed in his mind, a work of art to match his own personal idea of what was lovely, sensual, pretty.

To say that the woman standing in front of him now was the living embodiment of Ruben's *Little Fur* would have been an exaggeration, but not by much. Or, like that day in the museum, perhaps it was the light spilling onto her body, this time and this place, or that the Marcel at that moment wasn't the same Marcel of only a minute before.

Zazu was beautiful. Standing with relaxed ease only a few meters away from him, her body was rich and full. Sensual and inviting. Below, stockings. Above, a garter belt looped around an hourglass waist, canted over rounded hips. Above, the gentle dome of a plumy belly, winking eye of a playful navel. Farther above, heavy breasts spilled gently over the cups of more sable blossoms.

"Do you like?" she said, her voice soft, a throaty whisper.

I do, he wanted to say. You are lovely, he wanted to say — but he didn't, concerned not by what he might say, but that anything he would say would break the moment or ruin the spell.

Sliding down her hips, her fingers looped through the garter belt. Then around to the front, lingering over the snaps.

The right one was let loose as she said, "I like this. The perfect job, eh?"

The second one, the left, was then released, elastic bouncing up. Then her hands went behind, working hooks and eyes. Free, the belt hung in one hand. It joined her dress on the floor.

Josephine would have given him a glimpse, a flash. A teasing glance at what lay hidden. She would have held back, as he'd instructed. Remaining aloof and removed, she would have been as flawless as the ringing crystal, as refined and distilled as the champagne. Worthy of being hung on a wall, a creation to be displayed and admired.

He wanted to touch Zazu. He wanted to reach out, to feel her skin, to weigh a breast in his hand, feel a rubbery nipple between thumb and forefinger. He wanted to run his fingers over her. He wanted to drink her. Taste her. He wanted to hold this Little Fur tight, close, and feel her breath on his cheek.

But he didn't move. Even though for the first time in many years, he felt a bodily tug below his waist to do more, he was captured and held in place, struck dumb and pinned down.

"I love my breasts," she said. "I love the way they look, but I really like the way they feel."

Purple-painted nails slid over the slopes, stroked under, and deliberately hesitated over the rises of her nipples. One hand went behind, reaching for another clasp, preparing for another revelation.

More than at any time in recent memory, he was aroused. With Josephine it had been there, but more abstract, more a quality of the whole experience than a pulse-matched deep down, stirring where he wasn't Marcel the gentleman, the rich man, the owner of *L'Art*, but rather just a man and a very demanding desire. He might still be struck by silence, but he could move.

There was a good reason Zazu would love her breasts. They were phenomenal. Large yet exceptionally firm, they swept gently from the satin of her chest, ending in two saucer-sized, swollen areolas, topped by aggressively firm nipples the color of fresh strawberries and the size of gumdrops. As her bra joined her clothes at her feet, her breasts swung and jiggled, a mesmerizing display.

"Aren't they beautiful? I'm so lucky. But what's even better is that I like how they feel, not just how they look."

With thumb and forefinger, she tightly plucked at her right nipple, much harder than he'd ever seen a woman do before. She hissed, deep and languid, in response. Then the same, this time to the left, but now the hiss became a moan and her knees seemed to lose a bit of their strength.

"Oh, wow," she said through a sharp laugh.

Stroking himself, he realized he didn't care that he was or that she knew he was. It was too good. This woman was beautiful and sexy, and more importantly, he was enjoying himself more than he ever had before. How his zipper had come down, how he'd extracted himself from his underwear, he didn't know, but there it was and he wasn't about to stop. Again, the question — but this time only the barest of whispers in his mind and nowhere near a loud thought: what am I? The answer came immediately: I am me... and I like this.

The other nipple again; this time she had to catch herself before dropping all the way to the carpet. It took her some time to pull herself up and stand straight.

"I like this. It's one of my... things, I guess you could call it."

Peering through her purple bangs, she caught his gaze with hers. "Having fun?"

Even before he'd realized he'd broken the silence, he found his voice. "I-I am."

"That's good. I like to share ... what feels good."

The pause was the left nipple, this time more than a pinch, much more than a squeeze. Wide-eyed, he couldn't believe the force she put into the pressure on that sensitive part of her body. Seemingly overwhelmed, she dropped — unable to support herself standing — onto her knees. Face down, purple strands of hair falling in a curtain of bright color, she panted, heavy and fast.

In syncopation, he joined her, his breaths no longer a controlling, calming, steady in and out, but instead a rapid, ragged tempo. He could feel it. It was close.

Then, Zazu lifted her head and grinned again. Reflecting the lights in his office, her face was shining with her own perspiration. Arching her back, she slipped a hand inside the waistband of her delicate panties.

"I love this."

The world was that hand, everything followed her fingers behind the satin and silk. As her knuckles pressed out against the fabric, he tried to see exactly what she was doing. Out then, hand withdrawing, she took in a prolonged shuddering breath and held up two fingers for him to see. They gleamed.

It was there, strong and shattering — a body rush that cut all control, severed his mind from everything but a surging rush of pleasure from his penis to his testicles to his legs to his back to his chest and his mind. Focus gone, his lids slipped down over his eyes. Muscles sprung, he lowered himself in drops and catches, resting his cheek eventually on the slick marble surface of his desk.

Laying there in a pleasurably dazed stupor, unable to move, speak, or do anything but let the lightning of his orgasm fade into a hazy thunder, he was sure that she spoke. He was certain he heard Zazu's voice easing across the distance between them, a deep purr carrying the music of humor.

"All in a good night's work."

V

"I-I'd categorize that as a pleasurable interlude."

He coughed into his hand, but there hadn't been a tickle in his throat.

"I would even go as far as to say that it was more, almost much more, than I was expecting. I hope you won't take offense, for none is implied, but when I first saw you, I... didn't believe you would be able to provide anywhere near the service I'd enjoyed in the past. But I have to admit — no, I willingly admit — that I was wrong."

Blinking, he lifted his head from the desk, the surface of his cheek and the slick surface of the desk tacky, gripping one another. Running fast fingers over his lips, he was, in a hot moment, sheepish about their excessive moisture.

"Quite entertaining. Quite. Very pleasurable. Not that I have extensive experience in such matters, you understand. I may use your service periodically, but it really is more for a social form of recreation than ... than I guess you could say what happened this evening. Not that there's anything wrong in what we did tonight, not at all. I just don't want you to think that I'm the sort of man who does this kind of thing often."

While he was face down on his office furniture, she started to get dressed. Somewhere, starting when his strings had been cut and he'd descended to the desktop and he'd pulled himself away with a blush, Zazu worked herself back into most of her clothing. Putting on his own composure, he focused across the room and saw the purple-haired girl sitting on the edge of the sofa, patiently rolling a stocking up a well-turned leg.

Seeing him seeing her, she grinned and said, "Hi there. Have a good time?"

"As I said, I'm honestly not that familiar with how you or the agency might operate — beyond phoning to make an appointment, I mean — so I hope I don't, or haven't, committed some kind of egregious error tonight."

Then she spoke, smiling wider than she had before, adding to her earlier grin a muscle for each word too many he'd stammered. "Nope, you were a prince. Really."

"That's good. Very good. Back to my ignorance, I don't really know how to... well, request would be a good word, I believe, to ask for your company again. Shall I contact the agency and ask for you? Or can we make arrangements now for say, a week from tonight? If that's agreeable to you, I mean. Of course, it would be for the same remuneration as well. I do know that much about how things operate."

Eyes back down, she took a leisurely moment to examine that leg, smoothing imperfections in the silk he couldn't see. Without looking up, she said, "You can call me, if you'd like. Or you can call them and they'll pass it along to me."

"I will. I will. I do believe I'll call you, if that's appropriate. Do you have a card or something, a number where I can reach you? I know I may be in danger of repeating myself, something I hope you realize I rarely do, but this was quite a pleasurable experience for m-me."

From the couch she stood, smoothing her lingerie, making sure the garter belt was secure and adjusted optimally. Hidden once again behind twin cups of black flowers, her breasts made him stammer and trip over his words again. Obscured while he wasn't looking, they were as fetching and mesmerizing as they had been when she first revealed them. Memory fought fantasy and he almost asked her to undo hooks and slip off straps so he could see them again. This time he wouldn't do anything but look, capture them in a much more determined and studious way in his mind.

Still in black lace and little else, she turned, bent in such a way that his frustration momentarily deepened because he couldn't see more, and dug in the depths of her bag. From it a card, passed with very little expression to him.

"Here's my number. There's my email address, but I don't check that very often."

"Merci, merci. I appreciate this. I assure you I'll call very soon. Very soon indeed."

To this, nothing but a return to dressing. In the tight silence, he felt his mouth move, words tumble out without thought.

"This is a night for new things, I guess, for I find myself needing to repeat myself yet again. But as you've shown me — and I thank you — I shouldn't be so distrustful of new things. In any event, I do have something I'd like to ask you, if you wouldn't mind, that is."

Dressed, covered, hidden first by lingerie, then by her dress, and now, the curtain of her coat closing, she flipped out a bit of wayward hair from around her neck. Over her shoulder went her bag, the bag he suddenly remembered as being heavy, a blow to the back of his leg.

"Sure, whatever. Ask away."

"It's just that ... well ... I'm just curious, with someone in your profession ... do you ... I don't want to be inappropriate or rude in asking."

Close enough to touch, she stood in front of the desk.

"Sorry, no discounts. It's an agency policy, I'm afraid."

"Oh, that's not what I meant. I would never ask for so crass a thing, believe me."

The mention of funds was a reminder, but before he could ask, he was aware of the tacky moisture on his hand. Opening a drawer, he removed a tissue from a box within. Diligent swipes, his cheeks roasting hot, cleaning what had remained of his pleasure from his fingers. The rest — further shame — no doubt wet streaks on the carpeting. Its work finished, the tissue joined the printed pages in the trash.

Breaths, fast and deep, once again a regaining of control, a pulling in of himself against the shame of this physical remains of his pleasure.

In and out, out and in, pulse loud in his ears, but this time not for carnal pleasure, but instead for what he really wanted to say, wanted to ask her. Covering his shame of wetness and fear of what she might say, he reached into another drawer to withdraw his checkbook.

As he wrote out the date, the agency's name, and the amount, he said, "No, what I meant to ask was whether you ever — how should

I say this? Do you ever feel there's something unique, special that happens to you occasionally in situations like this? That is to say where you may also experience a certain amount of enjoyment?"

"Did I have a good time, you mean?"

"Well ... yes, I guess that's what I mean."

She accepted the check. Folding it neatly, she slipped into her bag. "Absolutely, mon cher. Absolutely."

But words, posture, lips, cheeks, eyes, color said the opposite — all of it adding up, but resulting in a minus rather than a plus. A negative rather than a positive.

Breathe in, breathe out. He should get up, should kiss her cheek, or at least shake her hand. Should say one last pleasantry. Should regain his composure, his elegance, or maybe some dignity. Should try and be a gentleman again.

Instead, all he said was, "Please show yourself out," and held himself very straight in his uncomfortable desk chair.

* * * *

Payments to arrange. Invoices to confirm. Insurance forms to fill out. Customs declarations to complete. All of it had to be done, might as well be done now, but instead Marcel sat and stared across the small distance of his office. Mind a storm, a riot, the possible distractions of paperwork fluttered in his mind, but never landed. He sat. He stared.

What he could do — should do — was that paperwork, the business of the gallery. Back to life as usual. But was anything *usual* anymore? Ten minutes ago he'd been watching a rough-edged, purple-haired prostitute undress.

An evening before, he would have been happy to watch, to be titillated and aroused by the elegantly abstract, the refined aloofness of Josephine. They'd had an artistic arrangement: gallery owner to art, wall to what was being hung on it. An arrangement involving payment for services rendered. At the end, there had been no messes, nothing remaining behind but restrained joy. A courteous game, a civilized entertainment.

Something lingered, hung around his neck, clouded his vision. He envisioned reaching towards the phone, his fingers dialing, the agency responding, Zazu coming back.

Dazed, he thought of what she would do again, and what he'd ask for this time.

"Touch me" "Like that" "Do this" "Do that."

But there was more beyond wanting to see her smiling face as she explored beneath black roses, hand coming up glistening wet. A request based on more than seeing her perfect breasts again. Josephine had been on display, a pretty thing framed for examination and appreciation, but Zazu thrummed with life.

He put his face in his hands, feeling flushed cheeks on his palms. Childish. Idiotic. He was a middle-aged, heavy, balding gallery owner. Of course she would come again if requested. She would stand across the desk from him. Drop her dress. Touch herself. She would do even more. If he wrote a large enough check.

Affordable, she'd give anything — everything except a true, honest, delighted smile. That was what he wanted, he realized, more than her mouth, hands, or body. He wanted her down from the wall, to be closer than across the room. He wanted her, her true smile, her real delight. He wanted the one thing from her he could never buy. Never have.

A sigh, deep and long. Up on heavy legs from behind the desk, he stepped slowly to one of the cabinets, pulled open a heavy metal drawer. Payments. Invoices. Insurance forms. Customs declarations. Sheets and printouts. Folders and files. Picking one at random, he walked back towards the desk, the uncomfortable desk, where the everyday and usual business of *L'Art* was conducted.

Then he stopped — short and quick. Folder still in his hand, he realized he hadn't heard the front door open or close with Zazu's departure.

* * * *

Vandal. Thief. Prostitute. Quickly to the stairs. Fast but still careful not to stumble and fall. Nothing to worry about. She'd gone and he simply hadn't noticed. Vandal. Thief. Prostitute. Down the stairs. He'd been more than childish, idiotic, foolish not to show her out, make sure she was gone.

Bottom of the stairs. Front door still closed, paintings still on the walls, spotlight still on and highlighting the lie, the new work — the one the painter should have brought to him to sell, the commission Marcel had been denied — still a meter square of color, form, and style.

She hadn't left.

In front of it, she stood. Only, just, merely standing. Coat on, bag over a shoulder. No vandalism, no theft. The girl with the purple hair stood there, and only, just, merely staring at that one painting, at that single work of art.

Mouth open, he was about to say something — what, he didn't know. Just something. Outrage. Anger. A condemnation. An accusation. Insults. Humiliations. But he didn't.

Unmoving, she looked. From where he was, at the bottom of the stairs, to her left, he could see her face, her expression.

Happy, blissful, enraptured. Warm, soft, and open. Appreciative, ecstatic, and elated. Euphoric, joyful, and delighted.

Seeing him then, her elfin cheeks rosy, long lashes dipped in shame.

"I-I'm sorry," she said, caught in the middle of honest delight. "I-I'll get out of here."

Then she did, moving to the door, fumbling with the locks, pushing on the heavy glass. Without a word or a glance back, she was gone.

Slow and heavy, he followed behind her, lagging enough so that when he put his hand on the handle, she was nowhere to be seen. Flipping the bolt, arming the alarm, he moved across the white box of the gallery, towards the stairs and back up to conclude his business of the night. On the way, from the front to the back, he paused and looked up at the painting on the wall.

"You bastard," he said, reaching towards it.

* * * *

"Gerard? I apologize for telephoning so late. Who is this? It's Marcel. Marcel from *L'Art*. I don't know why I should sound so different. I need to ask something of you, Gerard. Yes, it's about the auction. Oh, I'm sorry you worked so hard getting the big five together because there's been... Well, Gerard, there's been a change and I've decided to cancel it. Yes, the whole thing. Like I said, I do apologize, but ... you see, I've decided that rather than sell the work, I'm going to ... well, to keep it for myself. I know it's sudden and like I said, I do feel sorry for putting you through this. Thank you for understanding. Me? No, I'm all right. I appreciate you asking. We'll talk more in the morning. What? I'm sorry — an interview? An American from Le Monde? No, I didn't see your note. I'll deal with it, don't worry. Gerard ... I-I'm sorry again for making such a fuss. I apologize. Yes. Thank you. Good night."

Back on the cradle, a chirp of Japanese electronics, functions he didn't need or want to understand. A sigh then, deep and slow, out

through compressed lips, in a single hiss. After the girl had left —
after he'd done what he did — he'd come up the stairs again, back to
his office. A glass at his desk, a taller one than he'd served her. Then
another. And another. But the bubbles and alcohol hadn't seemed
to dull or lift him at all. He might as well have been drinking water
from the tap.

The first call was one of duty, to Gerard. The owner/operator of
L'Art had picked up the phone and made the call. The owner/operator
of *L'Art* had apologized.

Pink. Her card was pink. That seemed odd — it should have been
purple. Maybe purple was too hard a color to reproduce, or perhaps
that shade was for certain clients, pink for others. What was one of
those clients like? It didn't bother him, for some reason.

Phone again, but this time his finger hesitated over the first
buttons. Marcel was holding the phone, Marcel was going to make
the call.

Marcel began to dial. With the last numeral, a purr of ringing
then her voice, but not her live voice.

"Bonjour, this is Marcel, the gentleman you just ... saw, at the
gallery. Remember? I just wanted to ... I wanted to apologize if I
seemed abrupt with you, towards the last. It's just — It's just that
things have been difficult lately and I'm afraid that may have affected
me rather negatively. But I wanted to say that I had a very pleasant
interlude with you and would like to make an appointment to see you
again. In fact, I am available tomorrow, the night after that, anytime
actually."

Fingers to the bridge of his nose. *Hang up*, he thought, but didn't
perform the action.

"In fact I have a request for when I see you again. I don't know
if this is an appropriate place to say it, but I'd like to change our
interaction somewhat. It's not that you didn't do a superb performance
tonight, but I think I'd like to do something else. I'd very much enjoy
... that is to say, I'd like to..."

Beat, beat, beat in his chest. Sweat on his brow.

"I'd like to... touch you, if that is appropriate. I'd like to touch
your body, your breasts. I'd like it if you could touch me as well, put
your hands on my penis. I would also like — excuse me, something
caught in my throat. I'd like, most of all, and again if this is beyond
your boundaries, I understand and apologize, but I'd like ... to make

love to you. If that's agreeable. I want this to be enjoyable, pleasurable for you as well."

Hang up. Said too much. Hammer, hammer, bang, bang of his heart.

"Anyway, that's all I wanted to say. I do apologize if I've said too much or made you uncomfortable. Please call me when you can, this is Marcel... Marcel of the gallery."

Then he gave his phone number, and the one at home, at his place on Rue Condorcet, and, finally, he hung up.

He hadn't said what he wanted to. *Whatever it takes, I'm going to make you grin, make you pant, give you what he gave you, and more. I'm going to make you forget about him, and remember no one but me. What we will do together will make his painting nothing but garbage to you.* But he'd said what he could.

A glass, then another. Bubbles climbing always upward, starting at the bottom of the champagne glass, working their way to the top. Finally, the world seemed to be tilting, began to be swabbed in invisible cotton. More alcohol than blood in his veins, a victory for the fine vintage. Home soon — home and bed.

But before, he looked to the side, looked at the trash. Crumbled and ruined, folded and crushed, pigments damaged, frame broken. The painting. In spite of it all, or because of it, a grin for himself. It wasn't the same kind, perhaps, but he'd still have his revenge.

"You bastard," he said down to it, and the painter who'd created it.

CHAPTER FIVE

I

"Artists, they make beauty out of some paint on a piece of cloth. That's special. That's why they should thank God with it, 'cause to not would be a disservice to the greatest creator of them all."

That was peppermint.

"You're nothing. Nothing at all. Go away."

That was vodka.

"You have it. You have it, son."

That was peppermint.

Peppermint and vodka. One of them a tiny green leaf honed by mysterious processes — chemicals no doubt — to a painful edge sharp enough to cut his childhood sinuses whenever Uncle Sasha had turned, grinned, and exhaled.

The other a dirty lump, like a turd pulled out of the ground rather than being left beneath the earth where it belonged. Squeezed, crushed, mashed, until it wept a foul water that was dribbled into bottles, sold for a few jingling coins — then drowned millions. After his uncle sipped, swallowed, drank, then drained, his breath had burned Dimitri's eyes, tears at first from the vodka, then what the vodka made Sasha say, and sometimes even do.

A few years, that was all it was. A bit of his childhood. But maybe they were just the right number of days, just the correct number of months. Right and correct on peppermint days, when Sasha grinned or laughed or did his impression of Donald Duck, which wasn't good but made Dimitri laugh every time he heard it. Not right, not correct, when they were vodka days, when Sasha slammed doors, banged furniture, and Dimitri tried not to make a sound.

Rain. At least it wasn't the cold variety. Stepping out of the brightly lit store, thin plastic bag hushing as he moved, he pulled up his collar and did the quick math of how wet he might get trying to get from the University back to his apartment. It wasn't pouring — more like a hazy mist that fogged the streetlights and made rainbows out of rushing headlights — so the formula came out in his favor. He decided to walk.

Even though he had enough money, the idea of a cab didn't enter his mind. Old habits died very hard, even the habit of poverty.

Spray making his face cold, making his vision blur, he ran it through his mind one more time. Math again, but not getting soaked, instead a run-through, a mental inventory — did he get the right combinations?

A quiet street, a slow bend of narrow houses and dark storefronts leading from a busy avenue of heavy traffic, the spray fading as he walked, the night clearing a bit. One of Prussian Green, three of Transparent Red Oxide, one of Sap Green, five of Titanium White, six of Raw Umber. That was it, wasn't it?

Under a bright street lamp, now dry night air no longer ringing the bulb with primary colors, he opened the bag and flicked a finger through the tubes. Yes, that was it. That's what he got.

But he didn't keep walking. Instead, he stopped for a second. Gray houses next to black ones. The night taking away any other colors, a gentle blend of only Titanium White (23%) and Lamp Black (78%). A voice, a muffled, harsh voice, pulled his eyes up a bit to an intermittent row of windows. Yellowed shades, some up, some down, running from Cadmium Yellow Light (62%) to Cadmium Yellow Medium (21%), the rest sweeps and indistinct blotches of familiar Titanium White. One of them, the closest window, and the one maybe belonging to the voice, had a vein, a streak of something from a bad dinner maybe once thrown across it, or simply water that had dripped. Brown Pink (42%), Cadmium Red Deep (7%), and Cobalt Rose (51%).

The next window was clearer, only half a shade drawn there. The half-pulled fabric was cleaner, no vein of dripping water or sauce. Just Cadmium Yellow Light (14%) to Cadmium Yellow Medium (5%), and even more white. Beyond, Dimitri could see the Cobalt Rose

(71%) and Alizarin Crimson/Gold (29%) of what could almost be a Tiffany shade.

Clouds having parted, the night sky was even more Lamp Black (100%), speckled with a scattering of the universe's gently twinkling Zinc White (100%) of stars.

"We don't look at the world the way other people do. We walk with them, but we don't see just the sky, only a sunset, a rose, a house, a face, or someone's eyes. No, no, we see what else is there, the beauty of them, or the ugliness. We see it all. Comes with the painting. Comes with the art," said his peppermint uncle, a smile and bite in the memory of Dimitri's sinuses.

The street was percentages and formulas, window shades of math, bricks of mixtures, cobblestones of proportions, a sky of composites, a night of calculations.

What was worse was that when they were all added up, the correct tables calculated, some carried over, some remaindered, the result wasn't his, but someone else's work.

"A drink is what I need," Dimitri said, mumbling to himself. Then he took a step, added two, added three — and he was walking towards home.

"People are no damned good. No damned good at all. Fuck them before they can fuck you."

That was the vodka.

* * * *

He wasn't that close, but he still stopped on the next corner and — after a moment of indistinct thought — made the unconscious decision to go that way.

As he approached he saw a young man, maybe a student, standing in front of the big plate glass window. He didn't stay that long, which made Dimitri relax a bit, made his strides more fluid, less tense. Having him be there as well would be too much like sharing a confessional.

Then he was there. The place was closed and dark, the owner long gone. That was good, too. Having him be there would have been like sharing a confessional with God himself, or maybe the devil.

In the back, revealed by a powerful white spotlight, was the painting. Seeing it made Dimitri feel like the light was shining on him. How could anyone not see it for what it was? It wasn't that good, after all. Looking at it again, he could see all kinds of flaws, places where Dimitri's hand hadn't followed Escobar's formula. One corner in particular, where the Cadmium Red Deep mixed way too clumsily with the Cerulean Blue background. The Red was much too loud, yelling, screaming in all its bloody shame that this wasn't a great painting by a celebrated master, but instead something else, something slopped and splattered by a no one, a nobody.

"You know why I'm full of the anger? Do you want to know?" Sasha had said one night, after loosening one of Dimitri's teeth with an unexpected backhand. "Because I'm also full of the shame, boy. I'm ashamed of what I am. But I can't hit myself, so you'll do."

Afterward, Sasha had drained a whole bottle, collapsing in a rag doll heap in the doorway, unable to even make it to his bed.

Yeah, the shame. Yeah, the anger. He didn't want to think about it, but Sasha was right once more. Looking at the painting hanging in *L'Art*, Dimitri's hands became fists. If he could, he'd punch something, anything. The next man who said the wrong thing, he'd kick a stray cat or dog, break the glass, take the painting in his hands and bend it, break it, tear the canvas, smash the frame.

And the owner. Him especially. Fat and refined, slow and intellectual. Anyone that stupid deserved to have his face bruised, his hands stepped on, his stomach punched, water thrown on him while he slept.

Breathe in, breathe out. With effort, Dimitri let go of the tension in his hands, fanning them out, knuckles crackling with release. The deed was done, the check had been cashed, and there was nothing he could do about it.

Besides, even though he couldn't hurt Marcel, he'd done the next best thing. It was one thing, after all, to paint a forgery— but it took a whole new kind of fool to pay so much money for it and then hang it on a wall in a gallery for all the world to see.

He just hoped the dealer would never find out the truth. Not for himself, not for Dimitri, standing angry and ashamed in the street. That would be a relief, an absolution.

But because Dimitri had to do it again.

* * * *

"The only thing a man really has is his work. The rest is just waiting for more work."

Walking home, he paused at that memory. The corner was busy, late night traffic roaring by, people out and about, either going from an early supper or looking for a late-night place. Next to him was a little café, the patrons inside stirring their coffees or chocolates, the tiny bubbles of their conversations lost against the rumbles and roars of the cars, buses, and trucks. Had that been peppermint or had it been vodka?

He couldn't remember.

For a moment, he played with the idea of going in, toasting his hands round a cup of something steaming.

But he had work to do. No time for warmth.

Sasha had trained him well, he had to give the man that. A few teeth, lots of bruises, and a knee that sometimes acted up — all in exchange for a set of skills Dimitri swore he'd never use, if just to spite the man who'd given all of them to him. Of course, that was easy to say, as Sasha's talents were specific, and the market for icons diminishing year by year, helped along in its decline by Sasha's sips, then swallows, then emptying bottles. No one wanted icons anymore, and those that sure as hell did, didn't want sloppy forgeries.

One day the peppermints had run out. The vodka had won. It had been cold, an angry winter that resented any kind of heat, any kind of life. You had to keep moving or the ice would stick to your face, and mountains of snow waited on every corner to trap you, freeze you stiff.

He'd gone out — sent out by his uncle for something. Maybe paint, maybe more vodka, too many times for each to say for sure what it had been that last time. Dimitri came back, ice on his eyebrows, fingers blue, feet numb, miniature drifts of fresh snow on his shoulders, and found his uncle even colder, even stiffer, next to his bed, empty bottle in his hand.

Had Dimitri been younger he might have tried to track down another relative, the same way he'd been passed to Sasha after his parents had packed their bags and vanished, leaving him and an address of an uncle in St. Petersburg behind. But he was just old enough to discover where Sasha's money was hidden, where his supplies were kept, and how to contact a few of his remaining buyers. His plan was that after a few quick jobs to give him enough, he'd put most of it in the bank and spend the rest on a ticket south. Create a life that had nothing to do with paints or wood, stains and varnishes, soaking things in tea, or brushing away modern truth and replacing it with false age.

Find work in a café maybe, pouring steaming milk into bubbling brown coffee, taking orders for pastries or sandwiches. Get a job in a bookstore, perhaps, telling people where to find the art books, the romance novels, putting heavy volumes on high shelves. Sell cars even, thumping the bonnets of Volvos and Saabs while telling prospective buyers all about this new feature or that new statistic of the cars' high-octane performance.

But in the bag gently banging against his leg were tubes of paint, and back at the apartment were an easel, brushes, knives, lights, and canvas stretched tight on frames.

Dimitri never thought he'd do it. A few years or so ago, when he'd put together enough to finally leave what had been St. Petersburg, then Leningrad, then finally St. Petersburg again, always remaining a city of rabid winters, the thought of using the skills Sasha had beaten into him would have made him sad, pushed him also to drown himself in a bottle.

But he'd done it, and while it was an ache at the bottom of his heart, and while he sipped and even sometimes drank more than he should because of what he'd done, he still would do it all again.

Because he was doing it for her.

II

"You paint?" was the first thing she'd said to him.

"Why? Why do you ask?" was the first thing he said to her in response.

His eyes narrowed with suspicion.

It was in Paris specifically. It'd been his first winter in the city, and it felt like a few months of brisk, clear-sky heaven. Even when other Parisians had retreated to the steaming safety of warm drinks behind well-insulated café doors, he'd stayed outside, sitting at a tiny table on the icy sidewalk, relishing with a wide grin on his face the fact that while he had been seriously chilled, it was a January that couldn't kill him.

Cocoa? Coffee? A cup, that's all that mattered. A cup in his gloved hands, clouds flowing freely upward from the stained wood-colored surface. He'd remembered sipping it, a liquid burn where it met his tongue. Delightful. Wonderful.

No knocking on car hoods, no taking the orders from snooty

theatre patrons. He had a job, and it had nothing at all to do with the world he'd left behind. Agreed, being a car park attendant wasn't a career with much room for advancement, but the tiny booth he manned was warm, people treated him — mostly — with deference and sometimes even a kind of respect, trusting him with the safety of their precious motors. He even had a kind-of friend, the Iranian who took over for him in the evenings. The man's name sounded like a series of Sasha's wracking coughs that had usually ended with a foul-looking globule of spit landing on or near Dimitri's toes. Dimitri nicknamed him Boris, with no real reason why.

Boris seemed to like his new name, pronouncing it in a way that made the common name — the Joe, Philippe, Jean, or Hans of Russia — sound like it was the title of some sultan. Whenever he announced himself, thumping his wide chest as he walked up to the booth, Dimitri couldn't help but imagine the Iranian in another life, or another century, calling for his belly dancers or favorite Arabian stallion for a moonlight ride.

Every so often, Boris would bring in some delicacy his unseen wife had prepared the night before. A greasy thing usually of wilted greens and grayish meat hammering Dimitri's nose with the punches of garlic and far too many onions. The food was rarely good, more often foul in some uncertain way, but because Boris presented it with such compassion and pride, Dimitri ate every last bit and made appreciative sounds while rubbing his own stomach.

In return, when it didn't make him remember living with Uncle Sasha again, Dimitri would take a piece of paper — an unused sheet from the logbook they used to keep track of the comings, goings, and parking of the cars — and would spit out a quick sketch. He'd never seen Boris's house, their friendship not quite close, but Dimitri had no doubt that it was wallpapered in ballpoint caricatures of the Iranian for the exuberance and pleasure his coworker showed each and every time Dimitri handed him one.

It wasn't a great life, but it was a simple one, free of shadowy men with dangerous eyes knocking demandingly in the middle of the night; or palpitating fear that the next night it wouldn't be the foot or hand breakers knocking, but rather the police, who — if they didn't receive their fair share of the profits — would not only crack the bones in their feet or smash the bones in the hands, but also throw them in jail for a few years.

"A good life is a simple life," his uncle had said between visits from the scarred and hard men and the equally hard, equally scarred men with badges, popping a smarting mint into his toothless mouth.

There was much he hated his uncle for — mostly the burns, cuts, and aches in his joints he got from the old man instead of from the mob or the cops — but Dimitri had to admit that bits of the sweet-smelling Uncle still emerged in the strangest places. When he saw his first apartment: the old Jew with the hacking cough opening the door with a monstrously huge brass key, pushing the stiff door hard with his sloping shoulders until it squealed in complaint and then finally opened, Sasha's words formed the chorus. It wasn't an elegant life; that was for sure. But the room was his, the job was his, Boris was his, and it was kilometers and kilometers, and many better degrees away from his old life.

There was just one problem with it. A problem he had never really expected. There had been an abundance of obstacles to overcome. The idea of actually enjoying the companionship of a woman, to maybe even marry, had been at the very bottom of a very long list. But one by one, after he'd crossed many items off his list, he did find himself — walking back and forth from work, perhaps, or when Boris unwrapped one of his unappetizing meals from its greasy foil and his dark eyes grew misty in appreciation of his wife — aching for a woman.

But never in his wildest fantasies could he have expected to find a woman like the one who spoke to him that night outside the café.

* * * *

Illuminated not from an interior glow but rather like museum lights on the purest of alabaster, her face glowed. Thin wrists shot out from the furry rings around the sleeves of her oversized coat, fingers lithe and nimble plucked at his own tattered cuff.

Thinking this was some kind of European crime he had yet to understand, he'd jerked back at the touch, sloshing the hot contents of his cup.

"Spilled some," she'd said, grinning, showing him tiny, perfect teeth. Her coat also had a furred collar, her pale blond hair tied severely back so her elfin face seemed to hover over a bowl of fake ermine.

"Eh?" Dimitri had replied, checking the tiny table for dribbles of coffee or chocolate, embarrassed at having made such a clumsy mistake in front of this young American woman. "I do not see it."

Bells, tiny ones: her laughter.

"Not your drink, silly. Paint, on your sleeve. You're an artist, right? Either that or a house painter."

Bells, tiny ones. He wanted to hear more of it, of her.

"Oh! I understand you now. No, no — this is an old coat. This is just old paint." He picked at it, as if to demonstrate that the cracked and chipping blue was as old as he'd said.

"Don't know how you can be out here like this."

Flapping her arms, a thin bird with too much plumage, she thumped her thin chest then blew a breathy steam into her hands.

"It's freezing!"

"Oh, no. This is only cold. I've known freezing."

"That looks like just the thing," she said, a nod to his cup.

A turn then, her coat swinging, one of her hands maybe a bit too close to the edge of the table, the fur of the fabric of it catching on a burr of rough metal, and the table moved just enough to rock his cup.

"Now it really did — or I did!" she said, the chimes of her voice ringing clear in the cold night. "Let me get you another."

"It's fine. I was about finished with it anyway."

"No way. I'll be right back."

And she was, putting down two cups on the little table. Coffee or chocolate, he couldn't remember what he sipped or she drank after she sat down next to him.

They chatted, simple things that two people say while sitting together at a café table. The weather (cold). Their drinks (almost too hot). Where he was from (up north), where she was from (America), and Paris (wonderful, they said, almost together).

Rings danced in his drink, his fingers shaking and rippling the steaming liquid. Did she like him? Was there anything in him this lithe woman would find attractive? Or was she simply just a friendly person and he just a rough-sided, young Russian with old paint on his coat that'd been sitting outside in the middle of winter?

"That was nice," she'd said, getting up and adjusting the vast folds and drapes of her oversized coat. "Have a good day."

Watching her walk away, cautiously on the icy street, there was a tug in his chest, near his heart: a sadness that she did not turn around to wave, just kept walking — perhaps to spend another hour with another man, one who didn't have a bad haircut, a dirty coat, stubble on his coarse cheeks, or hands that looked like they'd been left out in a hailstorm.

Watching her walk away, tiptoeing from one less-frozen bit of cobblestone to another, his heart skipped. His smile hurt his chilled face when she did turn around. It was just a little wave, a flip of the arm, a flop of the wrist, but that she'd done it back to him with his frayed hair, paint-dotted coat, shadowy beard, and laboring hands was what was important.

* * * *

It might have been foolish, but he did it anyway. The next day was even colder, a bitter wind sprinting down the narrow streets, kicking up plastic bags, dead leaves, and dancing up tiny whirlwinds of dirt and dust. Sitting at his table was less an enjoyment of *not quite freezing* in January, but instead a *very close to freezing* in January.

But he did it anyway, warming his hands around a cup of — this time he remembered because he'd picked it to sharpen his senses — coffee, and looking right, then left, then right again, hoping to see her.

Dimitri stayed until the streetlights stuttered on and the owner of the little café began hauling out the garbage, unnecessarily banging his bins in a loud and wordless language, telling the Russian it was time to go.

Returning the next day was probably more than foolish, but he sat with his coffee and looked again right then left then right again for the girl to appear. The temperature and his hopes fell each hour he sipped and looked and watched. Was that her? No. Was that her? No. Was that her? The cans again crashed, bottles inside breaking in discordant music, so Dimitri got up and left.

Coming back each and every day that week *was* foolish. Definitely foolish. He could hear Sasha laughing at him, his breath foul with vodka: "You think you're worth something, boy? Your only value is to grow flowers on your grave." But he did it anyway. The next day, he promised himself as the owner spoke his trash talk, the next day he wouldn't come. He didn't know what he'd do, but it wouldn't be coming back to the café, wouldn't be waiting for her.

"A fool is someone who tries harder the more he fails."

Was that vodka or peppermint? Whatever the smell, it was true, because the next day he was there, at his table, with his coffee. Were her

111

eyes blue or green? Her voice … yes, like bells, but what kind of a bell? A tiny silver one or a large brass one? A chime or a gong? Sharp and sweet or deep and ringing? Her hair, he recalled, was pulled back, but what color was it? An American blond, an American brunette, an American redhead? Her body was thin, but how thin was it? A leggy stride down a runway thin or a thinness of hunger and desperation? Desire made her aloof and haughty in his mind, elegant and streamlined, legs sculpted and strong. Tight calves, perfectly turned ankles, tough thighs. Breasts like dollops of cream, tipped by dark pink gumdrops. A hard stomach, muscles beneath a lush coating of smooth skin.

But that was desire. What had really been there? The more he tried to remember, the more the memory slipped away, like something devious and quick, trying to sweep spilled vodka back into the bottle.

He had a pen in his pocket and a napkin on the table. Quickly, without thinking, he tried to hold what he did remember down in a few quick streaks of blue ink. Cheekbones, high and firm. Eyes, small but shining bright. Nose, sharp but also playful. Ears, close and tipped with bulbous points. A faery with her wings hidden behind her back, a dryad taking a stroll from her tree, an elfin queen strolling among the common humans, a merry sprite with laughter ringing with her voice.

"So, you *are* an artist," the girl said, looking over his shoulder at what he'd drawn.

III

Neither coffee nor chocolate this time. Instead, while they laughed together, she waved the waiter over and told him that they'd like wine, a bottle.

Olivia, her name was Olivia. Not Olive, nothing shortened. The full name or nothing. As he sipped the tannin-bitter cheap red, he nodded at what she said, trying to remember as much as possible yet fighting not to get lost in her blue, lightning-flash eyes. American, traveling through Europe. A nod. Family wasn't good, especially her father. A nod, he could more than understand that. Enjoying life, not thinking about the future, just letting things come or things go. No plans or fantasies, just one moment to another. A nod that he could not understand. Loving Paris, a city waltzing with the new and as well as the old. The modern shape of the ancient Louvre, madams doing what their mothers and grandmothers had done for centuries — buying bread, making supper, hanging sheets out to dry — while twelve-year-old boys raced by on Japanese motorcycles after wolfing down lunches of sushi or pad thai. A nod. He had seen that, though he preferred the smell and tender crush of fresh baguettes, a light dinner of cassoulet, and the sails of laundry hanging on wires connecting the ancient buildings.

They sipped, smiling more and more at each other. To what she said, he nodded less and less and instead smiled more and more, losing the fight not to fall into the clear cerulean depths of her eyes.

Then the bottle was empty and her hand was on his, slender fingers rising and falling with the slopes of his knuckles, traveling along the wrinkles he'd developed from working too hard on cold St. Petersburg mornings.

"You have to earn everything. Nothing is ever just given," said Sasha in his vodka voice then, a gruff and rumbling cynicism that pulled Dimitri for a moment out of her eyes and brought him back to talking to a woman who was only, just, smiling at this poor, simple Russian.

Only, just talking — the idea of anything beyond that a fantasy, a dream, a delusion.

A hostel ... that was where she was staying. A little place down by the Seine, full of brusque Israelis and stiff Germans.

"Where do you live?" she asked, twisting the stem of her empty wine glass, seemingly entranced by the sluggish red ink residue.

Ashamed, he said, "Nowhere special. Just a room, a place to sleep, cook sometimes, watch television, read books."

"The best things in life come when you pay attention," was what Sasha had said, opening a tiny tin box and flipping a small, yet very strong, mint into his mouth. Smiling, he'd patted Dimitri on the shoulder, a precious gesture that had made Dimitri return the grin with honesty.

Pay attention. Yes, not simple curiosity, but rather an inquiry, an invitation. To this, he said to Olivia, "If you'd like, I can show it to you."

"I'd like that."

* * * *

Burning with shame, hands fat and clumsy with nerves, he dropped his keys outside the door, the discordant chiming of their landing resounding in the narrow, dirty hallway. He was painfully aware of the mysterious brown stain on the lower wall by the landing, the non-working elevator, the daggers of peeling paint on the ceiling where the corridor turned, the gravelly screaming from the room across the hall that was either at some external unfortunate spouse or at some internal mental tormentor.

Then they were in, and his shame had a smaller arena: the pile of clothes in the corner, his underwear right on top. The dirty shuffle of dishes in the tiny kitchen. The stacks of books, threatening to tumble. The copy of *Zoom* with the bare black breasts of some African model on the cover, too near the unmade bed.

With quick, sputtering excuses and a flushed face, he stuffed the pants, shirts and — oh yes, his underwear — into a laundry bag, covertly kicking the provocative tiny breasts of the model under the bed. Olivia laughed, giggles ringing in the room, and helped him by making his bed. Tugging the yellow sheet, which didn't at all match the brown blanket or the blue comforter, she pantomimed with overdone gestures, a maid primping and smoothing.

"Is there anything else, sir?"

She ended the performance, curtseying before him, the furred edge of her huge coat momentarily becoming the illusion of a ruffled skirt.

Deserving applause, he gave her some. To his clapping, she bowed again, returning to her small height at the end of the graceful movement with a brilliance to her face that made the room clean, huge, and elegant; that made him younger, more handsome, stronger, and refined. It was a look, a smile on her delicate face that was more glorious than any face of any of the Madonnas he'd painted, sweeter than any peppermint he'd ever smelled.

It was then that he kissed her.

A peck, to begin: a gentle asking of permission. To his kiss, she kissed him back, reaching up — as he was just a bit taller than she was — to return it and more: added pressure, added duration, with her arms reaching around behind him and pulling him close.

Then even more, as he put his arms around her, feeling the shape of her slim and tight body through her coat and clothes. The heat of his soul rose as her lips slid velvet and silk across his. They did this, kissing and touching, while the world spun around them. Dizzy, he finally had to stop, frightened for a moment that he'd pitch over, and pulled gently away.

"That's nice," she said, hands flat against his chest, fingers between buttons and brushing his skin. His hands were still around her back, feeling her spine and the slow widening of her hips.

The coat came off, one shoulder then the other dropped down, the weight pulling it quickly down to the floor. Under it, she wore an oversized golden sweater, thick cords of yarn fuzzy with wayward threads, and American jeans, their tightness confirming his suspicions of tight thighs and elegantly turned calves.

Not for long. Reaching down, pulling up, over, and then off, joining the furred coat on the floor, Olivia revealed a bit of her mystery. The grin on her face still bright and shining, but now curled up at the corners with sly mischief. More revealed, but still holding secrets, beneath a simple black lace bra were a pair of small and very firm breasts. Amid the whirls and curls, he couldn't see anything but the twin rises of her nipples and the pure white descent of where her smooth chest rose outwards.

Beauty-blind, he could only stammer when she said, "You're wearing too many clothes," and pushed his own coat off his shoulders then began to pluck at his buttons.

When his shirt was gone, she ran one hand, fingers spread wide, down his black forest chest, delaying long enough for index finger rings around his nipples. It wasn't anything anyone had done to him before, and his face reddened and burned that this woman was not just beautiful, quick, and moved like a dancer, but that to her, he was a lump of coal, a pile of dirty laundry, a parking lot attendant, a bottle of cheap vodka — and could never be anything else.

They moved to the bed and he found himself kissing her again. Lips to lips, the world shrank to just that part of his body, only that contact between them. No performance, just a hot kiss passed back and forth. It was good. It was very good. If he had this, he thought, the rest was just learning.

Taking one of his hands, she put it on her breast. A simple gesture, and he thought his heart would burst. Just large enough, nothing spilled beyond his fingers, nothing was wasted. Touching his palm, a playful contact, was her nipple through the bra. Not wasting time for permission, unexpectedly brave, he let go just long enough to slip one strap, and then the other, off.

Lost and wistful, her eyes drifted half closed. Not caring if the delicate fabric stayed on the bed with them or slipped to fall on the dusty floor, he tossed the lingerie aside.

A ballet followed, a series of movements he'd see again and again in his mind for days, months afterward. Olivia giggled, cheeks and forehead beginning to reflect her desire in sweet sweat, and fell back onto his bed, her head barely missing the scuffed wall, and up and over went one of her still-jeaned, still-tennis-shoed legs over his head. Head too spinning, eyes too darting, breath too shallow, heart too thumping, he didn't do anything but sit and watch her.

Legs spread around him, tiny breasts firm and rising above her thin chest, topped by the cinnamon aggression of her nipples, she looked at him, spread her arms and welcomed him into another kiss.

Eventually, the leaps, twists, and pirouettes of this ballet long forgotten, the kiss was broken and it was his time to be on his back, staring at the crack on the ceiling, the lightning across a cloudy sky he'd always imagined, and she was bending over him. Hands for a time on his chest again, twirling the dark curls there into tiny points of almost pain, they moved steadily, teasingly, down to his belt.

Then his zipper. Wanting to help, he reached down, but all she did was kiss the back of his hand, the place where the wrinkles and scars seemed to be the thickest, and tut-tutted that this was something she wanted to do herself.

And she did.

With strength he didn't suspect she had, she gripped the top of his pants and pulled, revealing his cheap and too-used underwear. He flashed shame via red, warm cheeks. But either she didn't see his commonness or didn't care enough to say anything, because in the next moment, he was naked.

Kissing of one kind before, what happened then was a kiss of another kind. Not a blow, not a suck, nothing crude and rough and pornographic. Instead, a peck on the head of his penis. A taste, a sampling, almost a sign of kindness, of affection, and not just lust or mere desire.

Dimitri was gone, a moment away from everything happening to him. Luckily, his body was acting on its own and he stayed with her, aroused to the point of pain. But his mind went away. Sex, yes, he'd hoped for that.

Masturbating in this very bed for days after seeing her, thinking of exactly this moment — though with other actions, a slightly different body, new clothes — but he'd never allowed himself to think about anything beyond that moment. Sex was relatively easy, sex was a possibility, between this woman and himself. But he'd never allowed himself to think about anything beyond that. Anything else — well, that was for other people, not rough-edged Russians with bad pasts and no prospects.

Tears, he'd always believed, had a limit. Use them up and that was it, the well ran dry. He'd done more than his fair share, he thought, cold nights reeking of cheap vodka, mouth and nose red and bleeding from the old man's backhands, soul raw and bruised from his words. But there they were.

Covering them with a covert sniffle and a quick finger swipe, he came back to where they were: his bed in his tiny apartment, with a woman. A special woman.

Back to the sight, of her grinning up at him — lips more than curled into sexy mischief, now almost wild, hungry — and then the sight but also the feeling of her opening her mouth and carefully, almost cautiously putting her lips around him.

The feeling was intense, almost too much so. He had to breathe in and out to keep from coming too soon, but he also never wanted it to stop. The movement of her head, up and down, up and down, the sensation of her lips as they slipped up and down the length of him, the flicker and hot bath of her tongue on his sensitive head, the feeling of her hand wrapped around the base of his shaft or alternating with the gentle squeezing of his balls or even, in one shocking moment an almost-felt tickle of his anus.

As a performance, it was the best he'd ever have, but that's not what made him bite back his orgasm, try and then fail to think of anything but what was happening to him. What finally did it after a good, long time of her actions on his cock was when she pulled herself free of him to look up the length of his body, meet his gaze, then give him the greatest gift he could ask for: a nod of her head, a gentle touch of agreement that this was as good and special for her as it was for him.

* * * *

It wasn't so much what they decided, but what they didn't. Walking back through the city streets, bag of paints at his side, another evening spent at a canvas, trying to be anyone but himself, he couldn't really remember a dinner, a walk, murmurs as they cuddled when they weighed the options, considered the many alternatives.

It was clear that Dimitri's apartment was too small, so they found a little one-bedroom in the Levallois-Perret, near Rue Louis Rouquier. The front window rattled when the wind blew, which seemed like every night, the toilet ran night and day, and the kitchen always smelled of natural gas, but that didn't matter.

When he was at work, Olivia either stayed in their whistling, gurgling, reeking rooms, making them a little home, or she toured the city, bringing with her stories of mysterious corners, delightful shops, interesting architecture of the city he was beginning to realize he didn't really know at all.

The evenings were spent talking, she of life in the United States with the father she hated and the mother she hated for not standing up to him. With fluttering hands, she'd talk of the little hot dog stand that was a favorite childhood memory, of friends she'd had in college, of winters in a place called Vermont, of summers in the state of Florida. Stretched out in the bed they managed to get half-price because of too many broken springs, she whispered her dreams to him: an escape to Europe to walk the streets of Berlin, Amsterdam, Rome, Madrid, to be in a place that was new and different, strange and challenging, and no reminders of the life she'd left behind. Not in language, not in food, not in television, not in the way people lived.

Their nights were spent discovering other things about her. One night, a screaming rainstorm banging at their window, water trickling around the frame, pooling in a reflective seam where glass met wood, she lay on the bed and asked him in a tiny, little voice, just above a whisper if he'd lick her.

It wasn't anything he'd done before, his previous experiences being rushed fumblings with a barmaid, and a few dozen times with a woman more interested in his wallet than his technique, and whose idea of playful conversation had been to growl "hurry up."

Frightened, he did his best, afraid of hurting her or — worse — disappointing her. Slowly, though, he began to taste her excitement and, through hers, his own. He began not only to feel less confused and have fewer trepidations, but he began to enjoy it. He surprised her as she washed the dishes by dropping down to his knees and nuzzling her, playfully whimpering like an over-eager puppy, or tasting her as she still quivered from orgasm after she'd ridden him hard, or he'd push into her hard and fast as she lay on her knees, biting their pillows, making them cool and damp with her saliva.

"Uncle Sasha use to say —" he began one night as picked up their dirty dishes and carried them into the kitchen.

"Who? I'm sorry," she said, pouring them more wine.

It was then that he realized he'd never spoken of vodka or peppermint, never told this woman, whom he truly loved, anything about himself beyond the life he'd begun the day he'd gotten off the southbound train at the Gare de Nord.

Scraping leftovers into a trashcan, he considered creating a new uncle. A nice little tale full of innocence and discovery, a nice little childhood full of gingerbread and lemon drops, days spent skipping down clean streets, flying kites, or playing with puppies or kittens. The years he wanted to have, without cold, without backhands, blood, scorn, and shadowy men doing shadowy business late at night. No fakes, no forgeries.

That made him stop, the plate almost slipping from his fingers and falling down into the crusts and spoiled sauces. No fakes, no dishonesty. Not for her. Olivia deserved whatever he could give her, especially the truth.

Coming back into the tiny living room, he sat down at their even smaller table and picked up a now full glass of cheap red.

Swirling it, he watched the happily dancing reflections for a moment, then said, "He was my uncle. Sometimes he smelled of peppermints, other times of vodka..."

IV

It was simple. It was inexpensive. It was laughter and kisses, tender caresses and low moans of release. It was watching the sun peek over the rooftops with her, the moon impaling itself on the cornices. It was discovering new and wonderful things about her. It was freeing himself of the weight of his past, all between each rise and set.

Even though they never spoke of it — not even a whisper when they cuddled and spooned in their creaky bed — he knew they both might have wanted to eat better, watch color TV, make calls without watching the clock, go to the cinema, or buy nice clothes, but Dimitri was happy, and would do anything to make sure she was happy, as well.

It was simple. It was inexpensive. It was a life, and he loved it.

Then, she began to cough.

* * * *

"I'm sorry," she said.

Wrapped in her robe, pale wrists peering out from the sleeves, thin fingers wrapped around the chipped handle of her steaming teacup, she didn't raise her head.

"Do not say that," he said, taking her other hand in his. Wrapped by his rough sausages, hers was a shock of chilled skin, a steady tremor of shivers.

"I really am. I don't know what's wrong."

"You should see the doctor."

"We can't afford one," she said, finally lifting her head, giving him a sight of her pure blue eyes, quivering with barely controlled tears.

"Go. Please. We will find a way. Whatever you need."

A nod, her elfin face now ancient, creamy skin now pale and yellowish.

"I will. Thank you."

"You do not need to thank me, Olivia. I thank you. You are everything good for me."

"You're too good, Dimmie. You're too good," she said, a weak smile on her tired face.

* * * *

A used easel, some good lights bought cheap, money scrounged to buy paint, long afternoons in that tiny bookstore by the Seine turning page after page, free days in the Louvre studying every color and stroke. Sketches on brown wrapping paper begged from the corner store. Experiments with this color that tone, this shade, that tine, this hue. At night, when she lay curled into a tight fetal ball, forcing down a pint of broth or exhausting herself by just breathing, he rehearsed stories, trying to find faults in the lie as he tried to perfect his actual art.

Who to choose who was more a matter of science than art. Had to be contemporary, because he lacked both the true skills and materials to create a convincing ancient work. A man of the people, who used affordable and easily acquired materials. A private man, who wouldn't suddenly appear in a gallery, show up unannounced at an exhibition. A proud dealer, which was an added bonus, one who wouldn't say anything if the truth were exposed.

Leaden eyes drifting shut, just before sleep, he tried to understand the artists' choices, use what Sasha had taught him about observing the original with his studies of percentages and techniques. Never pure colors, instead always cut with at least 20% of a contrast. Composition rough, powerful, bold — almost primitive. Abstract but not angular. Representative but not literal. A master, occasionally called a genius.

Home from his job, Boris's friendship fading as Dimitri became more and more focused, increasingly desperate with the fading light in Olivia's cheeks, he played the role of husband by making her soup or simple pastas, then the role of lover with tender and slow times of lovemaking. Gone were the thundering movements, screams, and cries. Instead, they moved carefully together, he like she should break, she like she was frightened of getting sicker.

When she was in bed, or lying there unable to sleep and watching the evening's television shows in black and white, he worked his colors. 21% Burnt Sienna Deep as a base, followed by sweeps of 61% Rose Madder. 36% Ultra Violet mixed with fat globs of 71% Parylene Maroon. 91% Prussian Green smears with a soft kiss of 9% Titanium White.

Brush to canvas, Sasha in his ear:

"Artists, they make beauty out of just some paint on a piece of cloth. That's special. That's why they should thank God with it, 'cause to not would be a disservice to the greatest creator of them all."

Artists — famous artists — had money. A force more powerful than any god. The power of life and death. The difference between comfort and misery.

He tried not to feel guilt about what he was about to do. After all, he reminded himself with every stroke, every use of the brush or the knife — to allow Olivia to die would be the only true disservice to the greatest creator of them all.

* * * *

A jump in time, the fear of that single hour meeting compressing weeks of practice into a blur. One late night visit to the gallery with a bundle under his arm, heart shaking his fingers, making him catch his words, stammer his answers to the owner's questions.

Walking home afterward, hearing sirens behind him with every footfall, the thick gloves of French police on his shoulders on every corner, he came to realize that it had all been almost too easy, as if the gallery owner, Escobar's agent, had somehow wanted the mysterious painting to be true, had someone coming to him with a tale like Dimitri's.

But after he'd convinced himself that he wasn't being followed, that those sirens weren't coming for him, he discovered he didn't care.

He had a check. He had a check. *He had a check!*

He was a forger. A criminal — again. But he had a check. Medicines for her to buy.

Arriving home, they celebrated with careful sex, their motions joyous but controlled, their bursts of orgasm held in check against any rough movement. Afterward, they held each other, the room salty like a room near the ocean from their pleasure, and mumbled sweet hopes to each other, allowing themselves to laugh and share bigger dreams of the future.

There was only one thing, though. The next night, after Olivia made a trip to the doctor, she came home with her chin on her thin chest, eyes looking at the floor.

"Olivia?" he'd said, face burning with tension, with fear.

"The doctor," she'd started after he'd put a glass of slightly more expensive wine in her hand. "The medicine–"

A sip, another, a glass, another, and she told him. The money was good, the medicine would work, but she needed more.

More. He'd finished the bottle at the kitchen table, his impromptu studio, that night after she'd slipped between the sheets of their narrow bed. Once was one thing, a one-time crime of necessity. But another? Could he do it? Did he even want to do it? Even for her?

"Love is the rarest thing of all," said a memory of peppermint, Sasha looking out the window at the rare sight of a bright, sun-painted morning. "For it, a man will do anything, even the worst of things."

* * * *

And so, the next day — no warmth, no blue sky, just overcast and drizzling rain — a trip to the store for materials. A side trip past the gallery, the sight of his failure to leave his life with Sasha behind, hanging in the back of a white cube of exhibition walls. The want of a glass of something stronger than even moderately priced wine. Dimitri, who was not an artist; Dimitri, the forger, on his way back to his home to commit yet another crime for the woman he loved.

The bag of paints tapped against his leg as he walked the last kilometer or so, putting himself into Escobar's mind, the formulas and percentages he'd have to mimic: the math of that profitable genius.

Key in door, door shut behind. Stairs up to their floor. Keys, in another door. Door, again, shut behind. Into the kitchen, bag set on the table with his knives and brushes. A painting to create.

It was only after he'd poured himself a glass of unsatisfying wine that he realized there was something wrong. The living room — nothing. The bath — nothing. The bedroom — nothing. Olivia wasn't there.

And neither were her clothes.

V

Two days of waiting for a knock at the door or a ring on their phone. Two days calling everyone they knew (there weren't many), talking to their concierge (who hadn't seen anything), trying to track down her doctor (who didn't seem to exist). The police? No, too many questions.

At the end of those two days, he finally checked their accounts. Empty. Nothing. She'd taken it all. Afterwards, he sat in the kitchen, surrounded by books, hemmed in by easels, trapped by paints, cornered by sketches and studies, with a bottle of burning vodka and drank until it all swam back up his throat and he created a ruin of color, a spray of vomit all over a blank canvas.

Not two days but two weeks of crying, of screaming and yelling, breaking things. Two weeks of scouring the apartment for everything that might remind him of her — and failing. The old Jew who used to be his landlord liked him less but still found him a place to rent. That night he packed everything he owned and moved out of their apartment and into a small room of his own.

Not two week but two months later, Dimitri was finally able to try and return to the life he'd had before Olivia. Luckily the owner of the car park liked him, so he had a job again. Boris was a kind and sweet soul, and so he said nothing, did nothing, acted like nothing had happened, that Dimitri did not have a bleak pallor or haunted eyes, did not look out at the people passing by the car park for hours at a time.

"We hate our sores, but love to poke at them."

123

Peppermint or vodka? Not that it mattered. One night, the city beginning to yawn, Dimitri found himself walking the streets, his own sleep not soon coming.

A corner and then another and he found himself there, standing in front of the gallery.

* * * *

A pale room, walls neutral to better reveal the strokes and techniques of brilliance. At the end, revealed by a single, high-intensity, spotlight — was nothing.

Dimitri stared into the room, blinking fast, thinking that with each opening, the painting would reveal itself again. But with each, it didn't. It was gone. His forgery was gone.

"It's gone."

Too focused, wandering too lost and too alone in his own world, he hadn't realized that it wasn't just the street, the gallery, and himself. Young, a student-type. Dark hair, almost invisible in the dark, narrow yet richly soulful eyes.

"The painting that was there," Dimitri said, turning back to the bare wall. "Did you see it?"

"I did. I saw it," the young man said, joining him in looking down the length of the gallery.

"What did you think of it?"

The answer did not surprise him, but it did make the heaviness lift ever so slightly. It was true. No matter what had happened, no matter how deeply Dimitri's new scars cut, the painting was a fine work, executed with a master's hand, done out of love. It didn't matter that the signature wasn't his own or that the money he'd gotten from it was stolen.

It hung somewhere else now, on someone else's wall: a painting of Olivia, a forgery of a forgery, a lie in paint on canvas of a woman who had taken his money and broken his heart. But even though he hurt, ached, was in cruel pain, he felt a lightness. Sasha had put it well, sweet peppermint and not sour vodka:

"A touch of the heart is still a touch of the heart, no matter if it ends with tears."

"It was lovely," the other man said, the tone of his voice softly sincere.

To that, Dimitri nodded in agreement. Olivia, as well as his painting of her: they both had been.

CHAPTER SIX

Diego

I

A button? Because of a button on his uniform — no, not just a button. Less than a button. Because of a button that should have been on his uniform, Louis had crooked a plump finger, hooking him with authority and seniority into the passageway. Then with a sneer, then a frown, then a bullying roar, he had taken an average, ordinary day of punching tickets on the Le Havre line away from Diego, replacing it with a sour bellyache and an early evening of sitting on the dirty cement of a loading dock, staring out at a fat, rosy sun going down through tangles of phone and power lines, then finally setting behind rows of cheap apartments. And drinking.

One sip, he told himself as he hung his uniform up in his locker. One sip, he told himself when he brushed his own fingers — tough and straight and honest working — over the missing button. One sip, he told himself walking out the door, waving to the other conductors, nodding to a few greasy engineers, and then around the corner and back into the yards, to sit in his favorite forgotten corner of the maintenance bays, to stare at night arriving along with a few rumbling expresses and a pair of cooler, calmer local trains.

Louis, though, made him think of Uncle Santos's house — thick plaster walls, tiny paintings of even tinier Basque villages, decanters of thick, sweet liquors, and a brass serving tray. Sitting on filthy cement in his street clothes, he toasted the twists and vortices of memory, the cheap bourbon burning his throat; the way a portly supervisor complaining about a missing button could lead him to sitting, drinking, seeing a brass serving tray in a distant uncle's house in Northern Spain — and then drinking more while thinking of Elena.

That color. Not just blond, not 'almost' gold. Elena's hair had been the color of that finely polished metal. An assistant teacher at their small local school, she'd been only two years older but a world apart. An ideal carrying books and papers, a dream pointing to distant lands on a map, a fantasy correcting his division in red pen.

Ever since she'd arrived with those books and papers, spending days teaching the class where India was, and where to put an extra six in a math problem, she'd been supple and heated in his mind — especially late at night, after he was sure his brother was asleep. In a classroom after the other students had gone home, when she was bathing somewhere he could peek, she would welcome him inside her house, wherever that was, after he'd gotten caught in a pounding, blustering rainstorm. Too young to have his own fantasies, he'd borrowed from the crackling pages of the old magazines hidden under his bed, closing his eyes and superimposing her brass-haloed head over the black and white images, putting her imagined body into various positions.

No idea what would happen when she unbuttoned her stiff, starched blouse in that cool and dark school; or stood up from that pool or pond or stream or tub with water streaming down her thighs; or after she slipped his arms from the heavy sleeves of his sopping sweater and his hand accidentally brushed the plushness of a breast. The magazines were frustratingly chaste, tantalizing rather than informing him of the mysteries beneath the models' antique undergarments.

After, he'd sleep — hand sticky, sheet sticky, blanket sticky — wishing before other dreams came that she'd show him what the magazines teased, give him one of their wicked, inviting grins.

Elena. Yeah, Elena. One sip, then another, the cement hard and inflexible under his ass. Two sips, then three. The memory just as hard and abrasive as the loading dock. A new twist, a new turn. And, just as Uncle Santos's brass serving tray led to Elena, Elena eventually swung around to three sips, then four.

Another night, after dinner, with his own books and papers, trying to find Argentina, trying to find out how many times twelve fit into one hundred twenty-nine, all while his brother sat at the other desk in their room, doing what he always did: pad of paper, pencil in one pudgy hand, lines and curves, sweeps and rapid scratches of shading, tight concentrations of detail, hazy generalized backgrounds. But that one night, after that one dinner, the dark eyes were more focused than usual, one arm hooked around the pad, keeping the specifics of those lines, those curves, those sweeps and rapid scratches hidden.

Four sips. Then Diego took the bottle from his lips, rubbed a dirty thumb across the label. The lettering was elegant, fluid. Some work had gone into the design. He might not have had his brother's talent, but he still could recognize a skilled hand when he saw it.

Just like he'd seen it when Escobar had gone to bed, and Diego had stolen a look at what his brother had been feverishly working on. Too young to really appreciate it, at least not with an adult's vocabulary or cultivated sensibilities, he'd been struck dumb and still at what he saw on the pad. It was lovely, haunting, sensual, and revealing. It had smoothness of form, suppleness of texture. That was how it was haunting. It was full and rich, luxurious in its shading, solid in its realism. That was its sensuality.

And revealing. Yes, revealing. A naked woman, with nothing hidden, all her mysteries for the world — and the artist — to see. All the folds, the creases, the puckers, and the pelt of hair. But without being coarse or crude.

And revealing. It was a sketch of Elena.

Four sips, and Diego put the cap back on the bottle and returned the bottle to his coat pocket. Twists and turns. Things revealed that had only been a mystery before. A month ago he would have swallowed the whole bottle, thrown the empty glass at the gleaming tracks, and stumbled off to his little apartment to pass out on dirty sheets.

That was before. Now Diego had somewhere to go, something to do: find a gallery opening, and become a famous artist.

* * * *

Things had changed, but he still had to go back to his place. It was cold in the winter and steaming in the summer, the stereo in the little café underneath made his dishes and cups dance and jingle when it was played too loud, which was most of the time, and the design of his kitchen, bathroom, living room, and bedroom was a jumble of odd-sized steps and crooked walls. He'd been there for five years and never once thought about moving.

It wasn't that he dreamed of better, or that he'd grown too accustomed to sweating, shivering, listening to thumping bass, or stumbling from room to room, because after five long years, he hadn't.

Laying down in his too-soft bed, hands knitted behind his head, staring up at peeling paint on the sagging ceiling, he often thought about other twists and turns, a different sperm, a different egg: been born Escobar instead of Diego.

Nice? Definitely. To have a car instead of sore feet and a bus pass. Relaxing? Absolutely. To never have to worry about money, to be able to buy anything — *anything* — without a second thought. Exciting? Assuredly. Flashes of cameras, fawning interviewers asking how it is to be a success, models and actresses demanding your attention. Pleasurable? Positively. To see your handiwork hanging on so many very famous walls, on the covers of so many magazines.

At first he'd only managed to slip into restless sleep after swallowing bitter denial, rocking himself to sleep with sour fantasies: that his brother was too foolish to buy a really good car, or that the insurance premiums were insanely high, or even with chrome and plush leather, the car and its passengers would still have to sit and fume in constant, strangling traffic. That the taxman would take every other dollar, that bookkeepers clattering with devious calculators would take nibbles and then monstrous bites of his fortune, that for each thousand he made the cost of even the simplest thing would rise to meet and then surpass it — hundred-franc cheeses, thousand-franc glasses of red, million-franc vacations, when the best of holidays was sitting in the afternoon sun sipping excellent cheap wine and sampling robust and inexpensive fromage. That for each dazzle of a camera, for every sycophantic question, there was a little man in a trench coat following him down the street, pushing lenses into his tiniest, tightest, most private of private indulgences and screaming them in headlines on every tabloid from London to Tokyo. That for every thunderstorm of applause, every medal, every ribbon, there was the itch in the back of the skull, the fast-drumming heartbeat that the next might be the one received with frowns, shown with shaken heads rather than nods, or that one day another will walk into the spotlight and the critics and buyers will say to the mentioning of your name 'who?' instead of 'genius!'

Diego used to think all that, examining his sagging present, and drift to sleep relishing in the purity of his simple life, disparaging the maintenance of fine cars, scorning the weight of too much money, shocked by the prying eyes, or dismissing the precarious pedestal of fame. No, it was better, much better, to sip from the noble bottle of being a common man, loving the purity of an honest job, and sampling the earthly cheeses of life. He might be poor, but he was the salt of the earth, with a pride Escobar never could afford, and that Diego would never, ever sell.

But then something had happened, a night that had changed it all. Not that Diego had changed in the way he viewed his jumbled apartment, his miniscule paycheck, or anything else about his unpretentious life. Instead, it had changed the way he felt when sleep washed over him, still gazing up at the sagging ceiling of his apartment. No bitterness, not any more. If anything, he looked at his life with a true and genuine smile, and his brother with true and honest pity.

After all, Diego had found a way to have everything his brother had, and more, without any of the weights of luxury, fame, money, or exposure.

It was good. Very good indeed.

II

"Aren't you...?"

He'd been in a bookstore. Why he was in a bookstore, he couldn't remember. Maybe it'd been raining outside and the stacks had been a place to dry off, wait for the drops to stop falling. Maybe he'd stopped in to flick through magazines he couldn't afford.

Whatever the reason, he was in a bookstore — a newly opened bookstore — and a young man, a student, snot-nosed kid, bright button eyes under coal-black hair, pale face over fashionable sweater, portfolio under one arm, had asked him that. Suspicion and heart-fluttering paranoia had made Diego stammer something negative.

"No," "Not me," "I don't know what you mean."

Something like that. Whatever he'd sputtered, the student's young face sagged into middle-age from disappointment and he'd turned to fade back into the shelves of books.

Who had he thought Diego was? A criminal flashed on the late-night news? The newsreader's tone serious and heavy while telling the horrible story of this rogue who stole from the rich and kept it?

Or possibly his face was from a larger screen, a set of invading features from America: the newest rugged star from the plains of cowboys and Indians. Did he share the slope of a nose, the penetrating stare, the perfect coif of a new Brando, an original Victor Mature, a fresh John Wayne?

The question nagged at him, a persistent itch of thought, as he wandered through the brightly lit modern space from mysteries to romance, from science to the newsstand. Among the brightly, glossy, stylish cover models, he looked around but didn't really see any of their smooth faces. But then one cover caught his eye and he'd known whom the student had mistook him for.

The likeness wasn't good, but it was still there. A family nose, family eyes, family hair. Sure, Diego was five years older than his brother, but there were similarities in features nonetheless.

"Fucker," Diego had muttered, too loudly as one of the girls behind the counter, clicking keys on the register, had looked up with sour disapproval on her own bright, glossy, cover model face.

He'd wanted to rip *Art News* in half, reducing his brother's face to shreds, crushing his success down to litter, ruining his headline to garbage. Holding the magazine, the stiff paper of the cover cutting into his fingers and palms, though, he'd stopped. In part because he couldn't pay for it, but also because he'd realized that, yes, the student hadn't seen Diego, the railway conductor, but rather Escobar, the painter.

He'd stayed in that bookstore, drifting from one end of the building to the other, from music to politics, from history to games, but mostly around the section marked "Art," in simple sans serif letters. He even stood for almost half an hour with one of his brother's books in his hands, the base of the heavy spine pressing into his waist, turning page after page of masterpieces, hoping that another fresh-faced student, maybe even a bright, glossy, cover model aficionado would wander by and make the same mistake.

But none did.

* * * *

"Excuse me, but aren't you...?"

Standing, he'd craned forward slightly to show concentration; he hadn't turned around at the voice. Just as he'd rehearsed in his mind. Both he and the owner of the voice were in a tiny gallery in a less-than-trendy, less-than-important little neighborhood too close to a third-rate art college, too far from the first-rate one.

On two of the walls were a series of tiny lithographs, black-and-white frozen moments of classic — and very extinct — street life: men in top hats and cravats, women in blooming skirts and bonnets. In the back, a scarred and battered table with a visitor's book open only to its first page — the names written only halfway down — and a bottle of a vintage very ordinaire, a topple of glasses scavenged no doubt from a local café, a wedge of cheap cheese and a thickly sliced baguette that could very easily have been a day old. It was perfect. He couldn't have hoped for anything better.

"I'm sorry," he said after a carefully stretched minute, turning away from the idealized man, the perfect woman, to become who he wasn't to speak to someone not of dreams, but instead, just of the moment. "I was lost in this work."

"You were?" she said, eyes large, mouth bright with a smile. "That's great."

"It shows promise," he said, looking critically at the young woman, studying her shades, lines, contours, shape, and form.

Short but not too short. Full cheeks that got even fuller, redder, plumper when she smiled, which was what she was doing. Blue eyes, naturally bright and clear. Sparkles there, amazement and pleasure.

"Honestly?"

Black dress, dyed also, though less obviously than her hair, not showing much of her body, but from what he could deduce, it was full and rich and bountiful. Thick thighs, gentle round belly, full pendulous breasts, round little ass.

"Honestly," he said about her promise, sincere in his lie.

He was amazed he wasn't more nervous, it being his first time, or his brother's first time, or his first time as his brother. But he wasn't. What was the worst that could happen? A slap? A scream? But a slap to whose face? A scream about whose inappropriateness?

"That means a lot coming from you," she said, eyes even brighter, little goddess body shifting deliciously as she rocked back and forth on her heels in nervousness. "It really does."

Shrugging, he gave her a simple grin. He didn't have much to go with, his brother being shy, preferring his studio to the outside world. But by a week or so after that time in the bookstore, the first time he realized how much his brother and he had in common — at least with the position of noses, mouths, eyebrows, and eyes — he'd managed to put together a pretty effective costume based on his own knowledge of Escobar and a few paparazzi shots. Later, he'd refined his performance down to the smallest possible detail.

Still later, things had changed even more. Not in his costume or his acting, but the point of his performance: the kind of applause he'd asked for, and received from, various young and nubile artists.

But that was months after that first gallery, that first girl.

"I try to be true in all things. In art and in my life. Your work has true potential — as do you." Thinking that maybe he'd pushed it too far, he turned to the lithographs. "I see the possibility of great work here."

"I still can't believe ... well, you're you and you're saying that."

Looking to her, he saw dimples and full cheeks get even fuller.

"I am. You are a beautiful woman who does beautiful things."

Not a lie, not really, just the truth stretched, pulled out of shape. It wasn't that she wasn't pretty, which she was, or that her artwork didn't have merit, because to his fairly untrained eye it seemed to be good enough, but it wasn't Escobar who'd said it.

Where to go from there was another matter. Embarrassment, not for his costume or performance, reddened his cheeks and heated his chest: research, rehearsal, but when it came to truly exploiting the familial resemblance, he hadn't planned that detail, the finishing touch.

Ideas came and went: too rough, too smooth, too quick, too slow. Escobar wouldn't suggest a drink somewhere. Escobar wouldn't just stroke her hair. Escobar wouldn't give her a pinch. Escobar ... He'd no idea how his brother acted with a girl. He'd been there, of course, when his brother had begun seeing Constance, but as always, Escobar seemed more interested in his sketches and studies than sharing with his brother what they did together; and Diego, frightened of his brother's possible genius at love as well, certainly hadn't asked Escobar about it. Even when Escobar married Constance, there hadn't been a chance to study him, her pure beauty having turned Diego's stomach bitter and he'd spent the day in a haze of too-much wine.

Diego knew what to do with a woman. The older, rougher, brother knew. He just didn't know how to translate his experience into his disguise as his brother. Maybe that was it: an offer to pose, a suggestion to model? No, not enough time, and besides, where would he take her?

His failure to plan the final seduction for this initial impersonation, had made him ball his cleaned and buffed (for the night) fingers into fists. Fuck this. Fuck Escobar. Fuck his big house, his big car, his face in magazines, his artwork on walls. Fuck it all.

"This really means a lot to me," she'd repeated, but this time her hand was on his arm, fingers warm even through the thickness of his best coat. Looking down at her face, into her liquid eyes, he saw heat there, steam there, burning there, melting there, hot there. "If there's any way I can thank you…?"

The answer made him smile, bloomed his hands from a pair of fists into one hand spread across the small of her back, the other on her own arm. The answer relaxed him, the question of 'where to go from here' vanishing with it. Let her come to him.

Which is what he did, that first time, in that first gallery, still getting used to his costume as his brother. They chatted a bit more, Diego falling comfortably into his performance as the kind, successful, passionate artist. The chatting led to more cheap wine, the cheap wine led to his hand on her thigh, his hand on her thigh led to her leaning in close, her leaning in close led to their first kiss, their first kiss lasted for a long time — a moment of her soft moans and his deeper, harder ones — and finally led to the gallery owner telling them he had to close up.

It all led to a late night in a very dark city. A new question emerged as they walked away from the now-dark space: where to from here? His wallet was dry and dusty, a little money and a credit card he couldn't use. Escobar the great, Escobar the famous wouldn't have her pick up the tab for a room, nor would he stumble back to her no doubt tiny apartment somewhere.

The wine had helped. His hands didn't return to stressed clutches of fingers. This last question was merely a technical detail — a reservation perhaps in a nearby hotel, traveling into town as an excuse — as opposed to a larger, more difficult problem of how to get even close to that planned room, that final element in the seduction. If not that first time, then definitely later.

He'd almost laughed. Almost. He had smiled, though, when she'd held him tight, jerked him towards the tall, dark, narrow yawn of an alleyway, mumbling as she did, "Come here. I know you have a wife and all, but I have to do this. Just a taste, you know? Hope you don't mind. I really want to do this. Really."

In that soft darkness, her lips on his, then a soft feminine hand touched his tight, throbbing thigh. Then ... well, then a soft feminine hand between his thighs, gripping then massaging him into dizzying hardness, head-spinning firmness. Just when he was going to grab her, turn her, and lift those heavy skirts of hers, she stopped, breaking her grip and lifting her lips from his.

The power of fame, he remembered thinking, the clarity of the thought like a monster church bell in his head, rising above the bubbling, fuming, bellowing roar of his erection and its demand for release.

In that alley, in a darkness filled only with ghostly trash bins and pale veins of drain pipes, she carefully crouched down and began working on his fly. That almost brought his orgasm to its peak, just the thought, the concept, the idea of it: that she would get down on her knees in an alley for him — for Escobar, of course — but right then and thinking about it afterward, it didn't matter. What did was that she was on her knees, in that alley, and working on his fly.

Then it wasn't work — far from it. Then it was those plump lips of hers on him, beginning with a kiss, then a lick, then a swallow, then all of that up and down and back and forth, followed by her tight grip on his shaft.

It wasn't perfect, in fact, in the great scheme of a woman's lips on his dick, it wasn't even good. Her teeth grazed the so-sensitive head of his cock a few too many times, the teeth of his fly felt like they were going to saw through the thick shaft. She didn't put enough pressure in her actual sucking, too much saliva making sensation distant and too slippery. But it was still good, great, fantastic, wonderful.

Because she was on her knees, in an alley, and she was sucking his cock. That, more than her actual actions, was what boiled him, steamed him, tensed his back, and make him thrust back and forth in concert with her lips and hands and throat, until he felt it start — and not just start but begin too strong, too demanding, too powerful to try and push aside, to distract himself away from it, to prolong.

Yelling, bellowing, roaring, he came very hard, very fast. Dizzy when it ebbed, he put his hand back onto cold brick to steady himself. Panting, chest straining as it tried to get enough air, he felt even his braced legs turn to meaty jelly. A few more deep, soothing breaths returned his balance.

"Was it good?" she asked, rising to her feet in front of him, her wicked grin gleaming even in the dimness of the alley. Licking her lips, she ran her own quivering hand down his chest, a gesture that immediately made him think about doing it again, and again, and again.

But it was late, she was a young art student, and he was not Escobar. There would be other times, definitely. He knew that. Not with this girl, that first conquest, but with new ones. Now it was time to smile, to pat her head, to wish her the best, and to move on.

But first ... what would Escobar do? What would his brother do? It was easy, the easiest answer of that night, the comfort of it warm and welcoming around him. His brother was the role he was born to play.

"You are a beautiful woman," he said to her, lifting her chin and looking into her wet, deep eyes. "A woman who does beautiful things."

III

"So much for fame and fortune getting you a good room. I must apologize. This was the best they had available."

"Oh, I don't mind. It's kind of charming in its own way."

A narrow girl, a vertical woman: all leg and tight muscles, thin breasts and strong lines of cheekbones. Black jeans and a similarly charcoal-shaded silk blouse, parting here and there to reveal a thin strap that could very well lead to an elegant bra. She tried to costume her aristocracy, put her in the role of a proletarian artist, but her genetic precision betrayed her.

It was a bonus, not that he would have passed on the opportunity if her parents had been schoolteachers, grocery store managers, clerks, or even railway conductors. She was a woman, a struggling artist hungry for fame, and he was someone who had it. Or so she thought.

"You are too kind. Another trait one so rarely finds in the world of paint and canvas. Promise me you will never lose that," Diego said, closing the door behind him.

The night had been warm, touching hot, and so she had no coat he could gallantly offer to take from her.

"Can I order you something to drink?" he asked, hand on the old phone by the bed.

"That would be nice, but it's not really important," she said, eyes gleaming bright.

Tall and thin, narrow and upright, those eyes and the way she stood said that while her genes might be old and noble, tonight she was just a giggling girl.

"I still can't believe I met you."

"I could very easily say the same," Diego said.

It was at least six months after that first clumsy alley; he'd been practicing.

"But let me assure you, I'm just a man, like many others."

"Oh, no, you're not! I mean, goodness, just your work on the *Pieces of Infinite* alone ... is just incredible. I saw them in the Prado last summer when I was down there with my parents. All I could do was just goggle at them. *Zero Point Zero* is my favorite, though they all are, really, but that one with the streaks of rose, the tiny bits of gold leaf, the perfect placement of the two black triangles. I mean ... Shit, listen to me. I can't talk about them, but they are all just so damned perfect. I'm sorry. I must sound like a complete idiot."

He laughed, almost like a small cough.

"Nonsense. Not at all. I know what you mean. I really do. I feel the same way about Monet. It was fun to do, but ... Well, it's just paint and canvas, you know? Just art."

"Oh, no," she said, her emerald eyes bright in the poorly lit room. "No, no — I'm sorry, but I don't think that's what it is at all. I mean, with me, that's all it is. But you ... my God, what you do with it is so much more than that. When I saw your *Perfect Glow* in the Tate, I ... it was the best thing I'd ever seen. I mean that. It is just so powerful, and perfect, and elegant, and ... I have it in my apartment, you know. A poster of it, I mean. Sometimes I just sit and stare at it. The way the colors, the composition ... and here you are. I still can't believe it. I really can't."

His face was hot. The room was close, confining.

"Please, stop. I eat, breathe, and even shit. I'm no better than anyone else, not really."

"I don't believe that. What you do ... it's just too wonderful. I think sometimes I might be able to do one or two good paintings, enough to get me some kind of attention, but that's all. I know I don't have it and that's okay. You, though, you have the magic. You really do. I wish I could show you how stunning I think your work is, how much it's affected me, changed me. I just want to say ... I just want to say 'thank you,' Escobar. Thank you for your work. Thank you so much."

She sniffled once, then twice. Stretching out a long, thin arm, she pulled a tissue from a marred leather box sitting on a side table. Ladylike — a betraying, refined gesture — she dabbed at her suddenly pink nose.

"I'm sorry, I-I ... It's just..."

"Oh, stop it," he said. He reached down, hooked his hands where her narrow arms flowed into her streamlined chest, and pulled her to her feet. "Look ... I'm not some kind of saint, okay? Just a guy, just a man."

"N-no," she said. "I know that. I do. Sorry."

"It's okay," he said, the room feeling like a sauna.

Stepping back from her, he shook off his coat, tossing it at a chair after it slid from his shoulders.

"It is. I'm just a man. I'm not perfect."

"Okay," she said, looking suddenly very small and rather fragile. "I-I understand. It's just…"

She shook her head.

"It's what?" he asked, the temperature inside himself knocking up a few more degrees. "That I'm famous? That's bullshit — you know that. It's all bullshit. I could have been a fucking cab driver, punch tickets on a train or something. I was just fucking lucky. Just because I paint fucking pictures doesn't mean I'm any better than any other asshole. Fuck, you think I got you up here to talk about painting?"

Shaking her head, she squeaked out a tiny noise of negativity.

"No, Monsieur Escobar," she finally said, voice soft and small.

He touched her breast. No, not accurate. Not the scene and not the way he was feeling, the way he acted. Better: he grabbed her tit. Small, his hand cupped the entire rise of it, the kernel of nipple poking at his palm. He kneaded, hard and quick, feeling blouse and bra and soft skin slide against each other.

"This is why I brought you up here, okay? You got that? You understand? I want to fuck you. That's all. Not to talk about my fucking painting or how fucking great I am. You made my dick hard, that's all."

Nodding her head, she gasped out a miniscule sound of agreement.

"Okay," she said, her tone supple and passive.

It made his face burn. Even though she'd already begun to work free the first button on her blouse, he pushed her fingers away.

"You're too fucking slow," he said, the room very tight, way too small, his voice way too loud.

The next and then the next and the next, resisting with each one to just yank it off, bounce buttons off the too-near walls.

Her bra was white and simple, everyday wear. No lace, no satin. Between the pearl-colored straps, her chest was smooth, the slow rises of her breasts below the cups revealing that she bought a size too big. The insecurity made her seem even smaller, more delicate, more fragile. Fingers sliding along her shoulders, then under those straps, he slipped them free. Tight and small, the arrangement paused then dropped down, a loose belt of cotton and satin around her narrow waist.

She was whimpering. Those shoulders rose, her hands climbed but then slowed, finally stopping short before she could cover herself — a gesture agreeing with his hands, his eyes, his thundering heart, the persistent erection in his suddenly confining pants.

No, an agreement not with him, and that burned him even more. The bra came off with an assurance that surprised him; the hooks usually far more cryptic and confusing. It went somewhere behind him, tossed with strength but its trajectory encouraged by its near weightlessness.

Hard was not an accurate way to describe her nipples. This was the first time he'd seen a body like hers: peaked and firm, breasts of pure alabaster, a form from classical sculpture. Grecian, Roman, but fresh and new, just cut from young marble with none of the rough soil or cracks of history. The tips of her breasts were bright rosy swells of sweet skin, less nipple and more large, puffy areola.

Exotic, unusual. For a time, he could only stare. The room was quiet, not even the sounds of midnight Paris coming through to him. Her breathing, though, was loud: a steady, deep in, slow out of air.

The anger was gone, the sight of her draining it away. Its only legacy was his rigid cock, originally raised in fury but now determined at the sight of her.

Bending, he brushed his lips across the hot, smooth swell of one areola, a controlled movement painfully stately with restraint. Not just turning the graze into a kiss and then a firm suck was a form of torture, directed completely towards his erection.

She responded, even if he held back. With the first touch of lips to skin, her breathing went from steady in, slow out to a gasping intake, a sigh of exhalation. Hands previously at her side rose to the sides of his head, firmly grasping his ears, and with a determined pull, she did what he held back: pressed his mouth completely to her puffy nipple.

His suck was firm, passionate, as was her response — guttural sounds from deep within, then knees sagging, her descent pulling the silken skin from his mouth with a soft, wet sound.

Gasping, she carefully regained her footing. A hand to her forehead, she giggled and sighed. He reached down to her hand and pulled her even further upright with a single word.

"Bed."

She responded with her own solitary one: "Okay."

On the way, she shed the rest of what few items of clothing remained: a trotting strip revealing more and more lithe skin. Finally, standing on one side of the bed, she was naked and glowing, a tender rose of excitement. As she moved, falling in a cascade of arms and legs to lay on the bedspread, he caught sight of the moistness painting the insides of her thighs and felt his already hammering heart fist-hard in his chest.

His own clothes fell away and he was suddenly aware and frustrated by the number of zippers, belts, buttons, and elastic he had to deal with. But soon enough, he'd joined her in bareness.

And soon enough he'd joined her on the bed. Arms, legs, skin, heat, wet, hard, tongue, nipples, breasts, cheeks ... a cascade of one to another to another to another, all to a melody of equal and mutual deep noises.

Then he was on top of her, then inside of her. Her heat and wetness were an electric bolt from his erection through his body to somewhere between his eyes. Fighting the need to shove himself up and over into a bolt of orgasm, he struggled to focus on something, anything, but what he was actually doing. Pushing and pumping, his attention darted to a painting hanging over the bed: a street scene of Paris, somewhere around the turn of the century. He didn't know the technique, but he did see its commonness, its cheapness, its averageness. It was just one of a million, all of them perfectly the same.

Then she bent up with athletic, blind passion, her eyes out of focus, her face shimmering with sweat, to lock her lips around his own nipple. She may have used her teeth, might have actually bit him in her blind drive, but he never knew because what focus he had was gone and he found himself screaming and groaning in a whole body-shake orgasm.

And down, a puppet with its wires cut, to fall onto her heaving belly, forehead grasping the plushness of breast. Time elongated, became a moment of unknown duration, only broken when she started to play with his dark curls.

"That was wonderful," she said in a tender voice.

Responding with a kiss to a nipple, he smiled at her.

"Mutual, darling."

"I still can't believe..." she began, face beaming at him. "That it was with you ... Escobar."

That wasn't the one that changed it all. That wasn't the one that moved his whole world around. But, still, her reminder of what he was — just a cheap thing, just one of a million, and not a masterpiece — was an ice pick, a short, sharp shock that brought him up and out of a near-dozing bliss and to his feet, caused him to say "Yeah, whatever," and fish for his clothes, to put them on, and leave that small hotel room as fast as he could, slamming the door behind him.

IV

Months later, he was getting ready to go out again. Once again, he assembled his studied impersonation, moving his hair this way and that until it came close to the picture of his brother he'd taped to his bathroom mirror. He carefully trimmed, shaved, and primped himself until both faces, one real, one a copy, were as close as he could make them.

Then came the clothes. Expensive, but when one is creating something, one should use the right materials. He wondered, sliding his arms into the coat, if that was how his brother felt: picking and choosing his paints and canvas, his brushes and paper? A few months ago, the question would have made Diego punch his bed, maybe even the wall, in rage. A twist of fate, one sperm, one egg different, and he and not his brother would have been carefully selecting just the right pigment, the perfect weight of parchment that could — no, *would* — hang on a famous wall someplace. The great, the famous, the talented, the celebrated Escobar ... and his unknown, distant, forgotten brother.

But that was before that one night and the woman who changed it.

Thinking of her brought an echo, a wave of déjà vu. Another night, another ritual of preparation turning one brother into another with a different kind of brush, working on the flesh and blood canvas of his own face. That night, though, his plans had been very different.

A hotel? Absolutely. Reservations, in fact, made for a moderately expensive one. He wished his paycheck could afford a better one, to help the illusion, but he'd gotten very good at all kinds of explanations. "Only thing in the area" was his favorite. Research? Accomplished. Even though Escobar had avoided much of the spotlight he'd stepped into, its penetrating glare was enough for Diego to put together a convincing depiction.

Goal? Into the mirror he'd leered, changing his portrait of a middle-aged man from an artist of incredible ability and noble bearing to a beast out for one thing.

He'd gone out with that in mind. Theft via impersonation might have been how he'd begun, to have a taste of what his brother no doubt feasted on every night, but that's not how it had progressed. Instead of seduction, he'd gone out that night — the night when it had all changed — to, yes, enjoy sticking his dick in some poor art student's hungry cunt, but more to stick it to his brother.

More exactly: his brother's reputation.

* * * *

"Aren't you...?"

He'd been standing there, looking intently at her work for what had seemed like hours, but was probably just a few minutes, his time sense multiplied by impatience.

"Why, yes. Yes, I am — if you mean someone looking at your art."

Carefully refined, it was a line practiced many times in front of the mirror. Designed wit, perfected charm. A little gallery near the college, just like a dozen or so before. No surprises there: a wooden-walled box, window in front, table with wine and cheese in the back. Arriving late, as he'd always done, to avoid the crowd, and with it, too many eyes.

"Do you — do you like them?" she'd asked, just as others had.

A question warbling with hope. That little student, the young artist, wanting more than anything for the great artist to look down from his genius, his wealth, his fame, to pat her on the head and say that she, too, could join him on the covers of magazines, to maybe walk into a life like his.

"Not all of them, no," he said, also meticulously honed, another thoroughly crafted performance.

To say he liked them all would be unrealistic, too smarmy. To say that some of them had potential implied an honest standard.

"But some show promise."

"T-thank you," she'd stammered, like they all had stammered, paralyzed by his lights.

"No," he'd said, grinning with the appearance of warmth. "Thank *you*. This one, particularly, shows serious promise."

"The Arc de Triomphe?" she'd said in a low, hushed voice. The obvious stated, she'd blushed, a petaled glow rising to her cheeks.

"Yes."

Turning away from her, he pretended to study it. The play was for him to praise one work, say that it was as good as anything he'd done — that Escobar had done — at her age. To say she had potential. From there, he would walk her around the gallery, nodding at some, shaking his head at others, all the time sliding intimacy between his lines, hints, and suggestions that she was special not just because of her talent, but also her beauty, her passion, her sensuality.

From there ... from there, to an alley in some cases, to the hotel in others. An hour, or two, or three, or perhaps even waking in the morning to tangled legs, tangled sheets.

Alley, hotel, or the morning after — all to end the same way. Praise for the artist, adoration for Escobar, his brother — all to end the same way, a new line practiced in front of his mirror: "That was nice enough. But you understand that a man of my position has to be careful of the company he keeps." And the like, and more of the like, and still more of the like, until she was in tears, great heaving sobs of disappointment and shame.

Pleasure for Diego from a night with a young and eager woman. A reputation shadowed, rumors whispered, for Escobar. Pleasure, as well, for Diego — because of those shades across his brother, the rumors that would be whispered.

Business as usual. Fun as usual. But not that night.

That night he looked at two things. The first was the sketch she'd made of the *Triomphe*.

Art had been Escobar's land, Diego's brother's territory: surrendered to him with bitterness and resentment after his first acknowledgement of talent. But that wasn't to say that the elder brother didn't know "good" when he saw it. Before he'd watched Escobar sail off into fame and success, Diego had even thought about going in that direction himself. But, as said, and as even more deeply felt, that was gone. But also said, also felt, he still had a connection to it.

He'd lied to her, not just about being his brother, or his reasons for being at her showing. There was another sin, one of not quite omission, but rather one of degree. The sketch wasn't just good, it was incredible. With only a few carefully chosen lines, a few darkened patches, she'd captured not just the appearance, but also the power and importance of the Arc de Triomphe. It had weight, it had texture, it had dimension — and for including all of that in a small square of paper, this girl had talent. He should have told her the truth, that she really had talent.

"It is excellent. Truly," was what he did say, moving away from it. "Better than anything I could have done. I'd like to have it, in fact. If I might."

"I-I ... of course. Absolutely. Please, take it. I don't know what to say."

Then he looked, really looked at her — the second thing he saw that night. And everything changed.

It wasn't that she was pretty. He knew that already. It wasn't that she was young. He also knew that. It wasn't that she could be easily pushed into being pliant, led to being eager concerning a quick affair with a famous artist. It, too, he knew by experience and simply looking at her.

But for the first time, Diego really saw her for what she was: a pretty, young girl who wanted nothing more in this world than for someone, anyone, to hold her hand, look her in the eye, and say that she was good enough, that she had it, that she was really, honestly, truly an artist — and could be a great one.

"You don't have to say anything," Diego said, grinning at her.

Wanting to be something. Wanting it more than anything in the world. Wanting to know that you are special, wanted, desired. It was something he knew all too well.

"You have true talent. Never forget that."

"T-thank you," she said, eyes softening with the proximity of tears.

"But I can't take this for free. Do you have a piece of paper I might have?"

"Certainly," she said. She ran quickly towards the back of the gallery and picked up a large sketchpad she'd propped against the food table. Bringing it back, she presented it to him.

Art was his brother's domain, his brilliance blinding Diego from ever following. But just as he knew good art when he saw it, the elder brother also knew enough to be able to put a pencil to a pad, bring something out of it. It was not good, he knew that. But it was something he wanted to do for her — something he wanted Escobar, the great and famous painter, to do for her. Because it made him happy.

What to draw was a matter of convenience: the door to the gallery, in a few quick dashes of line. As he did it, he cursed himself for not being good enough, but he still didn't stop. As he did it, and felt frustration, he decided that he'd have to practice. Yes, practice.

Giving her the sketch, he accepted hers — an exchange that had both their eyes heavy with tears.

"Thank you," he managed to say as she presented it to him, wrapped in that day's newspaper.

About to shake her hand, he stopped, instead leaning forward to kiss her on the forehead. It was what Escobar would have done, he thought. No, that was not quite true. It was what the Escobar of her hopes and dreams would have done.

And what he would have said. So with the kiss, he left her one more gift before stepping out into the night.

"Always remember: it's not about what you do, but why you do it."

* * * *

Another night, another gallery. After that girl, it had all changed. No more hotel rooms or alleys. No more tears. No more bitterness.

Tonight's gallery was across the city, a tiny venue for big artistic dreams. The show, according to *Periscope*, began in a few hours. His disguise was perfected, the illusion as complete as he could make it. He'd better get moving.

But before he did, Diego paused and looked over his shoulder, at the sketch hanging on his wall. A button missing from his uniform, a tiny apartment with crooked walls, even being the forgotten brother — none of it mattered. Tonight he'd become Escobar, the famous painter; but not to seduce and ruin, or to steal a bit of his brother's success.

For them, for the hungry artists needing help, support, or just simple kindness like a kiss on the forehead, he'd be the Escobar of their dreams. That was his own great work.

All because of one young woman, the one who'd changed everything.

"Ciao, Madeline," he said, saluting the sketch she'd given him.

CHAPTER SEVEN

I

Passport, residency card, or American Express … slid right across the countertop, right under his nose. He didn't even so much as glance at any of them. Instead, the manager's pale blue eyes — twin spots of early morning sky — held on her face, long enough to be uncomfortable, making her pretend to cough.

"Is there a problem?"

Broken out of his stare by her voice, he leisurely shook his head, laughing lightly.

"No mademoiselle, there is no problem. Excuse me," he said, bending down under the counter.

But as he did, he still managed a quick glance up at her, a grin curling the corners of his mouth.

A registration book to sign, a brass key to take: the hotel had completely escaped the twenty-first century. Fortunately, she'd had the last-minute smarts to pack a phone line and her kit of international adapters. The free Wi-Fi of Paris almost spoiled her into traveling back in time with no way to reach the present.

The desk clerk at least seemed to have had his fill of her. During the signing, the passing of the key, he'd behaved himself, though perhaps with a bit more formality, a touch more elegance, than he'd show for anyone other than an American woman traveling alone.

Up a creaking lift the size of a phone booth and down the hall to her room, she went, her rolling luggage behind her.

Home for the next week or so wasn't claustrophobic, at least not until she'd opened the window. Swinging out the window revealed a view of twisting, narrow streets, smooth plaster walls where new and chipped brick and stone were old. Flower boxes under wood-framed windows fogged with lace curtains. High-peaked roofs with tiles the same shade as gravestones.

Lourdes was close, but obviously not near enough for its radiance of tourist money to have an effect. Even though Sheri's existence in Paris was as much bars and cafés as it was web sites, email, and her cell phone, she was glad she'd driven back a few centuries in her rented car. The past *felt* better than the modern throngs of gaping tourists.

Suitcase on the bed, she unpacked what was important first. She cleared the narrow wooden desk of a ugly lamp with a shade the color of sick goldfish scales and then set up her laptop.

The sight of her desktop — and the usual stream of new messages once she got online — and she was home, or at least the only kind of 'home' that was usual, stable, during her travels. Even her small Parisian apartment in Le Marais wasn't really *hers*, at least not until she opened her computer. Most of the messages were predictable: a few dribbles and drabbles of spam, a stupid joke from her father, a bit of friend-of-a-friend folklore from her mother (who still seemed to expect Sheri to be hauled off to Marrakech by white slavers), a message or ten from various Parisian friends wanting to hook up with her (and who clearly forgot she was out of town for the week), and a message from her editor at *Le Monde*.

That was important; everything else could wait. The email was quick and concise, two sentences in too-formal, textbook English wishing her luck and telling her not to be nervous. At the end of her reply, she wrote that the trip down was uneventful and that she was checked in. She added: *Am I ever?* Five years of working for David and he still seemed to expect Sheri to be hauled off to Chechnya by Slavic gangsters.

The rest could wait. The suitcase was damned heavy. When she shoved it off the bed, it landed with a deep drum beat, the impact firm enough to cockeye a postcard-sized picture of the Madonna over the twisting whorls of the carved headboard. The diaphragm voice of the impact, and the quizzically tilted Holy Mother, questioned why she'd brought so many damned books.

Laying on the bed, the mattress soft enough to pass for pastry but not hard enough to qualify for furniture, she tried to will herself to get up, unzip her bag, and get out her heavy reading.

No, not yet. She stayed flopped out on the duvet-wrapped éclair and stared vacantly at the jagged lightning bolt crack in the ceiling. She should read the books, should surf the web, should do her research, should take notes, should try again to prepare herself for tomorrow — but she only sighed, slow intake and equally slow exhale. She *had* read way too many books, *had* spent long hours going from site to site, *had* taken pages and pages of notes (both by hand and into her computer), and felt as uncertain and nervous as she had when David first handed her the assignment.

With a snort, she dismissed inexperience as the basis of her anxiety. If she could wrestle with Luc Besson, Michael Gondry, Jean-Christophe Grangé, and Serge Gainsbourg, she could take down just about anyone.

What was it then? While her eyes examined the intricacies of fragmented plaster, she let her mind fall back. What *did* she know?

The books talked about style and composition, form and color, and execution and technique. The web sites discussed early versus late period, various schools and influences, and future possible directions. Her research had produced copious notes, but every single Post-it and Word file was shallow and empty, giving her no real handle on the man himself.

What *did* she know? Born in Igualada, Spain. Son of a teacher and a construction worker. This show, that gallery, this magazine, that exhibition. Medals. Awards. How much made at auction. But where it mattered, where the man was, there was paint. Just paint.

While he wasn't a hermit, he certainly didn't live to be on stage. Other interviewers had been precise and inquisitive, fencing with barbed inquiries and circuitous foils, and had published fascinating accounts. Fascinating if you were an artist. Riveting if you were a collector. Exciting if you were a salon gadfly. But none of them had come close to drawing honest, true, sincere, blood.

The only thing she'd managed to come up with in all of her data mining was hardly vivid, barely crimson. Fogs, vapors, mists; hearsay, rumor, and tittle-tattle. Whispers of affairs, the clever seductions of bright, young artists. Nothing unique in that, nothing really juicy about a Picasso who was as deft with his ... *brush* as much as he was with his brush.

Yet. Yet. Yet. Returning to her apartment with the first batch of books — a tumble of spines, fans of pages out of her arms — one fell open on her own, much more comfortable bed, exposing a brightly colored plate.

Art, to her, was art. Just. Only. It wasn't nothing, but it also wasn't everything, not invisible but also not an obsession. Painting, sculpture, collage, sketches, installations, exhibits, shows, galleries — they were all a part of her world, but never really powerful enough, important enough, to occupy more than a multicolored backdrop.

A book on her bed, a page revealed. It hadn't been a ray of light from God, or a bolt of revelation. It hadn't changed her life, or elevated art in her mind to more than just art. But she hadn't looked away from that page, either. Hadn't just closed the book. No, she'd crawled across the comforter to get closer. Then she'd moved to be flat on her back, the heavy volume balanced on her knees, the lithograph filling her field of vision.

It wasn't a matter of liking what she saw, because she liked many pieces of art. It went beyond *that's nice*, to a thoughtless absorption, a kind of eye-drinking trance. It was abstract, but not. It was a nude, but not. It was bright, but not. It was meticulous, but not. It was stylish, but not.

Eventually, she'd put the book aside, made herself a chai. Sitting and sipping in front of her TV, she'd watched first the news and then the middle and end of a very violent thriller, full of spilled red of the more literal variety. Supper had been simple, Middle Eastern, microwaved, spicy, and private. She hadn't wanted to jangle her pre-interview mind with the small-talk of company, or even the babble of other diners.

After sleep began to put lead weights on her shoulders, she'd slipped under the comforter.

But before closing her eyes for the night, she'd made another bookstand out of her thighs, and again had fallen — until her vision began to blur and her lids started to sink — down into the painting.

Books and research, web sites and notes, numbers to call for background interviews — all of it not as revealing as a single picture in one book. She just wished she knew *what* it depicted.

It had been a long drive and tomorrow was the big day. Even though she didn't have lead on her shoulders and her eyes were sprung wide open, she rolled off the bed and unzipped her bag. Clothes would go in drawers, on hangers, and her toilet kit placed on the sink in the bathroom, in preparation for an early night.

But first the books. One by one, stacked on the floor next to the bed — the desk way too narrow for antique as well as modern tools. With the last book, heavy in her hand, she hesitated, a pause accompanying a thought about opening it again. A flick of glossy page after glossy page, until one ... *that* one ... one last look?

No. It joined the others, at first threatening to topple the pile. So it was slipped in at the bottom, preceded by a quick balancing act with the rest.

Yet. Yet. Yet. If he was adept with more than his brushes, if Escobar had as much fire in his body as he put on the canvas, if he was equal parts passion for art as well as ... Well, she thought with a ghostly grin, she'd have to be more than just very focused, very rested, or very prepared.

She'd have to be very careful.

II

It didn't look like much, which meant the world of art had been especially kind to the artist. Winding her way out of town, she'd had as much of an eye on the houses passing by as she had on the small-town motorists. The traffic had been light, just a few battered Citroens and a delivery van or three sharing the road with her. The houses were identical from her view the night before: plaster and wood snapshots from the previous century.

Leaving the town, she found her face muscled tightly with a scowl. One more turn, she imagined, one more kilometer, and there it'd be: a monster of glass and steel, a modern architectural eyesore. Welcome in twenty-first century Paris, here an arrogant display of fortune.

When she did get there, the grimace stayed. No gleaming glass, no polished steel, no rosy copper, no minimalist fountain, no precision lawn. Up a gently rising, softly undulating private road, passing periodic tableaus of gnarled trees forcing burgundy roots through cracked granite outcrops, over a precious bridge above a gleaming crystal stream, passing intermittent walls of ragged stone laced with lush velveteen moss, and then arriving at a house that was perfectly placed, expertly disguised, masterfully constructed to fit into the region's aesthetic. That, she thought to herself, takes *real* money.

Pulling into a gravel driveway, the crunching pebbles echoing back at her from the baby smooth plaster walls of the house, she stopped and yanked up on her Fiat's parking brake, but she didn't get out, not quite yet. First her ritual of pad, pen, recorder, digital camera

— all there in her work bag. Possible questions — all there on the pad. Even though she preferred to work by herself, photographers doing their stuff before or after, she wished she had some company.

But she didn't. So she got out, walked to the door, rang the doorbell, and waited. She looked up and down the length of the house, checked her bag again, looked at her shoes, glanced up at the blue sky, then at her nails, but mostly she stared at her watch.

At five minutes past the first ring, she pressed it again, listening carefully for the chimes, which definitely chimed, and then for any movement, of which there didn't seem to be any.

At five minutes after the second ring, she pressed it again, promising herself that if there continued to be no movement, no sounds beyond the echoing chime of the doorbell, she'd get out her cell and call the number she'd been given.

But she didn't have to. With a rush, the door swung wide, so fast she involuntarily stepped back, stumbling momentarily on the loose gravel.

"*Si?*" Wild hair, dark russet, freely bouncing curls. Below the hair, a pair of wide coffee eyes, pupils quivering in bloodshot whites, clearly visible behind simple, brass-framed glasses. Below the eyes, a well-shaped but rugged nose: honest, without the self-consciousness of lotions, salves, or crèmes. Below the nose, a broad mouth with ripe plum lips. Below the face, a thick chest in a frayed denim shirt. Below the shirt, a pair of jeans. On his feet ... They were bare, the toes very hairy.

"Monsieur Escobar?"

Sheri yipped in French, in a flash disgusted by the amateur shock in her voice and that she should have used Spanish.

"I'm from *Le Monde*. We had an appointment? An interview?"

Puzzlement: a quick dance of eyes, eyebrows, and lips. Racking memory: a pondering tango of face and body. Recollection: a rumba of welcoming arms, swept wide.

"Ah, yes! So sorry. I completely forgot," he said in the same language back to her. Stepping down, his bare feet crunching down on the gravel drive, he gestured for her to enter.

"Come in, come in."

"Th-thank you," she managed, and with it another flash of embarrassment at her unprofessional stammer.

Inside was a carefully wrought reflection of the exterior, an elegant reinterpretation of a local home: curl-legged heavy tables, mahogany cabinets with meticulously displayed crockery, iron-backed chairs, pots with sprays of dried flowers, a floor made of glassy tiles, lace curtains as brightly laundered white as the shining sun outside.

"So sorry," he said, closing the heavy door. "I was busy working, completely forgot."

For emphasis, he slapped his forehead, an abrupt and meaty sound in the pristine room.

"Here, here," he added.

He squeezed past her, heading from the foyer towards a doorway to the right. In passing, his body filled the space between front door and living room with swinging shoulders, expressive hands, slapping bare feet.

"Come this way," he added, shooing her towards the other room.

Lead by his wide grin and sweeping gestures, she followed; but halfway there, the perfection of the living room gave an extra push. Pretty, yes; handsome, for sure; but not welcoming. A person with all the imperfections of humanity just didn't fit with the décor.

But the kitchen was different. Here people lived: more plants but bottle green instead of dehydrated, tile floor but scuffed and worn, tables and chairs warm with lived-in comfort, a counter-top of glowing wood, a cream-enameled refrigerator more fifties than new millennium, a stove rough with thickly bubbled grease, and glass-doored cabinets full of pleasant meals to come.

"Here," Escobar said.

He waved her into a far corner, towards a pair of wooden chairs and a petite table, all of them baking in warm daylight flowing in from a pair of huge, curtainless, windows.

"Have a seat. You want something to drink? I have coffee, I can make tea."

As she sat, he rounded a cutting board island and threw open the door to the fridge with a rattle of jars and bottles. After a second of pondering the contents, he called out from inside,

"And Orangina. You want an Orangina?"

"No, no thanks," she said, still trying to actually *be* in the house, to settle his whirlwind. "Water would be just fine."

"Water it is, then."

A bottle came out of the refrigerator; a tumbler came down from a shelf. One poured into the other, he came back to the table, put the glass down in front of her, and sat down.

"Here you go."

"Thanks."

Resisting the urge to take a drink, a classic stalling reflex, she did the next best thing. Reaching down under the table for her bag, she began to rummage.

"And thank you for agreeing to see me."

"No problem! I haven't spoken to a reporter in a long time. I'm probably out of practice. You're American? My English ... not so good. French ... okay?"

The ending in English, stumbling and jagged with misplaced vowels.

"French is fine. Do you mind?"

From her digging, she brought out her recorder, pad, and pen.

"I don't want to miss anything you say."

"But sometimes I like to be missed."

He liked the joke, his laugh sharp, loud, and quick.

"Sorry. No, I don't mind your recorder. Not at all."

Both chairs and the table were small, but he made them seem even smaller.

"This is a wonderful house," she said, trying to focus.

Switching on the recorder, she tried to begin again.

"Have you been here long?"

"Thank you. Constance will be happy you like the house. It's really her hand — not that I don't think it's pretty. It really is. Oh, and four years. We bought it four years ago."

"It must be interesting being here. I mean how your career has gone."

"I really don't believe it."

There was gentleness there.

"It's wonderful, it really is. Like a dream, but I keep expecting to wake up."

There was sleight-of-hand there, slipping honesty up his work shirtsleeve.

"Insecurity? That's hard to believe considering what people have been saying about your work."

"Oh, you can't tell me other people haven't felt the same, waiting for it all to come to an end."

"Got me. I *have* heard that before. I just have a hard time accepting it. But then I've never been where you are now."

"Have a secret for you."

Conspiratorially, he leaned forward.

"It feels the same. There's no difference. Sure, the furniture is new — and the house — but to me ... I'm still just an amateur. Oh, but people are telling me I'm great. That's very new."

There was pondering there.

"You sound like you don't believe them."

"I don't, or at least, I try not to. People lied to me all the time when I was just starting out, but I knew why. Not that I wasn't grateful; my feelings needed protecting. Now all I get is 'oh, you genius,' and 'magnificent, maestro' and 'your best work to date' and I don't know why."

"Maybe you're just good?"

He laughed.

"No one can be that good. I wish someone would look at what I'm doing and say 'it's shit!' just so I know where the edge is."

He shrugged, wide shoulders rising up towards his tanned ears.

"Right now, I am whistling in the dark."

Opening her mouth, she was about to talk about the book, the plate, the painting, but then she didn't. The *why* behind it was complex as well as furtive, making her feel uprooted and wavering. To cover it, she cleared her throat, sipped her water, and pulled a stupid question out of her hat.

"How do you hope people think of you?"

"Don't care," he answered with another laugh. "Honestly. Like I said, I feel like I'm still just beginning. All of this isn't real."

The last back behind him, addressing the furniture, the decorations in the living room.

"People are just ... out there. They don't feel real."

"What does feel real then?"

An immensely bright spark lit his eyes: "The work, of course. What else? Do you do anything — creative I mean?"

"I'm a journalist. My boss frowns on being creative."

It was a lie. David cared about his people, but in regards to their work, it was always deadlines and sales figures over what was actually in the pages of his publication.

"It's like ... merde."

The profanity rang clumsily in French, clearly not his favorite swearing language.

"It takes up a lot of room. In my mind, I mean."

He let out another deep laugh, as if accidentally stumbling across a fond memory.

"Constance says it takes up too much, that it doesn't leave space for anything else. She's right, of course. But it's worth it. Well, sometimes it is. When it's good. When I *know* it's good. It's like having all the best things in the world at once, but even better because *you* did it."

"I've heard other artists say it's like having an orgasm."

Too blunt, but she threw it out there anyway, hoping for a nibble. Sex sold — and there were those rumors.

"Yes. I think the two are very closely related. It's always intimate, between subject and me. Like this..."

He knitted his fingers together.

"But also in my mind. When it's good, I can feel a deeper part of myself coming up to the surface, the part of me that really sees light and color. I guess I'm fucking with my subconscious."

"That's great," Sheri said, quickly writing it down. "Sex and art and the brain."

"Exactly! It's like when two bodies are moving together, at first you might be feeling your own body against the other person's, filling your senses, but at the same time you're still thinking, still in your head: worried about performing, hoping that things go well, all of that. But then it gets going, and then you aren't *there* anymore. You're off to somewhere else in your head, the sex taking over. When it's good, I mean. Good sex, good art. Same kind of thing."

Again, she wanted to talk about the painting. Again, she didn't. When it came to mind, she felt herself become fragile, vulnerable. Like confessing an intimate fantasy to a lover. Not yet. Not yet. Not yet.

Yet. Yet. Yet.

"I-I've heard about that part of your allure, your art, I mean. I've heard that it's very sensual. People feel things when they see it."

"Thank you! I don't even think you are lying to me," he said with a broad wink. "I think that is because I put a lot into it. Work, yeah, but other things as well. It's exhausting, but it can be worth it. Like sex again!"

The room was warm. Sipping her water, she bought herself some thinking time.

"How do you start — with a painting I mean?"

"Well, I look. Take a good long look at what I'm going to do."

Leaning forward, he demonstrated: dark eyes wide, the spark gleaming there.

"Try to see it as much as I can. Light, shadow, color of skin, those kinds of thing." Demonstration concluded, he leaned back, the spark still bright.

"Is it *just* looking?"

Escobar shrugged.

"I have my eyes, but I also try to see beyond that. Yes, I know how that must sound. But I mean it. Really!"

He grinned, recognizing how he sounded.

"That's the trouble, I don't know how to say it. As a writer, you might be able to. Words are your tools. A musician, maybe, too. Me? I have my eyes and my brushes. I just don't know how to explain it."

"Well, you did say it was almost sexual. The process. Fucking with your mind, you said."

"The process, sure. But there's also what starts it all. The looking. I mean, I can look at you now, but there's something wrong. Maybe the light, or this room."

With quick swings of his head, he looked for someplace better. Then a thought clearly displayed on his face.

"Here, come with me. Come on."

Standing, he put out a hand, brought her up to her feet. The sound of her chair skidding back could have been what made her shiver.

Pulling, leading, he took her from the kitchen, through the pristine living room, and to another door.

"Here, right through here."

When he opened the door, she walked passed him and in, without thinking. Once inside, she thought: *Oh.* It was the internal sound of a revelation, a little non-word connected to the feeling that here was where he lived.

It was obvious. Left behind was a decorator's sterile interpretation of living. She had walked into glass and light, life and passion: Escobar's studio.

It was a mess. Three walls and the ceiling were glass, rectangles of clarity set in a grid of greened copper. The one wall that didn't show a view of gently rolling green hills and distant, fractal trees — the one shared with the exterior wall of the house — was an eye-aching chaos of stacked virgin canvases; sloppily piled sketchpads; columns of teetering reference books with well-worn spines; a low mound of discarded rags; and a massive table of thick, crude lumber sprayed with a spectrum of paint tubes, encrusted pelletteknives, jars and bottles of cloudy liquids, cans of turpentine, and fans of thick, thin, vibrantly used as well as shiny new, brushes.

Pressed against the right-hand glass wall was a smaller chaos, a more intimate and immediate collection of tools, books, sketchpads, shuffles of virgin canvas, around and on a smaller and taller table — made from no-less crude or thick wood — a battered and knife-scarred stool; and an empty easel.

In the middle of the room was a green-carpeted platform, a half-meter-high stage.

"Much better," Escobar said from behind her. "Sorry for the mess."

The last sounded like a too-common ritual, a gesture said so many times that it had just about lost all meaning.

"Stand up there," he said, waving her towards the dais.

As she approached it, he slipped neatly through the clutter and confusion, a movement he clearly had done so many times that it had become a dance step. Retrieving a sketch pad from where it rested between the glass wall and a tilted roman numeral III of battered portfolios, carefully choosing a charcoal from a bouquet of similar ones in a mason jar, he sat down behind the easel.

With a soft chuckle, he said, "With my ass on this stool, I guess I see better than I do with my eyes. With a pencil and some paper, and in this room ... It just feels ... right, you know?"

His hand started to move. Even though the room was large, the scratching sound carried clearly to her ears. She was a good twelve feet away when his dark eyes peered over the paper, yet she felt like he was standing right in front of her.

"Much better," he mumbled, more to himself than to her.

Self-consciousness made her face warm, her cheeks blush.

"Do you want me to do anything?"

In the center, elevated, her body was instantly not worth looking at, let alone sketched by a genius.

"Hmm? Oh, I'm sorry."

Blinking large brown eyes, he shifted focus from the pad to her.

"Your shoulders are lovely. Very nice. There's an angle there, from your neck to your arms. And your neck — you really have a pretty neck. Very slender, very supple. Just stand as you normally would."

He chuckled.

"I know, it's like being told not to think of apples — then all you can do is think of nothing but apples. Just try to relax, think of something else. You had a good drive here?"

Halfway through a nod, she caught herself, involuntarily stiffening the neck he seemed to think was good.

"It was very nice."

Even her voice was self-conscious, her vocabulary sounding average, her grammar ringing ordinary.

"You live in Paris?"

"Yes, I've been there for the last ten years or so."

A dull life, not worth speaking of, let alone being immortalized in pencil on paper.

"That's where Constance is. My wife. She loves the city. I like it as well, but not as much as she does."

As he chatted, his hand kept moving, scratching continuing as a background to his voice.

"Your French is excellent, by the way. I am still self-conscious about mine. Constance says there is too much Spain in it."

Again she wanted to move her head, but resisted.

"I can hear a bit, but not a lot."

"You are too polite."

Attention diverted to the pad, he trailed off, surfacing after a minute.

"Very nice. Very pretty — sorry, that's not good for me to say."

"No, it's okay," she said.

The sunlight coming in, her burning cheeks, she was hotter than ever.

"I mean I don't mind."

A laugh came out, not forced but not easy either.

"It's not something I hear all that often."

"Well, you should. All women should hear that. Men, too. But women especially. All those magazines, TV shows, movies, they are telling you what you should be, and if you aren't then no one will ever want you. So stupid. Everyone has beauty in them. Eyes, shoulders, her neck, her feet, her hands. The only thing I don't like in women is when they think that all they should be is pretty. Models, they can be like that, worried about what they look like, that people think they are beautiful."

Returning to his pad, he scratched down some lines, capturing further details of her. Looking at his head, his face focused on his work, she felt her consciously set mouth slip gently into a grin.

"I prefer women like you. Honest. Real. True. A body that ... I am so sorry. I shouldn't talk like that."

Shaking her head, forgetting that she probably should be holding still, she said, "No, really. It's okay."

"It's not, but it's good for you to say that."

"I like what you said about women. I see a lot of that, working for the magazine."

The moment it was said — a reminder of what she was there for — two feelings hit her: happiness that she was back in control, but also disappointment that she'd broken the spell.

"I'm sure that you do. Just as I see it in some of my models. Others, though, are more like real women. But even though I love them, the public doesn't seem to see them that way, so I paint more peacocks than doves. So is life, I guess."

"Am I a dove then?"

"You are better than that. You have ... a glow. I saw it in the kitchen. It's just brighter here. That sounds silly, doesn't it? I wish I could say it right, but I'm not that good ... with words, at least. I prefer to talk with this," he said, holding up the pencil.

"I don't know, I think you've been making perfect sense."

"Merci."

A few more strokes to the pad followed.

"I wish I could see better. That's more important. When I get it right, it's like I'm getting everything down, getting it right. God, again. Seeing with everything. Other times I look, I see, but all I see are colors and shapes — not what's really there. Like you. I can see you, but I'm missing something."

Warm again, hot again. Caution vanished, fear went away — hope appearing in their place. Caution that he was smooth and slick, an acrobat who'd nimbly try to work his way into her panties. Fear that he'd push, twist, leverage her into posing — and then much more.

Hope that ... She remembered his painting, the one in the book. The one she'd stared at for hours and hours. The colors, the shape, the beauty of that woman. Hope, yes, but special forms of it, sweet and special kinds of longing: to be the lover of such a great artist, but also to be more than that.

Heart-racing thrill and giddy lightness came the moment she said, and then did it, committing herself with a sentence and a gesture.

"Well, I didn't come expecting to pose in the nude," she said, fingers reaching up to the top button on her blouse.

"That would be..." he said in a ghostly stammer. "Excuse me. I mean I wouldn't want you to be uncomfortable."

"I'm flattered."

Meaning it, she steadily unbuttoned. On the last one, she hesitated, a slowness of doubt and concern. What was she doing? Possible answers, but nothing definite. Posing for a famous artist? Yes. Allowing his seduction to proceed? Yes. Walking into his world of fame and sex as a participant, not just an observer? Yes.

The last button and the blouse slid off her shoulders. Looking up from watching the fabric, she caught him peering over the edge of his pad. His expression seemed complex, penetrating.

Kicking off her shoes, she put her thumbs into the waistband of her skirt. Stretching the elastic, she hesitated, a pause of introspection and understanding. Pushing down and stepping out, she began to talk without being aware of what she was saying.

"I saw a painting of yours in a book I bought. *Woman in Moonlight.* I-I think it's beautiful. Really beautiful. The way she looks — the way she looks back at you, and the shape of her body. I keep looking at it, thinking about what she was thinking, what you were thinking, too. It's just ... I really want to know."

Bra and panties, then braless and panty-less. Bare and exposed, she stood naked in sunlight. No longer self-conscious, she tried to imagine herself reflected out of his vision, to see herself the way he saw her, the way he'd also seen that woman who stood in moonlight.

Like her, her thighs were heavy. Like her, her breasts were too large. Like her, her ass was too big. Like her, she was short. Like her, her hair was dull earthen brown. Like her ... she wanted to radiate like her, gleam like her, be powerful and sure like her.

Even warmer, even hotter, Sheri felt her body act on its own, thrilled by exposure and his examination. Between those just right thighs she felt herself liquefy and melt, at the tips of her perfect breasts she felt her nipples stiffen, behind her she became aware of her full, soft cheeks.

"So beautiful," Escobar said, almost too low to hear.

The room was silent, his sketching stopped.

Still warmer, still hotter, she became aware of her breathing, how with each slow, steady breath her body moved, shifted. Her breasts began to ache. Her nipples began to ache. Her ... Everywhere she began to ache. Distantly, she knew what she was doing was foolish, reckless. A seduction by a fellow student was humiliating, a seduction by an employer demeaning, a seduction by a stranger in a bar shameful, but a seduction by a master of color, shape, and form, who saw her not just as a woman to plow, but an object of true beauty — that was, would be, wonderful.

The studio began to echo with the sound of his pencil again. Each audible line was like the ticking of an irregular metronome, mirroring her tripping heartbeat. With each one, she wanted to step down off the platform, walk to him. With each one, she hoped she wouldn't, the protraction being her intensity.

Step down ... yes. Step down and walk — her wetness painting her thighs, her breasts swaying gently, her ass bobbing — over to him. Or maybe she wouldn't have to. Maybe he'd come out from behind his easel, his sketchpad, instead. Yes, that could be it. He'd come around and up to her, moving steadily, slowly, until he was standing in front of her. His hand then ... Yes, his hand would rise to her breast, lifting and cupping and then raising nipple to mouth. His other hand then ... yes, his other hand would fall between her legs, parting and reaching and stroking her clit.

On the floor ... yes, he'd lower her to the floor, gently easing her down until they were a tangle of arms and legs. How big was he? How would he taste? Slow and fast, or deep and slow? She on top, or he behind? How long would they go? Breakfast or a late night snack?

Pencil still going, he looked and looked again over his pad, at her. Face red, his eyes were very wide, the pupils large. His dark skin glistened faintly, he clearly as hot as she was.

The *Woman In Moonlight* ... no, the woman in sunlight looked at him, feeling pleased and proud and hopeful, wanting the moment to last forever, but also to finish with hands and bodies, come and sweat and laughter.

Then it was over.

"I'm ... sorry. This ... this isn't going to work," Escobar said, shaking his head. "Please leave."

III

Clothes put on. Door to kitchen opened. Purse, notepad, recorder (still running), retrieved. Door outside opened. Door outside slammed shut. Key put in door. Key turned in ignition. Motor started.

Drive. Going away — going back — was at least unfamiliar, landmarks that could have reminded her of that morning now in the past of her rearview mirror.

The hotel. Park. Car door opened. Car door shut. In the front door, not looking if it shut behind her or was left yawning open.

The clerk, lost in a paperback book, not noticing her, not seeing her.

Crying. Blurred vision submerged the lobby, rippling her sight with distortion. To the lift and then up, wetness finally rolling down her cheeks. The clerk hadn't even noticed her, hadn't even seen her.

Not even the clerk.

The room. Not home, but safe enough for her limbs to go from clenched tension to loosened collapse, falling to the bed, curling up. Sobs, then. Heavy wracks, then.

Sleep also betrayed her. Tired, yes, body drained, yes, but every time she closed her eyes, she was back in the studio, back on the platform, and there he was, ghostly, superimposed on her vision of the bedspread, the hotel room wallpaper. In her ears, an auditory hallucination of his voice: "I'm … sorry. This … this isn't going to work. Please leave."

What did I do wrong?

When she opened her eyes, blinking away the gritty, gummy residue of her tears, night had come, the day gone from her view, if not her mind. Pragmatism became a good distraction, a way to lose herself in the mundane.

She should wash her face. Into the bathroom, she went. Hot tap, cold tap, a cup made out of her hands, she splashed and then rubbed, dried.

A mistake followed. Putting the towel aside, she looked at herself in the mirror, a black iron-oval framing a chubby-faced woman, eyes bloodshot and puffy, lips chapped, cheeks chaffed and raw.

Turning away, fast enough to twirl the bathroom rug around her foot, she left the image behind.

She should get something to eat. Breakfast was a long time ago,

161

without a lunch between then and now. She thought about leaving the room, going down in the lift, out into the town to try and find a good place. Her stomach was sore, still knotted up, but not from hunger. Not yet.

What did I do wrong?

She should check her email. Sitting down at the desk, she opened the computer, waking it up from its recharging sleep. A minute later, she was dialing, the screech of mating modems too loud in the small room.

Messages appeared. Still predictable: dribbles, drabbles of spam, her father asking if she got his stupid joke, more warning folklore from her mother, even more messages from various Parisian friends wanting to hook up — still not remembering that she was out of town for the week, and a new message from her editor at *Le Monde*.

She should read it first, and with a tap of the keyboard, she did. *Hope it is going well for you. Here are a few people to interview for background.* After were three names and three sets of international phone numbers. Constance, the wife. Jacqueline, a model. Marcel, the dealer.

What did I do wrong?

She should respond, and tried to, but by the third sentence of each try, the room felt colder, she felt smaller, and her eyes began to tear. So she only answered with two only lines: *Well enough. Draft soon.*

She should start to outline the article, frame what she could of the interview. For fifteen minutes, she simply stared at the screen, unsure of what to say, let alone how to say it.

Another attempt at sleep? The first try had been a failure, and she was uncertain if the second would succeed either, but the only other thing she thought she should do was to dig the recorder out of her purse, begin to transcribe. But the thought of hearing his voice again ... Better to try and sleep.

So she carefully crawled onto the bed, still coolly damp, rolled onto her back — even though she preferred to sleep on her stomach — and closed her eyes.

Breaths in, breaths out, waiting for that moment when her interior voice, the attempts at the article in her mind, began to make less and less sense: *How do you define 'genius,' for the world of art? We have all seen his work, but few have tried to know the man behind the paintings. They say that writing about art is like trying to sketch music.*

But then the work faded away, replaced by the louder voice of the heart rather than the head: *What did I do wrong?*

She knew she was a bit too heavy. She knew her nipples drooped a bit. She knew her belly was a bit too obvious. She knew her pubic thatch was too large, the black hairs pointing too much towards her navel. She knew her feet were ugly. She knew her ass was too big. She knew ... but he'd said, he'd said, he'd said...

He'd said I was beautiful.

What did I do wrong?

Eyes opened, once again she examined the fine tracery of cracks in the antique ceiling. She didn't know. She had no idea. She doubted she'd ever know. She could already feel that one moment hanging over her head, a weight of burning humiliation, a cloud of sad disappointment.

She got out of bed, movement better than hearing her mind race over it again and again. Her foot hit against something on the floor, the pain of it shooting up her leg. Sitting back down, she massaged her toes until the pain faded away.

She'd walked right into her reference pile, sending the books tumbling. One of them had fallen face down, exposing a momentarily unfamiliar back. Curious and desperately needing a distraction — any kind of distraction — she reached down and flipped it over.

Now it was familiar. Looking at it, the moment became even louder, the weight heavier, the cloud thicker. She might not have thought it, been completely aware of it, but she'd driven down to this little hotel, driven out to his house, talked with him in the kitchen, stepped into his studio, for that painting, that one image in that one book. She'd wanted to meet the painter, but she also wanted to be seen the way the woman in that painting had been seen, to be made as beautiful as she was.

But she wasn't. She wasn't. She didn't know what she'd done wrong, but the outcome was clear: she wasn't good enough for him. Not for his cock, not for his brushes.

The anger came like a sunburn to her face. The book suddenly in her hand, she first tried to tear it in two, but the hard cover stopped her. Flipping it open, she began to rip out pages. With each one, a new — fatter — tear rolled down her cheeks. One of the plates must have been *that* one, but she didn't see it in her hand as she crushed it down into a ball and threw it across the small hotel room.

Back in the bathroom, she heaved into the sink, her mainly empty belly trying to get rid of whatever was in there. When it finally stopped, she wiped her mouth, gasping for air as she dabbed at her lips.

It didn't go away, but it did die down a bit. The humiliation faded to hot smoke, the weight lifted, the cloud turned into an iron gray overcast.

Yes, she decided, kicking through the balls of wadded book pages, she had to get to work. First, a few calls — to the wife, the model, the dealer — and by then she'd be ready to listen to his voice again, transcribe his words.

Pulling her cell phone out of her purse, though, she already knew what she'd write. With her words, she'd paint him, show everyone what kind of man Escobar really was.

CHAPTER EIGHT

Escobar

I

Brush to pallette, a swirl of transfer from latter to former. A moment to examine the end, see if the bristles had become too wild, irregular. They hadn't. A moment, too, to ponder once again the mathematics of color, wishing one more time that he could have the assurance that an exact formula of Cadmium Yellow Medium, Brown Pink, Cadmium Red Deep, with Cobalt, would be exact, perfect, ideal.

As always, though, he'd had to touch, smear, and dab until they all mixed, randomly getting it right — or as close as he could get. There was no assurance. There never was.

The light was dying, fading towards night, but he kept working. Letting his hands and eyes do the work, he looked, studied, tried to deeply *see* the nature of his subject, the inner workings of it, the brilliant spectrum it cast in his mind. That's what they said he did, anyway. The critics. His dealer. The press.

He just hoped he didn't mess it up.

Too yellow, he thought, bringing the brush down, lowering the volume of the shining oil. Then, *not yellow enough*, and so more put back, the loudness increasing.

His subject didn't mind and that was refreshing. No concern, for once, that when the work was done, his model would be disappointed.

On a stool in the center of his studio, in a beam of ebbing light, the flower didn't care if he succeed or failed.

Too red. Brush to pallette, he dabbed up a darkening shade, lowering it until he felt it came close — or close enough — to matching the petals of the rose.

Then he failed. Not in the work, because that was going well, but in why he'd sat down to paint. Despite his efforts, he still hadn't been able to push aside his nagging, chattering, disparaging mind.

What, he wondered, *would be the color of guilt?*

* * * *

Muscling concentration, brush to canvas, color revisited composition, technique returned to capturing his subject.

A sweeping movement became the basic shape of a petal. A following gesture turned into a revealing depth of texture. A turn of his wrist created another element of the flower, a puzzle-piece snapped into place. In the few minutes that he painted, a flower would soon be perfectly evident. In an hour, it would be clear he was painting a rose. At the end of the day, when the sun had finally set and his precious light was completely gone, he may very well have made something that would last far beyond the wilting, browning, curling, fading, life of the flower. A preservation of its beauty, or a theft of its life, depending on the angle of the viewer.

But he was still failing. Sunflowers, not roses. Candytuft, not roses. Periwinkle, not roses. Daisies, not roses. Violets, not roses. Honeysuckle, not roses.

He still couldn't help but think, memories filling his head, shame reddening his cheeks. The first one, the loudest, largest one — the person he'd hurt the most. Not roses, but a field of grass, emerald save for sprays of golden dandelions. The two of them, young and innocent. The two of them, beginning life.

And then he...

No, don't go there. Don't think about that. With a shake of his head, he dislodged the field of green and yellow, forcing himself back to the present and a single red rose.

Roses. He didn't like roses. So ubiquitous, any of their splendor having been washed away by sheer numbers, by commonality. Seen every day, even loveliness can fade into a shrugging background.

True *beauty* — in the rare, true meaning of the word — was always bright, always brilliant, always dazzling, always radiant, always unique, and gloriously special no matter how many times it's seen.

The brush slowed, stopped, was pulled away from the canvas and the steadily emerging flower. The field again, as vividly jade and preciously yellow in his mind no matter how many times he wandered back there. The field of grass and daisies, *their* field, *their* sunlit place, where he'd *known* — in the rare, true meaning of the word — what love was.

Until he'd destroyed it.

No, don't go there. Don't think about that. Don't think at all. Back to the work, back to trying to submerge himself in stealing the rose's life: shape, color, value, texture and space, perspective, emphasis, and mood.

Sunflowers, not roses. Candytuft, not roses. Periwinkle, not roses. Daisies, not roses. Violets, not roses. Honeysuckle, not roses. At least when he failed, he didn't wander to where the real pain was. This time he fell back even farther, long before that field, before Constance.

As he worked, as he painted, he couldn't help but think about Diego.

II

There were flowers back then, of course. But they had also slipped into ubiquitous invisibility, or more than likely because children never notice things like that. Until they are old, that is, and nostalgia makes them look back more than forward.

Old? Yes. He guessed he was, because sitting there in the here and now, success supposedly all around him in recognition and expensive real estate, Escobar instead found himself back in Igualada with his brother.

It had been good. The two of them running home from school, Diego transformed into a dashing Spanish pirate, Escobar having become a foolish Englishman in pursuit. Diego, a handsome resistance fighter, Escobar, a stupid Nazi. Diego, an intrepid European astronaut, Escobar, the evil alien. By the time they'd wound down the narrow road from the school, up the roaring main road with its huge trucks and dust-swirling buses, went through the fallow field, over the rough-hewn fence, under sticky-leaved fruit trees, and up the hill to their house, the pirate had made off with the treasure, the Nazi had been defeated, the alien disintegrated. But no matter how many times Escobar had lost the booty, gotten shot, or ray gun zapped, they'd both came home accompanied by brightly sparkling bubbles of laughter, lit from within by glowing smiles.

On the weekends, if they weren't in the backseat of the family car on the way to one or another set of grandparents; or traveling away from Igualada to some museum (not fun), café (could be fun), or amusement park (always fun), there were other adventures to be had, other movies, television shows, and comic books to leap into.

Then, a summer — *that* summer: the heat wave days of Elena's sunshine hair, the humid weeks of her trying to teach them against the demanding roar of their breaking voices, aching joints, and knocking erections.

Humiliation, embarrassment, self-hatred: one, two, three through his mind in the present, one, two, three down through his arm, into his hand, onto the canvas. A mis-stroke, a clumsy action.

Ruined? No. After a few minutes of examination, he decided it could be saved. Other things, though, never could be.

One pencil had done it, one sheet of paper had done it. A sketch, a fantasy of bare Elena. It changed everything. After, the pirates never sailed; the Nazis marched unopposed; and aliens overran the universe. Diego stepped back, moved away. Brothers to strangers with a few strokes, family to acquaintances with one clumsy depiction.

With Diego gone, Escobar had only one place to go. Composition became pirates, colors were the Nazis, texture served as his own alien menace. His playground was paper, at first, but as he got more and more comfortable, he moved to the more adult world of canvas. It was all a new game, one he had to play alone.

In the now, he fixed the rose with a few deft strokes, but in the past, Escobar watched Diego walk away. Fading with each difference between them: special classes for the artist, special tools and toys for the artist, special treatment for the artist.

By the time of that field of flowers, that sunny hillside with Constance, Diego had already left: luggage packed, farewells given to friends, kisses on the cheek, hands shaken. For everyone but his brother.

For Escobar, his brother had left years before.

* * * *

The rose had begun to live. With a sigh of relief, the artist shifted his attention to making it do more than that, to trap in oils what the critics said was his supernatural ability to capture the essence, the soul, the true substance of his subject.

He didn't know what they were talking about.

A wry grin as he worked, a self-mocking smile. He talked a good game, a performance honed with a different kind of talent. He didn't exactly lie when the journalists asked, much of what he said about the process was true, but he also didn't really understand how it all happened. He just knew that it did, for now.

Thinking of reporters, questions, lies, brought her to mind. The American had left, the door slamming behind her. His … desired subject gone.

No, don't go there. Don't think about that. Work on the flower, work on the art, work to keep it all at bay. A hillside of bright green grass and vivid yellow flowers, an American reporter, put aside, forced down, compressed by concentration.

Yes, he wished he understood it, where it all really came from. Then maybe he'd be able to touch brush to canvas without his heart tapping, sweat beading his forehead, legs losing strength. Then maybe he wouldn't feel failure standing behind him, its axe ready to cut his career down with the sharp edge of a single, botched work.

Again: he couldn't help but think about Diego.

He envied him.

* * * *

Bad enough, he thought. *But can always be worse.*

A small place in the city, an apartment just the right size for a simple life. No filigree, no fine woods, no immaculate paint, no gleaming appliances, no geometric precision where floors met walls, no alarm, nothing decorated. The floorboards would be bowed and warped, plaster bulging or cracked, windows jammed or barely held in, kitchen stained and burnt, bathroom brown and fragrant.

Down one street a grocery store, friendly owner always ready with a *bonjour* and a slap on the back. Down the other a café, where everyone knew everyone else's name.

Periodically, he'd pick up the phone, finger hovering over the numbers, thinking that this time he'd actually dial. But he always put the phone down, closing any possible connection.

They were too different now. Too far apart. Money, fame, talent, respect between them — a gap Diego hadn't tried to cross, Escobar too frightened to.

The flower was almost complete. It would be good, Marcel would smile, it would sell, the critics would applaud, Constance would approve, and Escobar would be safe — until the next painting.

The small apartment was a retreat, another life he'd sketched out for himself. Day after day of tranquility, honesty, and ease. The world he imagined his brother living in, what the famous artist secretly wished *he* had.

The phone was *always* put down. The connection would never be made. His brother would always be on one side, he always on the other, *both* of them jealous of the other's life.

III

The sun had left for the day, a thin curve of moon taking the next shift. There were lights, naturally, the best money could buy. With a flip of a switch, he could snap on the morning. Ideal light for an artist. Perfect light for painting.

For a second, he thought about doing it. Over to the switch, flip it up, blooms of high intensity lamps, the choosing of a new flower to paint, another five hours of work, another five hours of distraction.

No. Making sure the drying work was safe and supported on his easel, he stepped out of the studio, into the still quiet of the house — leaving it all behind. At least for the night.

What to do? Now that the rose was flattened by oils onto canvas and he had his stay of execution, a hand fisted in his belly. Food? Yes. He hadn't eaten since that morning.

He winced when he opened the refrigerator, an unasked memory of a few hours before, an offering of coffee, to make tea. Shame when he looked in, guilt while trying to decide what to cook, remorse taking out eggs.

The rose had been beautiful, a perfect distraction. Cooking would be good, but not good enough. Cheese came out, too, as did butter.

Business might work. Clanking around in a cabinet for a pan, lighting up the stove, crackling plastic wrap off the cheese, taking the top off the ceramic butter bowl, he also tried to busy his mind with what to do next.

Fresh light in the morning, and with it, a refreshed look at the painting. Had it dropped any of its painted petals during the night? Was it really successful, or had it all been a trick of hopeful desperation? Perhaps some touching up would be in order, perhaps not.

Other artists had totally embraced electronica: cell phones, Photoshop, and digital photography. He preferred a simple handshake of a cell phone, an Apple laptop, and a digital camera. With the last, he'd take a few dozen shots, hoping that at least one of them would be sufficient to capture the right colors. With the first, he'd call his dealer to let him know that he'd finished a new work.

Other dealers had completely bought into a digital life: web sites, email, and eBay. His, though, had a rental kind of commitment to it all, preferring to see work in its pure paint rather than on an LCD screen. The rose would be wrapped, padded, and boxed up for a trip to the city.

Or maybe it wouldn't go to Marcel at all.

* * * *

Stirring eggs — his dinner hissing, the omelet puffing up steam — Escobar fussed with the recipe. A pinch of salt, a twist of pepper ... shallots? Yes, shallots. He went to the refrigerator for a quick rummage, a reward of a might-actually-be-fresh green addition to his meal.

Constance had tendered once again, before her trip to the city, the idea of a cook or a maid. Someone, she said, who could just 'help them out' when they were too tired (such as herself) or busy (as Escobar frequently was). As before, he'd made a few possible noises, then quickly changed the subject.

Constance ... thinking of his wife cramped his belly, almost clenching away his appetite. *No*, he thought, *don't go there. Don't think about that.* With a shake of his head, he refocused on his dinner of green and yellow, the color of that special field, he observed, in spite of himself.

Back to work: to the omelet as well as a plan for the next day. Yes, in the morning he'd check the rose out, see if it was a success or not. If it was good enough, he'd go ahead and box it and send it to Marcel. But if it was beyond good, touching great, even close to special, then he wouldn't send it to his dealer.

Cheese was added to the mix, yellow on top of yellow. *A bright dinner in a dim house.* Thinking of cheating Marcel wasn't a pleasant thought, but thinking of Constance was far worse.

The food was becoming deeply tempting, the aroma relighting his hunger. Beer? Yeah, a beer. Sliding the omelet onto a plate, grinning privately to himself at his fine technique (or at least in not dropping it on the tile floor). Safe, he left his dinner on the small kitchen table and went back to the refrigerator. There was a God, His Sign being a beetle green bottle of German beer.

Maybe he would send off the rose. Even if it was beyond good, touching great, close to special — didn't his dealer deserve his part of it? Marcel was more than a path from studio to gallery, and from gallery to money.

Even with a few good sales, a few small exhibitions, most dealers were still hesitant about signing him. Marcel had been too big, too well known, and so Escobar had put him at the bottom of his list. Rather than play a long shot, he'd decided to play it safe — hit up smaller dealers first.

But one after another, they'd smiled, then shook their heads. One after another, he'd crossed them off his list, until only a few large — too large — dealers had remained.

No, no, no. The names had gotten fewer. Marcel hadn't been the last remaining name, but he was close to it. Close enough to make Escobar feel small, fragile, and desperate when he walked into *L'Art*. Marcel had been cool, but polite; professional, but interested; all business, but also enthusiastic.

No promises had been made. Marcel was clear about that.

But he also put out his hand, shook Escobar's, and said, "I see great things for you."

He hadn't been wrong. Which was what made Escobar's betrayal of his trust ache that much more.

* * * *

The omelet was edible, good. No, it wasn't touching great, nowhere near special, but it did the job: it quelled his rumbling belly, occupied a space where a void had been before. Cooking wasn't a talent he'd spent time developing. At least he hadn't made a mess of it.

As he ate, he strolled back through his mind, revisiting his times with Marcel. Flashbulbs and champagne one night, signatures on contracts one day, meeting with journalists in the morning, television interviews in the afternoon. Always by his side had been the clout, the precision, the ordered mind of his dealer.

Escobar had more than a few illusions in his life — some out of desperation, a few others just simple fantasies — but Marcel's reality was as obvious as his presence. Escobar was a product, a route to fame, and through fame to fortune. But that confidence that he was seriously banking on Escobar was enough. Even if Escobar was painting dollar signs more than great art that Marcel believed he could deliver was enough.

At least Marcel left him to his art, which was rare, he knew. Other dealers pushed, prodded, forced, or bribed artists to be more colorful, more traditional, more commercial, to envision their work over a sofa and not hanging in the Louvre.

The only thing Marcel asked was for the painter to paint, and — his controlled voice even more controlled — for Escobar to bring him everything he did. *Everything.* Marcel was his dealer, and that meant he dealt with each stroke, each work, each painting.

It was an unspoken rule that Escobar had disobeyed. Eating slowly, sedately, savoring fork after fork of rich, creamy eggs, he also carefully, insightfully thought about Marcel, about his paintings, and again about his brother. And how they were all connected.

* * * *

Yes, he wished he knew where it all really came from. Chewing his soft dinner, he tried again to puzzle it all out. What he'd told that reporter was close, but only close. What he hadn't been able to say was how slippery it all was. How it could be there one moment, a burning, a blaze, a lightning strike, and then gone the next. Gone for an hour? A day? A month? A year? The rest of his life? He didn't know that, either.

When it happened, when it stopped or just soured, he found himself back in that tiny apartment, living the simple life of his brother, away from the terror of dropping down from the heights his work had lifted him to. The farther up you go, the more devastating the impact when you fall.

The eggs were more than half gone, the beer completely. A wind had come up, making a tree scratch against the window. Watching, hypnotized by the back and forth, up and down movement, Escobar steadily ate, finishing his dinner with a series of gestures as repetitive as the ghostly waving of the twisted branches.

Envy for his brother's quiet, simple life. That he'd stolen from his dealer, the man who'd believed in him. Both coming from his chilled terror, his constant fear of losing what the critics and buyers called his *talent*.

The plate clattered into the sink; the empty beer bottle hit the bottom of the trash with a flinchingly loud crash of shattering glass. Looking at the dirty dish, he thought about cleaning it, another activity to distract his buzzing mind.

Instead, he left the kitchen and entered his studio. With a flick of a heavy duty switch, the hated lamps flared on, blasting the glass-walled annex with unflattering, glaring light.

The rose was good. Very good. None of the petals needed touching up, the stem didn't require repair. It wasn't magnificent, but it was very fine, nonetheless. Form, color, shape, texture, and even a kind of life — it had it all. It was also different, a subject rare in his catalog of portraits and nudes. If it were not to go to Paris, if it were to disappear, it wouldn't leave a hole in his scope of work.

He owed Marcel. All that he had — the house, the recognition, the awards, the happiness of Constance — was because of his dealer. It was a debt that Escobar doubted he could ever repay.

But ... running a finger up and over one corner of the canvas, he wondered if he could produce another rose. Or anything else, for that matter. It could all be gone tomorrow. An hour? A day? A month? A year? The rest of his life?

No illusions. The rose was a picture, not a real flower. A commodity, not life with a stem and petals. Marcel had brought him success, but he'd only continue to bring it as long as Escobar's talent remained with him. The moment it left, so would his dealer.

In the morning, he'd wrap, pad, and box up the rose. But not for a trip to the city. It would never be delivered to Marcel.

Guilt? Yes. Shame? Yes. But he had all that his success, so far, had brought him to protect. The painting would be locked away, secreted in a private storeroom.

Attempting to pacify the accusing little voice in the back of his mind, Escobar tried not to think of it as betraying Marcel's trust. It was insurance, he justified. It was another commodity to be sold off when his gift had been returned to wherever it had come from, when the burning went out, the blaze died down, and the lightning had struck its last.

Leaving his rose, leaving his studio, Escobar flipped the switch, giving both back to the night.

IV

What to do? Now that the rose's fate had been decided, the stress of the decision relieved, if not liked, exhaustion dropped lead onto his shoulders. Bed? Yes. He needed some sleep, a good rest.

The house was dark, still, and quiet. It was a good house. Constance certainly seemed to enjoy it, but when she wasn't there, it was too big. The gray shapes of furniture in the barely lit living room seemed to be hazy from an extreme distance. Hardwood flooring creaked, the echo bouncing back after what felt like a long minute.

Carefully — trying to remember where that table, that chair, that vase, that cabinet, that bric, that brac, all was — Escobar moved through the space, towards the bed. Finally, after a long expedition with his hands outstretched, he felt the smooth plastic of another switch. He snapped it up and the main room shrank back to its real dimensions with the lights, and although still full of decorated perfection, remained too empty.

It reminded him of something, a memory that tickled the back of his conscious mind: a studied place, careful and immaculate. Not a table, a chair, a vase, a cabinet, a bric-a-brac out of place. It was a beautiful room, there was no denying that. But it was the splendor of frigid marble, the magnificence of a frozen photograph.

Not something, he realized. Someone. A beautiful person, obvious to everyone. But it was a splendor, too, of frigid marble, the magnificence of a frozen photograph.

It reminded Escobar of that model ... Jacqueline?

Yes, that was her name. *Jacqueline.*

* * * *

Her breasts. That was the first thing that leapt to mind when he connected the flawlessness of the room to her. Her breasts were quite simply perfect.

Large but not so large as to be sandbags sagging from her chest. They'd had a glorious shape, a pair of ideals that swept down, curved up, and slightly parted. When her robe had dropped, he could do nothing but look at her, look at them, and say, or not even think, anything at all.

Movement had not subtracted from her wonderful geometry. Dropping the terrycloth, she'd shifted her weight from one long, tapered leg to the other, flexing herself in preparation for the sitting. As she had, her breasts had bobbed, swung, rose, and fell, demonstrating youthful firmness, revealing porcelain fine skin.

Jacqueline had been special. But not just because of her breasts.

When the robe had fallen, she'd also revealed a body that was lovely: toned legs, flat stomach, a back that was like a classic Grecian slope, and a derriere with wonderful sacral dimples. Turning slowly, revealing herself on his studio stage, it had been obvious in her gleaming eyes that she knew what she was, knew her perfection, and loved the look she created in the eyes of her beholders.

Thinking of her, a tickle of shame raced up Escobar's own (though not as elegant) back and guilt flushed his ruddy cheeks.

Now that he could see, leaving the living room and entering the bedroom was easy. Turning back, he again stared into the living room, knowing the beauty of it, but feeling nothing.

Looking at Jacqueline as she posed for him on that bright Thursday afternoon, he'd felt something he'd never felt before, a unique feeling from being in the same room with a too lovely, very naked woman.

He should have been better. He shouldn't have done what he did. He wished there was some way he could make it up to her.

If he were a better painter, half the genius everyone said he was, he knew he would have done the right thing. But he clearly wasn't. When faced with her, with her superlative form, Jacqueline's ideal shape, he'd done no better than any ordinary man.

The sun had been bright, the day very warm — touching on becoming hot. As she'd posed, her skin had gone from cool granite to a glowing copper of perspiration. Between her well-built thighs, the petite feather of her carefully manicured pubic hair had begun to tightly curl in the heat.

Watching, he'd worked, studying her meticulously while he tried to conjure the intangible spirit of his talent. But no matter how hard he pushed, how much he twisted and turned his perception, he'd quickly realized that art just wasn't on his mind.

In the end, he did the unthinkable. He committed a crime against that beautiful woman.

Afterward, she seemed to be pleased with what had happened. Wrapping herself up in the terrycloth again, she'd grinned widely, beads of sweat like jewels on her cheeks and forehead.

"Wonderful," she'd said. "Quite wonderful, darling."

Wonderful?

No. It hadn't been. But he couldn't tell her that. Now able to look back, Escobar could see with better clarity what had happened.

Perfect. Superlative. Beautiful. Stunning. Striking. Lovely. Exquisite. Superb. Ideal.

But to Escobar, Jacqueline had been too perfect, too superlative, too beautiful, too stunning, too striking, too lovely, too exquisite, too superb, too ideal.

The sun might have been bright, almost hot, but to him it had been a cold winter day, a frozen afternoon. Shivering, teeth chattering from her frosty stone precision, he'd been unable to bring her to life on his canvas. That she was a living, breathing, sensual woman was undeniable, but to him, she'd been too ideal, her body for a pedestal, not for living.

In the end, he'd failed.

That had been his crime. What he'd created had been good, but it hadn't done her justice. Even after many months, he wished he could somehow make it up to her. Apologize for not getting her right.

That the painting had been sold, and even been on the cover of a magazine, did nothing to dull his ache. When his copy had arrived, he'd taken one look at it and thrown it in the trash.

The living room was a museum piece, elegant and refined. But it was cold and empty. As he'd done in his studio, he flipped the switch, making it vanish into darkness.

V

The bed was too big, but what made him feel even more lonely was that he was getting used to it.

It was there — the heaviness of his limbs, the weight on his eyelids, the slowing of breath. He could feel it, but not enough to make him fall asleep. So, stretched out in their bed, eyelids shut, he couldn't do anything but think.

Which was not a good thing to do.

Constance was in Paris. Constance was always in Paris, it seemed. So far away, and not just in kilometers.

Yes, he wondered, *what* would *be the color of guilt?* It had form, a mass greater than sleep. But, unlike sleep, when he dropped down into it, he slipped into a suffocating depression rather than dreams. Inspiration put a wry grin on his face: That was good, very good. If guilt had a color, it had to be various cerulean shades. Guilt was the blues.

He wanted to apologize. He wanted to offer himself to her. He wanted to hold her hand and explain. He wanted her to smile again.

Rolling over, he pressed his face into a thousand-thread-count pillowcase, sighing dampness into the fabric.

He wanted to make it right somehow. He wanted to unmake what had happened. He wanted to be someone else. He didn't want to be himself. He didn't want to *be*.

Mummified in sheet and comforter — held tight, held warm — he tried to calm his overcast mind, tried to push himself into finally sleeping.

But he couldn't do it. Too tense, he found his hand reaching down between chest and sheet, stomach and sheet, waist and sheet, and then even lower, down past his cock, to his balls. Cupping himself, the gesture comforting and basic, he again appealed to dreams to take it all away.

And again failed. But this time, embracing himself, wrapped in smooth cloth, he at least wasn't thinking about Constance and how he'd hurt her.

Sheri? Was that her name? The American. The journalist. The reporter. Bare, even more exposed than being naked, in his studio. With the memory, his cock began to harden, his balls began to warm.

He wasn't thinking about Constance. But what was worse, was that he began to think about that other girl and what he'd wanted to do with her.

* * * *

Other journalists, other reporters (but none of them American) had asked him about his imagination, speculating that an artist's must be more vivid, more complete, more widely sensory. One of them had even put forth that for a person like Escobar, dreams must be like an everyday man's waking life.

Escobar didn't know if that was true; he had no way of knowing what an everyday man's mental world might be like. But he often thought that if they weren't dull, ordinary, flat, lifeless, they might actually become happy — and since they rarely seemed to have smiles on their faces, they probably didn't, and so weren't.

That small apartment, the one he envied his brother for, was a private and complete cranial world behind his eyes. Often, when he needed to escape the pressure of being Escobar, he'd just close his eyes and wander through the safe little life he'd constructed for himself, adding as many details as possible to make it even more alive: the cheap plaster on the walls, leaving his fingertips chalky white when he stroked them; the faint ring around the tangerine-colored kitchen sink; the view out his bathroom window of lawn-green moss framing brown bricks; the way the front door would periodically stick, and how he'd have to tug it open to free it; and how the rain would blow when it was storming, making the thin windows rattle.

But there was another fantasy, one that was very much like his real life. Unlike Escobar in flesh and blood, however, in that world, he was not what he was but what he wanted to be. The house was the same, but not as frozen with too-careful decorations. His life was the same, but he wasn't frightened of failure. Diego was the same, but he was also a knock on the door, a bottle of wine, a hug, and warm, heavy laughs. Marcel was the same, but was not just profit and value, but rather a friend who cared about and understood the man as well as the artist. Constance was there as well, but was bright sunlight rather than chilly fog, a woman who loved him no matter what he did.

The reporter was there, too, come to interview him. But this time as they sat in the kitchen and talked, what he'd said had been honest and accurate.

Art was really like sex, really a release of a deeper, wilder, more passionate side of himself. His vision was penetrating, able to see the essential nature of a rose, a landscape, a cathedral, or even a portrait.

As in reality, she posed for him.

Between then and now, here and there, warm and safe, and one sheet above and one sheet below, Escobar squeezed his cock, savoring that as well as the weight of his body on his balls. Going from soft to almost hard to hard to very hard, he turned, the fabric hissing as he rolled onto his back.

Yes, she was posing for him.

The art, his talent, flowed — without doubt, without uncertainty. Brush to pallette, a twist of transfer from latter to former. A dance of perfect color and composition. A concerto of technique and execution. A banquet of skill and balance. Grinning wide, he felt the absolute certainty that what he was doing was great, good, and maybe even legendary.

The rest was just sex.

Memory overlapped fantasy: she posing for him. The details of her body recalled, used in his vision: the heaviness of her breasts, the way they gently sagged down, the glisten and gleam of sweat in the 'Y' of her cleavage; the tan saucers of her faintly wrinkled areola; the dark pinkness of her large, erect nipples; the inviting swell of her belly; the delicious peach of her bottom as she turned, moved, on his stage; and, of course, between her soft, plush hips, a wild tangle of black hair.

Memory again overlapped fantasy. Without doubt, without uncertainty, the young reporter had wanted him. While large, the studio was not so large that the salty bite of her perspiration could not reach him behind his easel. While roomy, it also wasn't roomy enough for him not to also detect the smell of her arousal.

She posed, nervous and self-aware, but also with a bold, dangerous sexuality: shaking, quivering, but also obviously wet. Moving from one foot to the other, she tried to balance in spite of her spinning head, eventually finding a kind of stasis.

"Beautiful," he said, unsure if he'd really said that to her.

If not, he wished he had.

In his hand, his cock was very hard. A rare kind of erection where the soft tissues felt more like a satin-wrapped bone. From his back to his buttocks, he was aware that he was tight, clenched, his body fisted as strongly as his sliding grip.

Behind his work, he was also very erect. In his jeans, the swelling was a sexual demand. But he refused to touch it, instead concentrating on bringing the earthen power of her to life. Carefully, teasingly, he worked on getting the color of those tan areola, those pink nipples, that dark forest thatch, just right. It was foreplay, or at least the painting of it.

Then it was finished: the best thing he'd ever done. What was even better was that he knew it. Knew it more than he knew anything in his life.

Back to the sex. Behind his easel, he was as hard as he was in reality, laying in the bed. In front of him, in his mind, she was breathing hard, skin reflective with gleaming sweat, her body also clearly demanding. Between her thighs, just below that tangle of dark hair, was a brighter reflection of moisture, a leak of slippery want.

"Can I see it?" she suddenly asked, voice quavering and broken.

"Of course," he responded., waving his hand over the top of the canvas, inviting her over.

In bed, his own sweat was making his cock slippery, but not slippery enough. Bringing up his hand, he gently spat into the palm. Then back, the sensation of hand on cock magnified by the better lubricant. Up and down, up and down, base to tip, body tensing, breathing gasping. It was going to be very good.

Towards him she walked, her breasts bobbing, her nipples swaying at the tips, her thighs sliding. Off the platform with a clumsy step, her mind on her wetness and not on her arms or legs, and then across to him.

"It's wonderful," she said when she moved around the easel, took in the sight.

Mesmerized for a good long time by the work, she eventually pulled her eyes away from his masterpiece and then turned to him and grinned.

"Magnificent," she added, but with it, her hand dropped to his leg, resting on his obvious bulge.

Gripping tight, she hissed in primal delight at his size, his firmness. She began to knead him through his jeans, working him with pure dedication to feel as much of him as she could.

Then, just when he felt he couldn't take any more, she fumbled for the zipper on his jeans and tried to take more. Fierce, hungry, she tugged at his pants, trying to get them off, battling against their tightness and the fact that he was still sitting on his studio stool.

To help, he stood. Smiling, her voraciousness slowed a small amount. With her treasure so close, she stepped back, slowed, and took her time.

Kneeling, she lowered his zipper as if she were helping to dress a burlesque dancer: steady, meticulous, careful. Then it was down, and after putting fingers through the belt loops, she began to do the same to the pants themselves.

When the pants had descended enough to expose his cock, it sprang free in a long, hard salute. Adoring it — and him — with hungry eyes, she returned the gesture with one of her own. Bending forward, she innocently kissed the tip of his cock.

In bed, as well as in his mind, Escobar's strokes became faster, firmer, his breathing became quicker and deeper.

The kiss became more passionate. From satin lips to the soft head of his cock, she moved up, wrapping her mouth around the end, washing that part of him with her hot, very wet tongue.

The wash then became even more passionate. From a hot, very wet tongue, she moved to sliding her mouth down the shaft of his cock until he could look down at the top of her head and see it touch the swell of his belly.

That alone would normally be enough. The thought of a woman, burning with want, getting down on her hands and knees to take his cock in her mouth — it was a special fantasy. But that night, in the big empty bed, he pushed ahead into something more.

Then came a jump, a disconnect: his own need too great to keep the fantasy in real time. In a blink he was naked as well, and they were both on the platform in the middle of the studio. Exposed to light, revealed by dozens of panes of glass, it was like they were performing for the entire world. No shame, no embarrassment, no fear of ridicule. He was in view and happy to be so, and she was ecstatic to be there with him.

Positions tumbled through his mind. A few he knew well, others were only from the small collection of DVDs he kept hidden in his studio. Even though he knew that better fantasies were out there — advanced images, video clips, web sites, and more — he felt left behind, an antique, when he saw them. Part of it was an early life of art, and submersion in the simple, innocent classics, but he suspected that for all his supposed imagination, he was a simple man at heart.

But it worked, which was all he wanted. So they were naked, on his platform, for the whole world to see. In front of him, she was on her hands and knees, offering to his eyes and body her plush and so-well-shaped ass. Rarely experienced, the novelty of visualizing her presenting herself to him, his view of the slickness of her from behind, the quivering of her anus, was almost enough to push him up and over the edge.

Not yet, not yet. Slowing his hand, pulling back from the edge, he tried to delay the inevitable. Distracting himself from the mental vision of her plush backside, he opened his eyes, focused instead on the plum-colored ceiling of his bedroom.

Heartbeat braking, inhale and exhale unhurried, his orgasm retreated. When he could think — make images with better detail — he began again.

The sun coming through the glass, the room sweltering, but like a good sauna, not a bad heat wave. The blond boards of the platform, the parade of bumps that was her spine, the way the light gleamed and glistened on her skin, the back of her calves below him, the smell of salt and sex, her murmurs and coos as she urged him, his knees pressing down against the unyielding wood.

As he became more excited, the elements began to heat, accelerate: his cock resting between her plush ass, the pearl bead of cum that had formed at the tip, the way she pushed herself against him to urge him in, the smell of her beyond perspiration, and the few dark streaks of wayward pubic hair between her cheeks.

Back to the top of his desire, he couldn't pull away anymore. In bed, his strokes got faster and faster. In his mind, he moved forward, easing himself into her hot, wet, tightness. Eyes down in his imagination, he saw his cock steadily, slowly, enter her one careful inch at a time. Not wanting anything but his body, she'd have no steadiness, no slowness. With a deep moan, she impatiently impaled herself on him.

That was enough. Details, position, feverish urgency ... Escobar's orgasm rushed through and out of him in a bolt of primordial happiness with a quivering, shaking, sticky conclusion.

As he trembled, and as his ejaculation filled his hand, he was in himself enough to try and make sure none of it escaped to stain their sheets.

Fading, diminishing until there was nothing but happiness and a bodily exhaustion, he carefully pulled the covers off and stumbled, stiff-legged, to the bathroom to clean up.

Done and finished, he returned to bed, and wrapped himself back into his tight cocoon of satin sheets and comforter.

Deep breathing, heart only faintly hammering, Escobar could see sleep on the distant horizon. But with the fading of his imagination, the urgency of his body gone, he was once again alone in their big bed.

Eventually, he nodded off. But not before tears of shame and guilt slid down his cheeks, wetting his pillowcase more than his breathing ever could.

VI

Morning and light. Rubbing the dried up dreams from his eyes, lucky or unlucky that he didn't remember any of them, Escobar eventually pulled himself from a comforting wrap of sheets.

The day was unplanned. There was always something to do, tasks from reviewing paperwork Marcel had forwarded for his signature to going through his paints, canvases, paper, brushes, and knives to see what he needed to reorder.

Dishes needed be washed. He thought again of Constance's desire to have someone come in. He opposed the idea, not because he didn't want her to have help, but because he selfishly didn't want any more people being between them, even if it was just to make dinner or clean afterwards.

Painting was also always an option. But painting was the last thing he felt like doing. His shame crushed down on his mind. What he'd done was inexcusable. Years of marriage, ruined. The image of himself as a kind, fair, and decent man, was gone. The love of his Constance was gone.

Constance … he shouldn't go there, shouldn't think about that. But this time there was no avoiding it. The beauty of her, the innocence of her, the affection she seemed to have for him, the years they had spent together. From that field of green grass and yellow flowers to one moment of weakness — all of it ruined.

It had been good. So good. If he could do anything, perform any kind of penance, it would be to take back his sin, erase the shame, restore her — and his — innocence.

He shook his head. *Can't.* There was no way he could redeem himself, no way he could show both his humility to her and his redemption to himself.

Pausing, he stood, looking out the kitchen window, and saw that the sun that day, the light it shone, was good, very good. Crisp, clear, luminous. A day for a walk. A day to sprawl under it and tan. A day to delightfully sweat at some simple, productive task. Light to live by, light — he had to admit — to paint by.

Escobar smiled. *Ah.* Not really a word. Rather a mental sound accompanying a lifting, a buoyancy, a release — or at least a temporary pardon of — weight.

It was a good day to paint. A very good day.

* * * *

Brush to pallette, a turn of shifting from latter to former. A moment to look at the tip, see if the hairs had become too mad, crooked. They hadn't. A moment, too, to dwell once again on the formula of color, yearning more than he ever had before that today — of all days — he could have the assurance that an exact formula of Cadmium Yellow Medium, Brown Pink, Cadmium Red Deep, with Cobalt, would be exact, perfect, ideal.

Today, though, he didn't have the luxury of self-pity and doubt. This painting, more than any other, had to be perfect. He couldn't afford a mistake, couldn't risk anything because of habituation.

What to paint was easy. The composition, the setting, and, of course, the subject had never left his mind. Eyes to the globs of paint, then, to mix and compare and mix again, pushing each of them towards the ideal capturing of his memory, his desire, his hope, and, most importantly, the most powerful emotions of all.

What, he wondered, *would be the color of regret?*

Green, he decided, which fit ideally with his reminiscence of that moment. A steadily rolling vastness of emerald, a sea of shushing grass swelling and ebbing in a playfully buffeting breeze, a meadow milieu of sweet growth.

What, he wondered, *would be the color of hope?*

Yellow, he decided, which suited perfectly his recollection of that time. Blossoms speckled here and there and there and here, tiny bursts of dazzling botanical allure, temptations and come-hithers with crooking petals and blown-kisses of perfume.

What, he wondered, *would be the color of love?*

Red, he decided, which matched, flawlessly, his memory of that day. A balmy sun fixed on a cerulean backdrop, an illumination casting dazzling mirrors onto her just-so angled cheekbones, shifting her shady curls into a playful cloud of wistful smoke.

Constance, that day in that field of flowers. Constance, the day he first sketched her. Constance, the moment he knew he wanted to be with her always.

If he was really a genius, if what they all said about him was true, then she'd *have* to forgive him. Forgotten would be his crime of being tempted by that young American reporter. That he'd resisted in the end wasn't important. His failing was that he'd come so very close to touching another woman.

If he was a genius — and the work showed it — then he'd succeed. She'd see a bright and beautiful love letter to her, a statement of everything he felt for her, a demonstration of what she meant to him.

But if he wasn't — and the image didn't — and she saw only oils and fabric, color and composition, technique and form, then he'd know that he wasn't worth being called Escobar, the great artist. Then he'd know that he wasn't worth being Escobar, her lover and husband.

Brush to pallette, a turn of shifting from latter to former. A moment to look at the tip, see if the tip had become too mad, crooked. It hadn't. Then back to the work, laying down pigments, pulling up details, adding texture, removing empty whiteness. Stroke after stroke, sweep after sweep, dab after dab, touch after touch, each movement revealing more and more of himself.

Strokes, sweeps, dabs, touches, and most of all, brushes — hoping with every one that she'd see the overwhelming splendor of his love in the color, shape, composition, technique, and texture.

That Constance would see, with perfect clarity, the truth of his heart.

ABOUT THE AUTHOR

Calling M.Christian versatile is a tremendous understatement. Extensively published in science fiction, fantasy, horror, and even nonfiction, it is in erotica that M.Christian is widely considered an acknowledged master, appearing in multiple editions of *Best American Erotica, Best Gay Erotica, Best Lesbian Erotica, Best Bisexual Erotica, Best Fetish Erotica*, and many other magazines, sites, and anthologies.

In erotica, M.Christian's respected for their passionate imagination and chameleonic ability to convincingly write for — and as — a diverse range of gender expressions and sexual orientations.

Of their work, Tristan Taormino said, "M.Christian is a literary stylist of the highest caliber: smart, funny, frightening, sexy—there's nothing [they] can't write about… and brilliantly."

M.Christian's short fiction is collected in many bestselling books in a wide variety of genres, including the Lambda Award finalist *Dirty Words* and other queer collections such as *Filthy Boys* and *BodyWork*; erotic science fiction like *Rude Mechanicals, Technorotica, Better Than the Real Thing, Bachelor Machine, Skin Effect*, and *Hard Drive: The Best Sci-fi Erotica of M.Christian.*

As a novelist, M.Christian further demonstrates their versatility with the queer vampire novels, *Running Dry* and *The Very Bloody Marys*; the erotic romance, *Brushes*; the sensual cyberpunk, *Painted Doll*; and the controversial gay horror/thrillers *Finger's Breadth* and *Me2*.

On top of all that, they're prolific and anthologists, editing over twenty-five anthologies, namely the *Best S/M Erotica* series, *Pirate Booty, My Love For All That Is Bizarre: Sherlock Holmes Erotica, The Burning Pen, The Mammoth Book of Future Cops* and *The Mammoth Book of Tales of the Road* (with Maxim Jakubowski); and *Confessions, Garden of Perverse, Amazons* (with Sage Vivant), and others.

M.Christian is also a celebrated sexual futurist, through his novels and short stories as well as Senior Columnist and Managing Editor for Future of Sex (www.futureofsex.net), which provides "insights into the fascinating topic of the future of human sex and sexuality."

Visit www.mchristian.com for further information.

www.ingramcontent.com/pod-product-compliance
Lightning Source LLC
Chambersburg PA
CBHW070505200726
48293CB00007B/2399